# THE FANGED & THE FAE

## A FAERY BARGAINS COLLECTION

## MELISSA MARR

# ALSO BY MELISSA MARR

### <u>Signed Copies:</u>

To order signed copies of my books (with free ebook included in some cases), go to MelissaMarrBooks.com

### <u>Adult Thriller</u>

*Pretty Broken Things* (2020; psychological thriller)

### <u>Adult Fantasy</u>

*Graveminder* (HarperCollins, 2011)

*The Arrivals* (HarperCollins, 2012)

*Cold Iron Heart* (2020; *Wicked Lovely* adult)

The Wicked & The Dead (2020; Urban Fantasy)

*The Kiss & The Killer* (2021; Urban Fantasy)

### <u>Young Adult</u>

*Wicked Lovely* series (HarperCollins, 2007-2012)

*Made For You* (HarperCollins,, 2013)

*Seven Black Diamonds* (HarperCollins, 2015)

*One Blood Ruby* (HarperCollins, 2016)

### <u>Middle Grade</u>

*The Hidden Knife* (Penguin, 2021)

*Loki's Wolves* (with Kelley Armstrong, 2012)

*Odin's Ravens* (with Kelley Armstrong 2013)

*Thor's Serpents* (with Kelley Armstrong, 2014)

### <u>Collections:</u>

*Tales of Folk & Fey* (2019)

*Dark Court Faery Tales* (2019)

*This Fond Madness* (2017)

## Co-Edited with Kelley Armstrong (with HarperTeen)

*Enthralled*

*Shards & Ashes*

## Co-Edited with Tim Pratt (with Little, Brown)

*Rags & Bones*

# BLOOD MARTINIS & MISTLETOE

A Faery Bargains Novella

Set after BOOK 1

# CHAPTER 1

Giant aluminum balls hung around me even though I was standing in the cemetery not long before dawn. I didn't know who hung the balls, but I wasn't too bothered.

Winter in New Orleans was festive. We might have *draugr* and a higher than reasonable crime rate, but damn it, we had festivities for every possible occasion. Gold, silver, red, blue, purple, and green balls hung from the tree. Samhain had passed, and it was time to ramp up for the winter holidays.

November--the month after Samhain--was uncommonly active for necromancy calls. Unfortunately, a certain sort of person thought it was festive to summon the body and spirit of Dear Uncle Phil or Aunt Marie. Sometimes the relatives were maudlin, and sometimes they were thinking about the afterlife.

Now, the dead don't tell tales about the things after death. They can't. I warn folks, but they don't believe me. They pay me a fair amount to summon their dead, so I always stress that the "what happens after we die" questions are forbidden. Few people believe me.

Tonight, I had summoned Alphard Cormier to speak to his

widow and assorted relatives or friends who accompanied her. I didn't ask who they were. One proven relation was all I needed. Family wasn't always just the folks who shared your blood.

Case in point, the faery beside me. Eli of Stonecroft was one of the people I trusted most in this world—or in any other. I closed my eyes for a moment, which I could do because he was at my side. I was tired constantly, so much so that only willpower kept me upright.

"Bonbon," Eli whispered. His worried tone made clear that a question or three hid in that absurd pet name.

Was I going to be able to control my magic? Did he need to brace for *draugr* inbound? Were we good on time?

"It's good." I opened my eyes, muffled a yawn, and met his gaze. "I'm still fine."

Eli nodded, but he still scanned the graves. He was increasingly cautious since my near-brush-with-death a couple months ago.

My partner stood at my side as we waited in the cemetery while the widow, her daughter, and two men spoke to their reanimated relative. Mr. Alphard Cormier was wearing a suit that was in fashion sometime in the last thirty years.

Why rouse him now? I didn't know and wasn't asking.

"Twenty minutes," I called out. I could feel the sun coming; I'd always been able to do so—call it in an internal sundial, or call it bad genes. Either way, my body was attuned to the rising and falling of the sun.

"When he is entombed, we could--"

"No." I couldn't force myself to glance at him again.

I was bone-tired, which made me more affectionate, and Eli was my weakness. Cut-glass features, bee-stung lips, and enough strength to fight at my side, even against *draugr*, Eli was built for fantasy. His ability to destroy my self-control was remarkable—and no, it wasn't because he was fae.

That part *was* why I wasn't going home with him. Trusting him, wanting him, caring for him, none of that was enough to overcome the complications of falling into his bed. Sleeping with a faery prince had a list of complications that no amount of lust or affection overcame.

"I won't get married," I reminded him.

"Are you sure that's a good idea?" Mr. Cormier asked, voice carrying over the soft sobbing women.

The man with them handed Cormier something metallic.

I felt as much as saw the dead man look my way, and then his arm raised with a gun in hand. The relatives parted, and there was a dead man with a gun aimed at me.

"Fuck a duck. Move!" I darted to the side.

Eli was already beside me, hand holding his pretty bronze-coated sword that I hadn't even known he owned until the last month. "Geneviève?"

"On it." I jerked the magic away from Mr. Comier.

It was my magic that made him stand, so I wasn't going to let him stand and shoot me.

*REST,* I ordered the dead man.

*"I'm sorry, ma'am. They made me. Threatened my Suzette if I didn't . . ."* His words faded as my shove of magic sent him back to his tomb.

I could hear the widow, presumably Suzette, sobbing.

"I do not believe those gentlemen are Mr. Cormier's relations." Eli glared in the direction of the men who had hired me to raise a dead man to kill me. They'd grabbed the two women and ducked behind mausoleums.

"Why?"

"They seem to want you dead, buttercream," Eli said. "If they were his family, that's an odd response."

A bullet hit the stone across from me. Shards of gravestone pelted me. Oddly the adrenaline surge was welcome, even if the bullets weren't. Nothing like a shot of rage to get the sleepiness out.

"Not why *that.*" I nodded toward the men who were staying

crouched behind graves. "Why go through the hassle? Why not simply shoot me themselves?"

"Dearest, can we ponder that *after* they are not shooting at you?"

I felt my eyes change. As my rage boiled over, my eyes reflected it. They were my father's reptilian eyes, *draugr* eyes. The only useful thing he'd ever done was accidentally augment the magic I inherited from my mother. Unfortunately, the extra juice came with a foul temper—one that was even worse the last few weeks. After I'd been injected by venom, my moods were increasingly intense.

I wanted to rip limbs off.

I wanted to shove my thumbs into their eye sockets and keep going until I felt brain matter.

Before the urges were more than images, I was moving from one spot to the next.

I could *flow* like a *draugr.* I could move quickly enough that to the mortal eye it looked like teleportation. I *flowed* to the side of the shooter and grabbed his wrist.

Eli was not far behind. He didn't *flow*, but he was used to my movements and impulses. He had his sword to the shooter's throat a moment after I jerked the gun away from the man.

"Dearest?" Eli said, his voice tethering me sanity.

I concentrated on his voice, his calm, and I punched the other shooter rather than removing his eyes. Then I let out a scream of frustration and shoved my magic into the soil like a seismic force.

The dead answered.

Dozens of voices answered my call. Hands reknitted. Flesh was regrown from the magic that flowed from my body into the graves. Mouths reformed, as if I was a sculptor of man.

"You do *not* wake the dead without reason," I growled at the now-unarmed man who dared to try to shoot me.

*Here*, of all places. He tried to spill my blood into these graves.

I stepped over the man I'd punched and ignored the cringing, sobbing widow and the other woman who was trying to convince her mother to leave.

And I stalked toward the shooter in Eli's grip.

"Bonbon, you have a scratch." Eli nodded toward my throat.

"Shit." I felt my neck where Eli had indicated. Blood slid into my collar.

I stepped closer to the shooter. "What were you thinking, Weasel Nuts?"

"Would you mind *covering* the wound?" Eli asked, forcing me to focus again.

His voice was calm, but we both knew that I could not shed blood in a space where graves were so plentiful. I'd accidentally bound two *draugr* so far, and blood was a binding agent in necromancy. Unless I wanted to bring home a few reanimated servants, my blood couldn't spill here.

I had to focus. And I didn't need an army of undead soldiers.

"Take this." Eli pulled off his shirt with one hand, switching the hilt between hands to keep the sword to Weasel Nuts' throat.

I stared. *Not the time.*

Eli's lips quirked in a half-smile, and then he pressed the blade just a bit. "And, I believe you need to answer my lady."

I shot Eli a look--his *lady*? What year did he think this was?--but I pressed his shirt against my throat. I did not, absolutely did *not*, take a deep breath because the shirt smelled like Eli.

Eli smiled as I took another quick extra breath.

"Thou shalt not suffer a witch to live." Weasel Nuts spat in my direction. "Foul thing."

I opened my mouth to reply, but Eli removed his sword blade and in a blink turned it so he could bash the pommel into the man's mouth.

Weasel Nuts dropped to his knees, and this time when he spat, he spat out his own teeth and blood.

If I were the swooning sort, this would be such a moment. Something about defending me always did good things to my libido.

"Geneviève, would you be so kind as to call the police?" Eli motioned toward the women. "And escort the ladies away from this unpleasant man?"

It sounded chivalrous—or chauvinistic--but it was actually an excuse. I needed to get my ass outside the cemetery before I dripped blood. Eli had provided a way to do so gracefully.

"Ladies?" Eli said, louder now. "Ms. Crowe will walk you toward the street."

The women came over, and the widow flinched when my gaze met hers. My *draugr* eyes unnerved people.

But then she straightened her shoulders and stared right into my reptilian eyes as if they were normal. "I do apologize, Ms. Crowe. They have an accomplice who is holding my grandson as a hostage. We had to cooperate."

My simmering temper spiked, keeping my exhaustion away and my focus sharp.

I stared at the women. With my grave sight, I saw trails of energy, the whispers of deaths, and the auras of anything living. These women were afraid, but not evil. They were worried.

The older woman grabbed the fallen gun and ordered, "Walk."

For a moment, I thought I'd been wrong, but she pointed the barrel at the man who had shot at me. "You. Get up."

Her daughter smiled. "Would you mind helping us, Ms. Crowe?"

Eli and I exchanged a look. We were in accord, as usual. He bowed his head at them, and then scooped the unconscious man up.

In a strange group, we walked toward the exit.

As we were putting the unconscious attacker in the trunk of the Cadillac the women had arrived in, the sun rose, tinting the sky as if it were a watercolor painting.

I paused, wincing. Sunlight wasn't my friend. I wasn't a *draugr*—luckily, because sunlight trapped young *draugr*—but my genetics meant daylight made my head throb if I was out in too much of it. I slid on the dark sunglasses I carried for emergencies.

"It was nice to see Daddy," the younger woman said quietly to her mother. "I wish it had been closer to Christmas, but still . . . it was nice."

The widow motioned for the other prisoner to get into the trunk. Once he did, Eli slammed the trunk, and the widow squeezed her daughter's hand. "It was."

The daughter handed Eli the keys. She was shaken by the shooting, and I was bleeding from the shattering stone. Neither of us was in great shape to drive. However, it wasn't great for Eli to be trapped in a hulking steel machine. Faeries and steel weren't a good mix.

"I'll drive my car," he said, popping the trunk and grabbing a clean shirt. Working with me meant carrying an assortment of practical goods—clean clothes, duct tape, a sword, zip ties, and first aid supplies.

I tried not to sigh that he was now dressed fully again. Don't get me wrong. I respect him, but that didn't mean I wasn't prone to lustful gazes in his direction. If he minded, I'd stop.

He walked to the passenger door and opened it. "Come on, my peach pie."

The widow drove her Caddy away as I slid into the luxurious little convertible that had been fae-modified for Eli.

"Are you well enough to do this?" Eli asked as he steered us into the morning light.

"One human." I kept my eyes closed behind my sunglasses, grateful for the extra dark tint of his windows. I rarely needed sleep for most of my life, but lately I was always ready for a nap. Not yet, though.

I assured Eli, "I'm fine to deal with this."

So we set out to retrieve the young hostage. We didn't discuss my near constant exhaustion. We didn't talk about the fear that my near-death event had left lingering issues for my health. We would have to, but . . . not now.

We arrived at a townhouse, and I *flowed* to where the captor held a smallish boy. *Flowing* wasn't a thing I typically did around regular folk, but there were exceptions.

The boy was duct taped to a chair by his ankles.

The captor, another man about the age of the two in the trunk, was laughing at something on the television. If not for the gun in his lap and the duct tape on the boy's ankles, the whole thing wouldn't seem peculiar.

When the man saw us, he scrambled for his gun.

So, I punched the captor and broke the wrist of his gun-holding arm.

Eli freed the boy, who ran to his family as soon as they came into the house.

The whole thing took less time than brewing coffee.

"Best not to mention Ms. Crowe's speed," Eli said to the women as we were leaving.

The younger one nodded, but she was mostly caught up in holding her son.

The widow looked at me.

"Not all witches are wicked, dear." She patted my cheek, opened her handbag and pulled out a stack of folded bills. "For your time."

"The raising was already paid," I protested.

"I took it from them," she said proudly. She shook it at me insistently. "Might as well go to you. Here."

Eli accepted a portion of the money on my behalf. He understood when it was an insult not to and when to refuse because the client couldn't afford my fees.

Honestly, I felt guilty getting paid sometimes. Shouldn't I work for my city? Shouldn't I help people? Shouldn't good come of these skills?

But good intentions didn't buy groceries or pay for my medical supplies. That's as much what Eli handled as having my back when bullets or unwelcome dead things started to pop up.

After we walked out and shoved the third prisoner in the trunk of the Cadillac, Mrs. Cormier said, "I'll call the police to retrieve them. Do you mind waiting?"

"I will wait," Eli agreed, not lying by saying we "didn't mind" because *of course* we minded. I was leaning on the car for support, and Eli was worrying over my injury. If he had his way, he'd have me at his home, resting and cared for, but I was lousy at that.

It was on the long list of reasons I couldn't marry him. Some girls dreamed of a faery tale romance, a prince, pretty dresses. I dreamed of kicking ass. I'd be a lousy faery tale queen.

But I still had feelings for a faery prince—and no, I was *not* labeling them.

So rather than head home, I leaned on the side of the Cadillac, partly because it was that or sway in exhaustion. "I'll stay with you."

Once the widow went inside, Eli walked away and grabbed a first aid kit from his car. I swear he bought them in bulk lately. "Let me see your throat."

"I'm fine." Dried blood made me look a little garish, but I could feel that it wasn't oozing much now.

Eli opened the kit, tore open a pouch of sani-wipes, and stared at me.

"Just tired. Sunlight." I gestured at the bright ball of pain in the sky. Midwinter might be coming, but the sun was still too bright for my comfort.

"Geneviève . . ." He held up a wipe. "May I?"

I sighed and took off my jacket. "It's not necessary."

"I disagree." He used sani-wipes to wipe away my blood as I leaned on the Cadillac, ignoring the looks we were getting from pedestrians. Maybe it was that he was cleaning up my blood, or that he was fae—or maybe it was that there were people yelling from the trunk.

Either way, I wasn't going to look away from Eli. I couldn't.

Obviously, I knew it should not be arousing to have him clean a cut in my neck from grave shards because someone was firing bullets at me, but . . . having his hands on me at all made my heart speed.

"Would you like to take the car and leave?" Eli was closer than he needed to be, hips close enough that it would be easier to pull him closer than push him away.

"And go where?"

He brushed my hair back, checking for more injuries. The result was that I could feel his breath on my neck. "Drive to my home and draw a bath or shower. I'll stay here and . . ."

"Tempting," I admitted with a laugh.

He had both a marble rainfall shower and the largest tub I'd ever seen. It came complete with a small waterfall. I admitted, "I've had fantasies about that waterfall."

"As have I."

I pressed myself against him, kissed his throat, and asked, "Ready to call off the engagement?"

He kissed me, hand tangled in my hair, holding me as if I would run.

I'd sell my own soul for an eternity of Eli's kisses if I believed in such bargains, but I wouldn't destroy him. Being with me wasn't what was best for him.

When he pulled back from our kiss, he stated, "Geneviève . . ."

I kissed him softly. I could say more with my touch than with words. I paused and whispered, "You can have my body *or* this engagement. Not both."

He sighed, but he stepped back. "You are impossible, Geneviève Crowe."

I caught his hand. "It doesn't have to be impossible. We're safely out of *Elphame* now. We could just end the enga--"

"I am fae, love. I don't lie. I don't break my word." He squeezed my hand gently. "I gave you my promise to wed. In front of my king and family. I *cannot* end this engagement."

We stood in silence for several moments. Then he held out his keys, and I took them.

"Meet me at my place. Maybe we can spar," I offered.

Eli pulled me in closer, kissed both of my cheeks, and said, "I will accept any excuse to get sweaty with you."

"Same." I hated that this was where we were, but I wasn't able to change who or what I was. Neither was Eli. He had a future that I wanted no part of, and I felt a duty to my city and friends. We had no future option that would suit both of us. I'd be here, beheading *draugr* and trying not to become more of a monster, and he would return to his homeland. There was no good compromise.

# CHAPTER 2

After the weirdness of handling the Cormier situation, life resumed normalcy. I was still unnaturally tired, still engaged, and still not getting any loving.

What passed for normalcy in my life was overrated.

The work part, at least, was a welcome lull. This was an annual tradition. I tended to think of it as the pre-holiday calm. By January, it would be hectic. Mid-Winter was always when I had the most downtime, but during the end of year holiday people would start deciding death was overrated and hunting down *draugr* for a shot at eternal life on Earth instead of natural deaths. I wasn't sure if it was depression, greed, or sentimental holiday moods.

Mine was an odd job, but I didn't ever want to give it up. I wasn't immune to *draugr* venom, but I was stronger than humans and could *flow* as fast as the *draugr* could. I had advantages, and I felt duty-bound to make use of them.

Tonight, I was enjoying a night out with my closest friends. *Draugr* weren't all trapped by sunlight, but the newly-infected, bite-first-think-never ones were. I tended to think that was a good excuse to stay in the bar until dawn's light

"Yule? Chanukah? Christmas?" Sera was holding up pictures of formal dresses. "Did you discuss it? Which are you celebrating in *Elphame*? I know Mama Lauren has usually had dibs on Chanukah. Do we call one? Or do we wait on Eli?"

Jesse and Christy said nothing. They exchange a look that spoke volumes. No one expected my first holiday season as the future queen of *Elphame* to go smoothly.

Running away to *Elphame* as if I could be fae wasn't an option for more reasons than just my issues with Eli—which was why I was livid when I received a beautiful handwritten summons to celebrate "the holiday" with the king of the faeries. Eli's uncle seemed to think there was *one* holiday. As a Jewish witch with Christian friends, I could guarantee that there were at least three of them on my social schedule.

The four of us were enjoying a night off at Eli's bar, the oddly named Bill's Tavern. No one called Bill had ever owned or been employed here, but whenever I asked "who is Bill," Eli simply laughed.

Fae humor confused me sometimes.

I still had my weapons, but that was like saying I still had on trousers. It would be weird and uncomfortable to go out for the night without them. One sword, two guns, and a dagger if I needed to draw my blood. It might seem odd, but my blood was my best weapon. One loyal army of the dead trumped most conventional weapons.

Christy, whose job was mostly pool-hustling—often here-- wasn't working tonight either. She and Jesse were sort of hand holding, but not being all couple-y in an obnoxious way. Sera was scheduling our lives. It was her thing. One of them, at least. She was why we were out tonight, too. She was our glue.

"I have received a summons from the king," I said.

"You'll need another dress," Sera said, as if dresses were the priority not the fact that some old dude had summoned me like I was his subject.

"That's what you got out of this?" I met Sera's gaze.

"Maybe we should get a couple of them."

"Or not," Jesse muttered.

"She cannot go before the king of *Elphame* in jeans." Sera gave us all a look, one that meant she was debating smacking one of us upside our heads. "Which holiday did he invite you for?"

"*The* holiday, as if there is only one." I was starting a list of grievances against the faery king—starting with the fact that he insisted on referring to me as "death" or "death maiden" and rolling right up to the moment. Honestly, the only thing I liked about him was his nephew, Eli.

Sera sighed.

In a game of chess, she'd be the king—maybe the queen. It varied. Christy was a bishop, influential and strong. She was impervious to Sera's quelling look and spoke her mind. Jesse was the Rook, the castle. He was *home*. Steady in whatever way we needed. And I was either a knight or a pawn, depending on the moment. I'd like to be a knight, but lately I felt like I was being played.

I just couldn't decide whether the player was someone I knew already or not.

I looked up and met Eli's gaze. If you asked him, he'd claim that he wasn't on the chess board at all. I had trouble believing that a faery prince was so innocent--and Eli was *the* faery prince, as a matter of fact. He failed to share that tidbit with me at first. Right up to the point where he'd spirited me away to his homeland to save my life, I thought he was just a guy: a very hot, infuriating, loyal, fae guy. So, maybe I was still pissy over the whole my friend is an exiled faery prince thing.

Now that we were accidentally engaged because of it, I was starting to think that he was the hand in the sky. Was Eli the chess player toying with my life? Had he always planned to trap me?

But based on the way my life had gone of late, he was far from the only one moving pieces. His uncle, the king I might have to wear a dress to meet again, and the dead lady I thought might be an ancestor or mine . . . and some unknown figure who hired a *human* to murder me a few months ago. The shooting at Cormier's raising was weird, too. The police had no answers, and all three of the men were suddenly dead. Too many people were trying to play with my life, and I was fed up.

I couldn't do anything about that murder-attempts thing, but I could handle the holidays. I was still me: half-witch, half-*draugr*. I wasn't a fae princess, no matter what the King of *Elphame* thought, and I wasn't pleased to be summoned as if his laws applied to me.

"Which holiday do *you* want us to celebrate?" I asked my friends. "Cocktails. Friends. Maybe we can do a formal meal. You want dresses, Sera? Fuck it. We do dresses."

Jesse and Christy both looked at me like I'd suggested we knock over a bank or gnaw on a witch's house.

"Gen, you can't just ignore the king," Jesse said. "You're engaged to--"

"Not on purpose! For an honorary brother, you're awfully calm. Eli is trying to *marry me.* Besmirch me." My voice was loud enough that several people looked our way.

"You like besmirching," Jesse said. Then he met my gaze and added, "And you're obviously not *besmirched* yet because you're surlier than usual lately."

I shot a glare at Eli. It took effort to glare at him, though. Logic meant I was still angry that he wouldn't free me from our engagement, but logic was a weak defense against him. I wanted Eli the way witches crave nature, the way the starving crave food.

And I was in definite need of being besmirched, preferably by Eli. Repeatedly. I'd been ready to ignore the risk to our friendship, tired of resisting our chemistry, over all of the very sound reasons not to lock the doors and get gloriously naked with Eli.

But then someone tried to kill me.

And Eli had to save me.

And in the mess that followed we ended up accidentally betrothed—which meant no sex for me. Fae rules of love and matrimony meant that if I banged him while we experienced true love, we were *de facto* married.

"Both holidays," I said, louder than necessary. "We'll celebrate twice. Fuck him."

"Oh, I do wish you would," Sera muttered.

Christy snorted.

Sera squeezed my hand fondly. "Eli is not without his charms. You're engaged—and please don't take this wrong, sweetie—but you need to burn up some sheets or something. You're on edge."

"Understatement," Jesse said with a shrug.

When I made a crude gesture at my friends, Sera held up her hands. "Fine. Eli is hotter than Satan's knickers are in the summer, and Geneviève is as tense as a kitten in a room of rocking chairs and Rottweilers." She took a long drink of her bourbon, and then she added, "The point, Gen, is that you *like* him, and he obviously loves you. Why not give it a go?"

Sera pursed her lips at me when I tried to interrupt.

"And he was willing to do whatever it took to keep you safe," she continued. "For the fae, that's a *lot*. So, go to dinner with the king, and try to be a little kinder to Eli. His greatest crime—as far as I can see--is that he wants *you*."

My temper fizzled. She was right. Hell, they all were. I wanted to give in to Eli, but he *needed* to have a child. That child had to be carried by his wife, or his line of the fae would wither. He—literally—carried his ancestral memory in his blood. A child of the blood was required to pass on the living memory of his family.

He had to have a kid.

And I would never ever be a mother. Some people just weren't meant to be parents, and that *should* be okay. Freedom of choice ought to mean freedom to choose not to breed.

Eli, however, had to have a kid. There wasn't really a compromise there.

It wasn't even that fae law was unreasonable. There were exemption options for infertility or if a person was gay or lesbian—

or if they had a sibling who was able to pass on the family memories. *Elphame* Law addressed most concerns. There were even Temple partners who were magical enough to have multiple children. That enabled the exceptional cases—gay, lesbian, or second children-- to pass on their genes.

Eli was neither gay nor a second son.

I'd be asking Eli to sacrifice his ancestors if he was with me. I wouldn't do that to anyone I liked even a little, much less someone I trusted and respected as I did with him.

"It's complicated," I said quietly.

I didn't have consent to share the fae secret of ancestry. I couldn't explain why I was refusing him. And no one quite understood my aversion to parenthood. It wasn't *just* that I didn't want to pass on my fucked up genetic soup. That was a huge factor, but when Eli explained how we could avoid that . . . I still didn't want to be a parent. I wanted my life. My mission in my city. I *liked* what I had.

The only thing I'd change was . . . adding Eli.

He'd always been the flame that drew me. His glamour hadn't ever worked on me—either because of my witch blood or maybe my *other* blood. I wasn't sure what he looked like to others, but he'd always been perfect to me.

If not for the whole royal requirement and duty to pass on his ancestral lineage, I'd be naked with him by now.

Without quite meaning to, I looked over and met his gaze again, and this time, he walked over to the table. I guess a guy could only ignore being stared at so long.

"Christy. Sera. Jesse." He nodded at each of my friends. Then he looked at me. "Geneviève."

My insides turned to mush, and I realized I was *still* staring at him. It had been forty-three days since I'd thought we could be together. Forty-three days that we had been engaged. Two weeks since the last job together when we kissed and sparred. For the first time in my life, I couldn't even pretend to want anyone else. I'd never been monogamous, but something about Eli had me embracing monogamy—without the sex that should go with it. It was baffling.

I licked my lips unconsciously, and then blushed at his responding smile.

"What?"

"I said 'Would you accompany me?'" he asked, eyes twinkling as if he was aware that I'd completely failed to hear him the first time. He added, "To meet Lady Beatrice."

"Beatrice?" I echoed.

Eli nodded. "Indeed."

I had been avoiding the *draugr* queen since she's saved my life. I was being ungrateful, but I had complicated feelings. I was, awkwardly, related to her, and as best as I understood, she was my maternal ancestor—but she was a *draugr*. My job was killing her kind. So, yeah, it was complicated. "I'm not sure I—"

"She has requested my presence, and I am unable to visit her alone."

I startled. Eli was the strongest person I knew--other than Beatrice--and they had no discord. She knew who he was and had no desire to start a war with the fae. And while Eli had no great love for her, they'd spoken almost cordially.

"It would be inappropriate to see her without you with me. A fae who has pledged devotion must not meet unchaperoned with anyone sexually mature." His voice was level; he always had the same calm tone when I was panicking or about to lose my temper.

"Like you can't see her because you might be overcome and marry her instead?" I stopped short of saying that would be fine. It wasn't—and everyone who knew me knew it. I might not be interested in making his babies, or a future in *Elphame*, but I was exceedingly interested in Eli.

"Geneviève—"

"Monkey balls. This is that whole faux engagement that--"

"Not faux," Eli interjected. "My hand is already yours, sugar cookie." He gave me the sort of look that could melt knickers. "This was a formal invitation, Geneviève, which means I cannot visit her without accompaniment of my intended, a relative, or a male friend."

"I can go, Gen," Jesse offered.

Eli smiled. "Your offer of friendship is cherished."

"Faeries are weird," Christy said when Jesse's mouth gaped open —presumably at the realization that he'd called Eli a friend. They'd been at odds before my almost-dying-thing.

At that Eli bowed his head to her and to Sera and added, "It means much to have your regard."

Christy toasted him. They had a strange dynamic. Their friendship was natural, equal regard but not sexual tension. Sometimes I envied them.

Sera opened her mouth, but before she could say anything, I blurted, "Let's go, Eli."

We said our goodbyes, and I walked away with Eli. In some ways it was less awkward than trying to talk to him and my friends. They had turned to his side when he saved my life, risked his freedom to do so, and now, I was left with no defense other than "I don't want to." It was weak—because I couldn't spill his secrets *and* because they were a lot more accepting of my *draugr* heritage than I was.

We made it halfway to the bar door before I told him, "Your uncle sent an invitation."

"I know. He has commissioned six gowns so far in hopes that one will please you." Eli had the carefully calm tone again.

"Six *gowns?*"

"Did the invitation mention the presentation of the future queen?" He tucked my hand into the fold of his arm. "It's traditional."

I stopped walking. "Presenting the future qu-- . . . you mean *me?* The event is about presenting me?"

Eli nudged me forward. "I suggested he order you a sword or

three to assuage your ill mood in his direction. Not that I'll give him all the answers, Geneviève, but in this case, I thought weapons might interest you more than gowns. The armory has been working on several pieces."

"Flaming monkey balls."

"Geneviève, there are laws. You are my intended. I cannot change that," he said, again.

I glanced back at my friends. I was to be out tonight enjoying life. Not off to see a *draugr* queen or navigate Yule plans with the fae king. I mouthed, "Help?"

Sera gave me an encouraging gesture, and Jesse smiled.

Christy mouthed back, "Get some."

"I do like Christy." Eli chuckled at seeing her. "Smart woman. Wise. Perhaps you should listen to her advice."

"If only it were that easy." I leaned in and kissed him quickly, just a butterfly brush of lips. "There ought to be perks to this clusterfuck, and you naked under me sounds like an excellent idea."

"Indeed, bonbon." He growled a little.

I shivered at the desire that little noise sparked.

Smiling, Eli open the door for me. "What do you say to a faery bargain, Geneviève Crowe?"

The last faery bargain was for a kiss, and that had led to this engagement. Was I fool enough to make a bargain with Eli? When he stepped outside, his hand pressed against my low back, and my fracturing resolve grew even weaker.

"What are your terms?" I was pretty sure that Eve had felt this same flutter in a long-ago garden.

"Ones that include pleasure."

"Tell me more," I encouraged.

He smiled. There were a million sins in that look, and I wanted to commit every one of them twice.

# CHAPTER 3

Chapter 3

ELI'S CAR was waiting for us. He opened the passenger door, and I slid into the little blue convertible. If my hand brushed his stomach as I did so, it was purely accidentally, as was the way I looked up at him.

"Temptress."

I grinned. "Says the faery who just offered me my greatest desire."

He closed the door and was silent as he entered the driver's side of the car and eased us into the nighttime traffic.

Once we were zipping through the ever-busy night streets of New Orleans, Eli finally said, "If I could avoid the traditional presentation of the queen, I would."

"I know."

Eli added, "And if I wasn't who I am—"

"A bar owner? A liar?"

"Geneviève, I do not lie," he stated.

It was true in a manner of speaking. The fae never lie. Omit? Distract? Trick? Those are a kind of mistruth, too, but they are not what the fae consider a lie.

"A man who desperately wants to tell my world and yours to go burn while I lock us away and start to slake the needs we have," he said, as casually as anything.

"Oh . . . So, this bargain--"

"I would have picked a fiancé from the women there if I could have," Eli continued. "That was too much of a lie to do, though. I want none of them. No one in *Elphame* or here. Just you."

"So, we're really discussing this, then?" I glanced over at him. "No longer avoiding it?"

Eli sighed. "The fae are not renowned for being *direct* without reason."

"What's your reason?"

"A bargain, love. I want to propose a deal with you." His voice was somehow even more alluring here in the dark as we zipped through the city. "Are you clever enough to make a bargain with me, Geneviève?"

It would be wrong to throw caution away while he was driving, but his voice did things to my body that some men couldn't accomplish with their mouths.

"I'm listening," I said. It was the most I could offer without destroying the peace we were building.

Inside the car, this small bubble of safety where the monsters were unable to get to us, where our issues were tucked away as we rushed off to jobs or meetings, I felt like we could exist outside of time. I wanted that desperately, to ignore the reasons we couldn't be more. I wanted a simple world. And I suspected I wasn't alone in that.

The city was alive with too many decorations already. Oak trees draped in cheap balls and tinsel. Mardi Gras beads repurposed as Christmas beads. There was a defiance to the way the city approached festivity.

That defiance made sense to me.

Eli added, "We will go to *Elphame*. We will present ourselves to my family and world. . . unless you can tell me you don't feel the same. Do you care for me?"

"Obviously." I sighed loudly. "But some people are not meant to have children. I am n--"

"Did I ask that of you?"

"No but--"

"So, shall I tell His Majesty that we will be there for Yule? Or am I wrong about your regard for me? I can sever our tie, return there, and allow my uncle to select my future bride." He sounded calm, but I heard the trickle of fear in his voice. "Or you can make a bargain with me."

The thought of it, of Eli bedding and wedding another person, made my jaw clench. I couldn't, wouldn't send him away. "We are a terrible idea, Eli."

"Do I go home alone or do you feel as I do?"

"You're . . . not wrong about my feelings," I admitted. I was the least romantic, least appropriate choice for a man like Eli, but for reasons that I didn't understand, he *liked* that he had my heart. "A wiser man would leave me."

"I've never claimed wisdom, my dear Devil's Cake." He reached out and took my hand, and I knew that he was relieved. He sounded happier as he added, "I like danger, passion, a foul temper, talent for violence, fierce loyalty. I prefer warriors."

"My sword is yours," I swore. "You have that. No matter the future, you will always have that."

"Then I'll wait for the rest. Your heart. Your body. All of you, love. I want all of you."

I shivered again. We both knew he had a lot of my heart, and the only reason he didn't have my body was this damned engagement. The trouble with faeries, I was discovering, is that they have the patience to go along with their longevity.

I twined my fingers through his, keeping hold of his hand, even though I felt like a child for wanting to hold hands. My reaction to this touch was far from childlike, though. Touching Eli made me flush and my heart race. We'd kissed and had the sort of heated admissions that ought to be headier. This, though, was about my heart. His heart. Admitting that we wanted to find a way to be . . . more. That was scarier than sex or lust ever could be.

"So"—I cleared my throat—"what's this bargain?"

He laughed, and the sheer wickedness in that sound had my thighs clenching against the instinctive urge to yell, "Take me now." Instead I took a steadying breath and said, "Eli . . ."

"Date me."

"*What?*"

"Date me until Twelfth Night, and you will earn a favor," he said. "Anything you ask of me. One request. Whatever you most desire on that day. I won't say no."

I rolled it over in my mind. Anything? I could end the engagement. It seemed so simple. I stared at him and said, "Faery bargains are never this simple."

"Maybe this one is. All you need to do is truly date me," he said. "Not think about forever. Just . . . date me as if the rest wasn't a factor."

Part of me knew what he was implying. Most of me thought I could manage it. No rules, no strings, meant that we could revel in the thing between us.

"So, no rules? Just no holding back. We . . . date."

"And on the sixth of January, you have one favor," he clarified.

I paused, rolling it over in my mind. Twelfth Night, the Masquerade Ball that started Carnival season, was on January sixth. That was roughly a month from now. Between now and then, however, were a lot of events. Chanukah began in ten days. Yule and Christmas were roughly ten days later, and then New Year's Eve in six *more* days, and then the Twelfth Night Masquerade Ball six days later.

"Why are you offering so many details?" I asked. The last bargain he'd offered me was without much clarity.

"Because, Geneviève, I want you to understand the terms." He steered us onto the bridge, taking us out of the city into the ghost zone.

Something about the ghost zone, what was once the suburbs of most cities, was eerie. It was simply a ghost town of sorts, one that existed beside most cities. If you were brave enough or foolish enough, you could scavenge there; those who left their homes there, did so without taking most of their possessions. But the risk of *draugr* encounters in the ghost zone was high.

After the ghost zone was the Outs. I grew up there. Nature. People with more guns than sense. That was where Jesse and I met, neighbors in the Outs. My mother, Mama Lauren, was still there. I thought briefly about Chanukah. I'd have to take Eli to meet my mother if I agreed to this.

"Date, as in I play nice at the Yule presentation and you are at my side for *any* event during those weeks," I clarified.

"More or less. I want you to be yourself, but without thought or discussion of the future," Eli added.

"But any event?" I pressed. "You mean you'd meet my mother?"

"I would like that." His hand tightened on the steering wheel. "That, however, is not my primary goal. I just want . . . to be in the now with you."

I glanced at him, enjoying the moonlight on his profile. There was something about those cheekbones that just made me want to touch. Something about Eli that I barely resisted. My voice felt too loud even though I was whispering when I said, "If I didn't think about the future, we'd already have been naked, *bonbon. . .*"

He grinned at my use of one of his pet names for me and said, "All the more reason to date me."

I sighed.

Eli glanced at me then. "Give me these days. Let me be in your life. We were so close to progress, and then this"—he gestured between us—"engagement stalled us. I want us to be as we were."

My throat was parched with the wave of need he brought to the forefront of my every nerve, but I still had to add, "Whatever happens is not precedent-setting. When January sixth comes, we . . . reset."

He chuckled. "Expected, and accepted."

"Agreed, then," I said shakily. "I agree to your terms, Eli. We will date."

"I look forward to courting you," he said in that damnably calm tone, which meant that he was hiding his emotions.

I knew for sure then that I was fucked somehow, but the deal was done. I was going to let Eli into my life.

I swallowed hard and tried to sound just as calm. "For tonight, let's see what disaster awaits us at Beatrice's door."

# CHAPTER 4

A little later when we arrived in The Outs, the region that was once called Slidell, I had to concentrate not to send out a summons to the dead. I was on edge, and my magic was akin to a malformed pipe lately. Sometimes, I tried for a trickle and ended up with a flood. Sometimes, I tried for a stream and received a few droplets.

If I let my magic out tonight, I would wake the dead.

Or beckon the again-walking.

My affinity with death was an affront to some people—the faery king included—and I couldn't entirely blame them. I had a pheromone that meant the not-living found me irresistible. Not in a weird lets-get-naked way . . . okay, sometimes that way, too. Mostly, though, that response was because I was powerful, and power gets many a motor revving.

"What do you feel?" Eli asked, his tiny little convertible was bouncing along a road that seemed to be cobblestone.

"At least twenty *draugr*," I said, feeling the minds of those re-animated dead notice me. "Scattered bones."

Even if I tried not to reach out with magic, I would still feel death, absences in pockets of space. Graves. *Draugr*. My sense of the dead was simply there, like hearing or sight. Near me now was a man. Recently dead. I let the magic roll out in several directions. Three woman in the bayou. Six more men in the ground closer to the house. A child in a grave.

And a tangle of bones in a field . . . sixty. . . maybe up to eighty bodies.

"The ground is filled," I said, the horror of so many dead trying to connect with me slid into my voice. I knew without doubt that Beatrice had summoned Eli in order to make me come here. I didn't know why, but this much I knew.

Eli stopped the car under a willow that looked like it was here before the Civil War. The trunk was thick and old, and the wind through the branches felt like a song. Nature. Soil. Plant. Sky. These were the parts that called to my maternal heritage, and they were the parts of this world that also beckoned Eli.

The fae have an affinity for nature that makes it atypical for them to come to our pollution filled world, but despite the parts of the human world that were flawed, the Outs were like that. Without people, the land there was increasingly pure. Alligators, raccoons, feral pigs, snakes, life thrived and blossomed now that most people had to retreat to the cities. Nature was where people *visited*, but to live out here meant to know that there were Alpha Predators that looked like you but thought you were more of a snack than a friend.

I stood, feeling the humid air and listening to night birds sing and mosquitoes buzz. I'd give a lot for more time surrounded by this. I grew up out here, and if I could, I'd have stayed here.

"Lady Beatrice will join you in the courtyard," a well-dressed, once-human girl said. She was young in appearance, maybe fifteen upon her death, and she was dressed as if we were at an expensive Renaissance festival.

She'd *flowed* in the way of most *draugr*. She, I would presume, had been at the door, but now she was at my side.

"The house is . . . unusual," I murmured as we approached what appeared to be a small castle. As far as unusual Southern homes went, this might be the winner for ostentatiousness. It was vaguely modernized—no drawbridge—but there was a long stone bridge between parking and the massive front doors.

As we were walking toward it, I could see that that the bridge was over a moat. Under the moat were resting alligators.

"The Lady Beatrice had a canal put in. That way the bayou waters come closer and the water dragons can swim around her home."

"Dragons?" Eli echoed.

The girl pointed toward the one enormous alligator. "We didn't have these in the forest at home. Sir George is always here. The others come and go, but Sir George is my lady's pet."

"Of course she has a pet alligator."

"Do you mean the dragon?" the girl asked.

Eli motioned us forward. "Are there more dragons in the courtyard?"

The girl giggled and led us to the main doors. Wide enough to walk an elephant into the castle, and tall enough to allow a giraffe with minor stooping. Wooden. Medieval. The doors opened with minimal noise at our approach, as if by magic, but in reality, there were two women there. One had obviously pulled each door open, and when we stepped into the foyer, they marched the doors shut.

No one else was visible.

To the foolish, the house would seem to be the possession of an eccentric and her all-woman staff. The two very muscular women at the door were human. The *draugr* escort spoke so clearly she had to be at least two centuries old. Young *draugr* were never so articulate. They were all Caucasian, female, and I was glad to see that the Southern tendency toward racism in staffing was not at play here. There were plenty of places in the South where things had begun to change in the years before the cities put up walls. New Orleans was a leader in that change.

But New Orleans was a city that had a rich history of finding its own path, so no one who knew the city was surprised when we led the way.

"Are there any men here?" I asked as we crossed the foyer to exit into a small passageway that was stone-lined and lit by honest-to-Pete sconces.

Our guide gave a smile that was disturbing on such a young face. "If we have use of them, we send out for them."

Eli laughed, but all he said was, "As I was summoned, I am glad I chose to bring my fiancé with me tonight, then. I have no desire to be besieged."

"You *are* a fine specimen." The girl nodded at me, though, not him as she opened another door. This door was average-sized, although there was a salt line across it.

The girl met my gaze. "If you must keep a man, the fae are a good choice."

Before I could ask what in the name of duck dongles *that* meant, she was gone. Her giggles echoed in the hallway, but Eli and I were alone. A part of me, a surly not-interested-in-bullshit part of me that was typically my largest deciding factor, wanted to *flow* after her and demand answers. The less reasonable sort wanted to simply leave.

"Candy apple," Eli began, his hand already reaching for mine as if he knew that I might bolt. "We are here to meet with Beatrice."

I sighed. "I know. No beheading the hostess' staff."

It pained me to admit, but this was not a new conversation. Sometimes clients for my job—which was typically only beheading *draugr* or summoning dead relatives to answer a few lingering questions—were about as charming as angry weasels. My witchy genetics should lend me calm, but I guess that was countered by the *draugr* side.

"Is she coming outside or intending to chase after Eleanor?" Beatrice's voice rang out, sounding amused.

"Geneviève?" Eli prompted.

"I am here." I stepped out before Eli did so, bracing myself for something wretched. Instead I was met with the only other witch-*draugr* I'd known of. I didn't know if she had been born *draugr* and witch, or if she'd been made so.

Right now, she was standing beside two feral pigs.

"Son of Stonecroft," Beatrice said with a moderately deep bow in Eli's direction. Then she met my gaze. "*You* have been avoiding me, Geneviève."

I shrugged.

Beatrice looked at the pigs and made a sweeping gesture. I could swear they bowed their heads before leaving.

"Are those regular pigs?" I asked.

"What else would they be?" Beatrice was dressed in the most normal thing I'd seen to date, a simple black linen pantsuit. Her feet were bare. "Do I look like Circe to you?"

"Witch with feral pigs who bow to her? Yeah. A bit," I admitted.

Beatrice's expression twitched like she was trying not to laugh. I couldn't decide if it was a laugh that I was *right* or laugh that I was wrong.

I glanced away. Her courtyard, where we were currently stand-ing, reminded me of my childhood home because of the nature, and for a brief moment, I could swear that I'd met her before this past year. I stared at her. I would've known, right? Mama Lauren wouldn't have . . . I chased that thought away.

"What do you want?"

"To catch a killer," she said.

"Lydia was—"

"A pawn. I want to know who held her marionette strings." Beatrice motioned to me. "And why something of *mine* was targeted."

"I am not one of your feral pigs."

This time she did laugh. "You must realize that there are those who are unhappy with my rise to power, Geneviève. I am a *woman.* Most *draugr* of any importance are centuries old, and you may not be surprised to hear that the transition was not bestowed on many women. We were food or playthings or servants. Not equals."

"Okay but . . . what does that have to do with me? Why would being pissed at you mean I get injected?"

She shrugged. "I trust you know that answer."

I steadfastly ignored that question. I had enough clues to have a theory but I wasn't quite ready to address it. "What do you want from us?"

Beatrice straightened in a way that was less casual, more regal, and said, "I need a small favor from the *bougie-man* that makes *draugr* quake"

"No," Eli said. "Miss Crowe is quite busy over the holidays."

"I can pay for your work or I can be in your debt, Geneviève," Beatrice said, as if Eli hadn't spoken. "A substantial amount."

I was busy, and I had just agreed to date Eli—but both Beatrice's money and her help had been of use to me lately. Her payments for my investigation into the *draugr* venom murders added up to the equivalent of several years of work, and her assistance had been immeasurably helpful when I was injected with venom.

"Someone shot at me a few weeks ago," I said. "Figure out who, *and* cut me a check for my help, and I'll help you."

Beatrice pressed her lips together tightly. "It may be connected, but either way I would investigate *that* without a favor owed. You are too important to me for that offense to go unanswered."

I squirmed, and Eli gave me a searching look. Apparently my attempts to ignore this topic were about to be thwarted.

"Did she not mention our familial tie, young prince?" Beatrice said lightly. "I would cross even the boundary to your lands for my granddaughter's safety."

Eli didn't reveal his feelings on that matter--or answer the implied threat--and I wasn't about to follow that topic if it was possible to ignore it.

So, I tried to steer the conversation back to the job she had, "What do you need?"

"I'll have a gathering." Beatrice motioned, and a fire started blazing. The courtyard was medieval in style, giving the fire more of a pyre feeling than I liked. "You will come and see what you can glean from the minds of the guests. I simply need you to read their minds, find threats, determine loyalty. I can read humans, but not fae or *draugr*."

"So, the guests are. . . all dead?" I prompted.

"Except you and your escort."

Eli, my likeliest escort, looked at me. The flickering of flames made him look ominous; at least, I hoped it was the firelight that cast such shadows in his expression. I didn't want to ask if it was the party, the risk, my continued exhaustion, or the relationship to the dead lady that had him looking so irritated.

"I find it fascinating that you can read one of the fae, granddaughter. I'd imagine it's too intense to read him without fornicating," Beatrice offered, possibly trying to be helpful. "That much magic must be difficult to engage with clothing impeding you."

I swallowed. Energy was woven into Eli's very fiber. As a witch, it called to me. Touching him was nearly addictive, and admittedly, sometimes I wanted to intrude on his mind as I could with the dead, but the few times I'd done so were sheer accident.

"Reading Eli gives me a blinding headache," I confessed.

Then I looked at him and added, "The only time it didn't was when you invited me. I don't *try* to, I swear."

"But can you read me if you want to do so now?" he prompted.

He'd invited me to do so, but this was not about that. What he wanted to know was if I could do so without his consent. I hadn't tried. It felt wrong.

I shrugged. "Stray thoughts about me or us."

"More often now?"

I nodded. "It's like you left a door open."

"I see," Eli said, calmer than before.

I, however, did not see what he had realized. Something had

been answered for him, possibly for Beatrice, too. Now was not the time or place to ask him, though.

I looked at Beatrice, who was smiling at us. "I have tried with my friends. They get headaches. I can read the dead as if they are speaking aloud, though."

"Most *draugr* cannot do that. Nor can witches. Lauren would never have mated with Darius if she could have read him." Beatrice frowned. "Had I known he was targeting my granddaughter, I—"

"Explain the granddaughter thing," I interrupted.

"I had a child when I was a human. She mated with a human. That child grew to adulthood. She mated, as well." Beatrice pressed her lips together and shook her head. "It's blurry. Centuries pass. Humans age, mate, age more, die." She turned to meet my gaze. "Eventually, there was Lauren. Darius found her, and he decided to procreate with her. Now, there is you."

Eli took my hand, and I realized I was trembling. Both my witch and *draugr* genetics were standing before me. She was my ancestor, and I needed no necromancy to ask her questions.

"So, Darius knew about my mother because of you," I clarified. "Because you were a witch."

"I am still a witch, Geneviève." Beatrice sighed. "Sometimes when you're powerful, people want that power or simply want to end your life because of it, more so if you are a woman. More so when you are a Jew. Their hatred of us has changed over time, but only slowly."

I didn't ask if by "us" she meant hatred of witches, women, or Jews. Historically—and now--all three earned violence for the sheer act of living. We were scapegoated, murdered, and despised. Adding *draugr* to the list probably had changed very little for Beatrice—or for me.

"I don't like you," I pointed out. "But not because of any of those things."

"You dislike me because I am a *draugr*." Beatrice shrugged. "How is it different than hating me for the other things?"

"I don't *hate* you," I stressed. "I just don't like anything that tries to bite me."

"I shall remember that next time I am called to save your life." Her voice held all the laughter she didn't show in her expression. "But I do doubt that Lauren would agree that you ought to hate me for such a thing."

Beatrice walked away, staring into the edge of her moat, and I was left with very few options. Did I apologize to my dead ancestor? Or did I simply acknowledge my bias?

I hated being an adult.

I released Eli's hand and followed her.

"I may have . . . issues with *draugr* because of my father." I stood beside her and stared at the alligator filled canal. There were a lot of gators there. "He wanted to, err, breed me to as many *draugr* as he could. Use me . . . whether or not I consented. "

She nodded. "They attempted that with me several centuries ago. It was how I died."

Her voice was calm, but she let me see inside her mind. A human Beatrice. A captive Beatrice. A group of *draugr*. She fought them—and lost.

"I killed them slowly," she said, shrugging as if it was no significant feat. "When I regained my senses, I killed every one of them." She shrugged again. "And now I am queen."

I thought she was insanely fucking strong to turn her rage into power. Beatrice was old; the sort of old that meant my bones ached at the chill she radiated. When she died, dust and air would be all that remained of her, so her assault was longer ago than I could fathom. Her rage was still vibrant, and her pride at avenging herself was burning bright.

I met her eyes and said, "Fine. I like you some."

And she laughed, peals of joyous laughter as we stared at the alligators.

Then she leaned in and whispered, "The pigs were men once, granddaughter. I tolerate no man injuring me or what's mine." She glanced behind us to where Eli stood calmly watching the fire and us. Then Beatrice said, "He seems to care deeply for you. Fae blood is more nourishing, but if he hurts you . . . I will not forgive that. Had you not killed Darius, I would have. Once I discovered what he'd done, I was not pleased. I did not live here then. If I had . . ."

Just to be clear, I said, "You came here because of my mother."

"And you."

In a tone as close to Eli's calm as I could manage, I said, "Eli is mine, Beatrice. To hurt him is to enrage *me*." I touched her wrist. "Blood matters. I am grateful that you care for Mama Lauren, but . . . do not ever threaten my family or friends, or I will find a way to sever your head."

Beatrice kissed my forehead. "I am grateful to know you, grand-daughter." Then she *flowed* toward her castle. Her voice drifted back, filling the courtyard in an echoing sound. "There will be a dinner to celebrate my granddaughter's betrothal to the crown price of *Elphame*. Hear and be welcome."

I shuddered at the realization that her magic was undoubtedly carrying that invitation to *draugr* in her queendom.

Eli looked at me and said, "This job of hers will complicate things, Geneviève."

And my few weeks of relative calm ended. I felt it as surely as a warning knell. I was engaged to the heir of *Elphame*'s throne, with whom I'd made a faery bargain, and now declared family to the queen of the *draugr*, for whom I was ferreting out a threat. The holidays were no longer simply about irritation over dresses and random witch-haters who shot at me.

"Probably," I admitted. "But complication is what we do. Nothing is ever simple."

I took his arm and walked through the passageway of Beatrice's castle. No one stopped us. No one did anything other than open doors and bow deeply. Now that Beatrice had made her little proclamation, all eyes were going to be watching us.

# CHAPTER 5

In the span of one night, I'd agreed to a Yule Ball in *Elphame* and an "early Yule" party with the *draugr* queen.

Eli was silent as we drove back to the city, and I decided to simply wait to speak.

Finally, Eli parked alongside at a building in the Garden District that looked like it could have been one of the first in the city. A fence, stone not iron, surrounded his house. The house was almost so plain as to be unnoticed—which required a lot of magic. There was neither balcony nor gallery, neither porch nor Ionic columns, just a nondescript house in a very expensive area.

His home.

When we were standing at the door, Eli bowed to me. "You are eternally welcome in my home, Geneviève Crowe. I offer you my hearth and lintel. May you find shelter."

"That's some formal sounding stuff," I hedged. "I was here before and—"

"I cannot answer the questions you have right now." He held out his hand. "You will have the answer on Twelfth Night."

"You're making me nervous." I didn't take his hand, and he didn't lower it. Whispers rose up from some knowledge older than the stone that protected this house or the magic that flowed in my veins. "What does it mean if I take your hand right now?"

"That you accept my protection, my shelter. That you willingly enter this house." Eli stood, waiting.

Some part of me thought he'd been waiting longer than I knew, longer than I wanted to know.

He stayed there, hand outstretched, and said, "Come into my home, and let me shelter you, love."

"Is this how you normally treat dates?" I tried for lighter tone, for avoiding this tension that was in the air like magic between us.

"I've never dated." Eli shrugged slightly: elegant and utterly telling all at once. It was often to avoid discussions—usually for my benefit. Tonight, that was not the case. He felt embarrassed or awkward.

My staring at him all agog probably didn't help matters.

"You will be the first," he added.

"*What?*"

"I've fucked. I've had sex. I've spent time clothed and naked with friends and acquaintances, but dating is only done with intent among the fae."

My mouth was drier than the desert. "Oh. . . *fuck*. What if we didn't--"

"You agreed to date me, Geneviève. Are you reneging on a bargain with one of the fae?"

No matter how much I'd thought I understood, once more, I was fucked by my own hubris. Every human in history who had made a bargain with a fae believed they were clever enough to outsmart the fae. That *never* happened. Ever. And yet, I'd tried it twice.

"So dating, to you, is a precursor to . . ."

"Matrimony."

I sputtered, "It's not what it is to me, Eli."

He smiled. "You are bound in promise to the fae, which means fae law applies to you. You've even agreed to a date for the end of our courtship."

I stepped away from him. "This is not how to seduce me, Eli."

"You have a month to find a way to end our courtship," he reminded me. "And I have a month to make you accept the inevitable. You said 'I agree to your terms, Eli. We will date.' So, I do believe, my Divinity, that you now must either date me or break our bargain."

"What happens if I break the bargain?"

"The king of *Elphame* would determine your fate, as he is chief in my familial line." Eli shrugged again. "So, I ask again, will you date me or do you break our bargain?"

"Fine." I took his hand.

He lifted me into his arms bridal style. The smile he gave me would probably incinerate knickers in at least a three-mile radius.

My voice was squeakier than it had ever been as I asked, "Eli?"

"You are eternally welcome in my home, Geneviève Crowe. I offer you my hearth and lintel. May you find shelter." He stood under the keystone of the doorway. "In this world and my home, you are mine to safeguard."

I felt magic swirl around us, as if we were in center of a firestorm. Each spark of magic brushed against us with butterfly wings. Whatever vow he'd made was one my body accepted-- loudly. Desire surged like lava in my veins, and a moan of need escaped my lips.

I wasn't sure I could stand if I tried.

Arms around his neck, I pressed my lips to his. I wasn't sure if it was magic or lust driving us, but I *flowed,* carrying us both into the house. I'd never moved a second person this way, but I did. In a heartbeat or three, we were inside, upstairs, and somehow entangled on the floor.

"Geneviève." Eli pulled back and stared at me. His already bee-stung lips looked thoroughly kissed. "How did you . . .?"

"You're not the only magic creature here." I removed my shirt. It was too much of a barrier. "Please?"

He looked at me like he'd never seen my half-naked body. He'd stitched enough of me that I wasn't sure I had many secrets, but the way his gaze burned me up now, I thought I might be wrong.

Our gaze was only interrupted by the removal of his shirt.

"Rules?" he asked.

"Touch me."

He laughed, low and full of the same needs I was feeling. "That's a demand, Geneviève, not a rule."

My hands were on his skin already. Muscle under silk. Magic under flesh. I wanted all of it, all of him—but I wasn't going to end up married.

I kissed his chest, his shoulders, his throat.

"*Geneviève,*" he said. "Rules?"

"No intercourse," I said between kisses. I couldn't call it fucking because it wouldn't be, and I couldn't call it making love because I was afraid to say that. If a faery made love, truly made love, to a person who reciprocated that love, they were wed. It was that simple. "No intercourse. No . . . I want to, but I won't end up accidentally wed."

He looked unsurprised by my demand, but disappointed.

I knew damn well that he wasn't going to remind me of that rule, but I wasn't going to forget it. There were other options.

"What do you want, Geneviève?"

"Touch me. Kiss me." I stepped closer. "Please?"

Maybe it was the please, or maybe he simply understood me better than anyone else ever had. Eli took my hand and led me to a bedroom.

He leaned down and kissed me speechless. Then he ordered, "Stay right here. Strip. No jeans. No shoes. Nothing."

When he returned, I was naked. I don't know what I expected. Ravishing? Hurried grasping? I ought to have known better. Eli was fae—which meant he had the patience of nature.

In his hand, he had a bowl. "Turn onto your stomach, love."

I rolled over, and soon I felt the hot drizzle of oil. The room smelled of the clean nature of *Elphame*, so whatever oil it was, it was fae in origin.

At a word in his language, the room became completely dark.

I could see nothing. "Eli?"

"You asked for touch," he said, voice low and rough. "No intercourse. Merely touch."

I felt him place my hands along my sides, arrange my body as if I was clay in his hands. Then I felt him touch me. Slowly, steadily, hard, teasing, he rubbed and caressed *almost* everything in some fashion.

Time seemed to freeze. I could see nothing. The world was reduced to touch, scent, and sound. His murmured words, sighed, groaned as he explored my body. It didn't matter whether he was caressing sensitive spots or mundane. Under Eli's touch, everything was erotic. My feet, my calves, my hips. He was leaning his weight onto me, his forearms and muscular chest brushed my body as his rubbed along my spine.

And I realized he was atop me.

Straddling me.

Naked.

Eli was naked.

I felt the hard length of him nestled between my thighs. Unconsciously, I parted my legs further, and he leaned down so his chest was flat against my back and his lips were by my ear. "No intercourse, Geneviève," he taunted.

Goddess help me, I whimpered. "We can't, but this is . . . nice."

"Nice?" he echoed. He was a voice and pleasure in the dark, and I was certain that no one had ever made me so desperate so quickly.

He thrust his hips against me, groaning. Not entering me, merely taunting me with what I was refusing.

"Still just nice?" he asked.

I moaned and admitted, "More than nice."

By the time he had me roll over, exposing my naked chest and hips to his touch, I was wishing I could find a loophole in the no intercourse clause.

He parted my legs further. "Shall I be thorough, Geneviève?"

"Please. *Please.*"

His hands danced between my legs, but only for a moment, sliding along my most delicate skin, and then they were gone. In the dark, he plucked my nipples, massaging my thighs, my belly.

I could only feel and beg. "More, Eli. Please. *More.*"

In that moment if he'd asked me again, I'm not sure I'd have refused intercourse. Damn the consequences, I was shaking in need. Maybe he knew that, and it was why he didn't ask.

Instead he asked, "Is it so horrible to date me, bonbon?"

"No." I took several breaths. "Not horrible."

He was quiet, breathing as needy as mine. I heard the strain in his voice as he asked, "Would you still only like touch or would you like a kiss? Or more?"

I knew what would happen if I agreed to *more*, and as much as I wanted his mouth on my body, I wanted to *see* him when we burned that bridge. So, I reached out into the darkness and trailed my hand over his hip. The oil from where his naked body had been against mine made my hand glide over skin and muscle.

"Touch," I asked, demanded, begged.

"Yes."

So, I stroked him as he touched me. We were nothing but hands and skin and moans in the darkness. I wanted more, but I wasn't sure I could endure it.

# CHAPTER 6

I'd slipped out of Eli's house in the night. I slid away from his embrace and fled. He said I was to be myself, and well, my self wasn't great at the softer side of dating. My world was tilted by the intimacy we'd shared—and in my usual way, I ran from emotions.

Honestly, sometimes I felt sorry for anyone who tried to date me.

I liked Eli more than I'd cared for anyone, and I suspected most of our conflicts boiled down to my innate panic at feeling tender things in his direction. Some girls had pretend-weddings as children, fantasies of gowns as teens, and thought about the future as young women. Me? I thought about monsters. I dreamed of swords or trips. I fantasized about the sort of sex that made grown men blush.

The odds of finding anyone who found my messed-up brain and monster-tainted body appealing were so thin that I never really expected to deal with it. I'd always been the person that nice boys and girls took for a spin before settling down. I was the mid-life crisis car, the thrill-ride, and not the sort anyone wanted to marry. I chose that. I highlighted my traits that kept me firmly in the "makes a great mistress, not a wife" box.

So, I was not prepared to wake up the next evening to a gift-wrapped faery-wrought dagger and antique bottle of the same oil Eli had rubbed all over me. I sniffed the bottle and couldn't help but smile.

The post also delivered a piece of parchment with elegantly written instructions for a "celebratory holiday gathering" hosted by the dead-chick-in-charge of the *draugr*. The dinner at Beatrice's castle was later that week.

No rest for the dead, or half-dead, I supposed.

BY THE TIME the gala rolled around, I'd procured a total of three dresses, contacted my mother to tell her that I'd be bringing an extra guest the next week for our holiday dinner, and managed to not feel completely overwhelmed by my fiancé.

The latter took a lot of effort. Eli sent gifts each day: a brooch, a poison ring and pendant set, a scarf with a beautiful wire embroidery that was perfect to garrote someone. When he saw me—a brief moment here or there—he bent me into a dip and kissed me, or he pulled me into a hallway and pulled me tightly to his always aroused body.

Every embrace he whispered, "No intercourse?"

My resolve was not . . . weakening. I would not be married because my needs were spiking so intensely. I was stronger than that.

By the time the night of the gala was upon us, I was ready to torment him until he was as maddened with need as I had become. I chose not one of the reasonable holiday dresses I'd planned, but an ivy column gown. My throat was covered by a high collar, and my arms were bare. The back had a teardrop cut-out, the bottom of which was scandalously low. The left slit exposed a long thin dagger—Eli's gift--strapped onto my thigh.

If I stood perfectly still, I was as covered as a matron. Only my arms were bared. If I walked or turned my back to him, bare flesh and weapons glinted at him. And if the light was bright, most of the dress was nearly translucent.

Eli met me at my home—and the light was, indeed, bright enough that his eyes dilated in desire. "You are radiant, Ms. Crowe."

I twirled, and yes, I'd practiced to get that twirl just right. My leg with the dagger practically winked at him, and the hair pins that he'd gifted me that day were holding my tumble of blue hair in place. Tiny little sheathed throwing knives with jewels at the top held my masses of hair in an elegant up-do that had taken Sera and I an hour to create. The effect was, mostly, to expose my back, but it also let me wear his gifts.

"Winter at her finest looks less lovely than you," Eli said, voice nearing reverence.

In fairness, my escort was gorgeous. Eli had elected to dress to his heritage. No glamour. No mortal attire. He was wearing leggings that made clear that his legs were all muscle, tunic, vest, and a circlet crown. The most unusual item was a codpiece that matched the crown. Although the codpiece was barely visible under the tunic, the glint of jewels made it challenging not to look.

"You test my resolve," I admitted.

"I *do* try, Geneviève." He looked my over. "Your loveliness and strength would shame the queens that came before you."

There was no reply that seemed suitable, so I brushed my lips over his gently and prompted, "Shall we?"

ARRIVING at the castle again was different. Everything felt different, tonight. This would be our first official outing as an engaged couple. A couple. The mere thought made my stomach twist in anxiety.

"You have been busy," I said as we parked.

Eli met my gaze. "I wanted to show you that I have no need to take up *all* of your time, peach pie." He offered me his arm, and we approached the massive doors. "Being with me will not consume your freedom."

I nodded.

"It's not you," I reminded him. "Any woman would be lucky to be chosen by you."

He stilled briefly, not quite bringing us to a stumbling halt, but slowing us. "I would remind you that we have a bargain, Geneviève Crowe."

I winced.

"You are not to be thinking of the future." He began to walk, and I stayed in step—even when he added, "If I have not satisfied you with my touch or my gifts, you will tell me, so I might correct my errors."

I blushed despite myself. "You have not failed to satisfy me."

"You left without word. One might find that worrisome," he said lightly.

I laughed. "It was that or fear that I'd fail in my own resolve. You are a very thorough lover. Already. Even with . . . not . . ."

The look he gave me was enough to make me well aware of my lack of knickers.

"You are remarkable as well, Geneviève."

Then we reached the door and followed Eleanor to a ballroom, where we were swept into Beatrice's soiree. Her attention was drawn to us as if she could sense our arrival. Perhaps, however, that was the ripple of whispers that carried through the ballroom.

I let Eli handle the speaking and mingling. I followed his lead as we danced. I meekly stayed at his side to enjoy hors d'oeuvres—and I slid in and out of the minds of the well-dressed corpses walking around the ballroom. Only about fifty people were present, so the search and scan wasn't terrible. I was as uncomfortable as a lamb invited to the side door of a restaurant.

"*You are a wolf,*" Beatrice said, her voice a reminder that she could read me, too.

I didn't flip her off, but I thought the visual at her and felt her answering laughter.

*"Hunt our enemies for me, wolf."*

I hated to admit it, but I was mollified by her faith.

As I let my magic roll out, sliding in and over the cacophony of voices, I thought that this was not that dissimilar to reading the dead in the graveyard. I'd expected minds like the *draugr* I usually encountered. They were nothing but feral needs.

Unlike the disjointed minds of the newly walking, however, these were orderly minds. Pretentious. Bored. Judgmental. There were thoughts of hunger, but it was more often hunger for power. These were not the *draugr* who would be found on the streets of the city. They struck me as the sort who had chefs or delivery or whatever service posh dead folk used for their food.

*"I would drink her dry."*

*"Why do we need to allow his sort here?"*

*"Vintage fae juice. What a lovely pet he'd make."*

*"Stupid bitch."*

*"When Guarin was in charge, we weren't so burdened by rules."*

The last one was the first that felt angry in ways that were alarming. I reached out with my magic until I found the speaker. He was tall, and from the look of him, he'd died before reaching full maturity. His face was soft, and he lacked the tell-tale texture of facial hair. He was trying to compensate for his physical appearance of youth with austere dress. His only concession to holiday frivolity was an ostentatious medallion-broach-thingy. A ruby as big as my thumb-nail was surrounded by emeralds.

*"Thou shalt not suffer a witch."* He glanced at Beatrice, at me, and then he started toward me.

"Harold," Beatrice said, *flowing* to my side as if she had intended to be there all along. She stood in front of me. Her assistant, servant, whatever-she-was Eleanor arrived with two more women.

The room felt charged, and the thoughts were weirdly gleeful.

*"How charming!"*

*"Entertainment!"*

*"Is it vulgar to accidentally cut the faery for a sip of blood?"*

I glared at that one, a rather regal looking woman who had been grandmotherly upon death, and growled. "Mine."

"Witch." Harold tried to push passed Beatrice. "We have no use for witches."

Simultaneously, Beatrice said, "Back up."

Harold drew a respectable-sized blade and tried for Beatrice's throat. Her guards were there, but I was literally inches from her, so I pulled her backward to safety.

Harold's knife sliced my arm from shoulder to near my elbow.

"Witches have no right—"

"Duck fucking weasel." I kicked Harold and snatched his machete. "I'm getting sick of hearing that nonsense."

It was too much of a coincidence to ignore. Harold was somehow tied to Weasel Nuts shooting at me. I pushed that thought at Beatrice, who transformed from elegant to feral in less time that it took to blink.

"Take her out of here," Beatrice said.

Eli had my hand, but we were jerked apart as Eleanor moved me further away from Harold. Then in a little more than a heartbeat, Eli and I were both outside.

"You are a gift," Eleanor said. "Her Majesty will dispatch with the vermin."

Then she was gone, and I was swaying precariously over ground that was filled with bodies, outside a castle where there were ancient *draugr* I very much didn't want to adopt.

# CHAPTER 7

I f I wasn't mistaken, there was a poinsettia petal in my cleavage. It was hard to tell because I was losing blood faster than the average tourist losing their dinner after midnight. It could have been blood, but I thought it was a petal.

Admittedly, it was a toss-up between bleeding and vomiting on my "things I dislike" list, but in this particular moment, I was thinking I'd have preferred puking.

"Are you well enough to stand?" Eli was at my side, looking more warrior than prince. He looked fierce, even as he stepped over the already-rotting corpse.

"I'm good." I nodded. I was standing. Well, I was leaning on a cooperative oak tree outside Beatrice's castle, but that was *like* standing.

"How bad?"

"I'm upright." I shrugged, clutching my new blade as if I'd be any use against the sort of *draugr* inside the castle.

"I want you to get me inside the car before my blood spills onto the ground."

So far, I'd held my arm so the gash was angled upward, so nothing had dripped to the soil.

Yet.

"I give it about ninety seconds." I shoved off the oak's trunk.

Eli scooped me up and all but ran to open the passenger door on his little blue convertible. I was ready to leave, not argue with whatever Thom, Rick, or Marie I summoned if I bled on soil.

Inside the safety of the car, Eli said, "Lower your arm, cupcake."

"Can't. I'll ruin the seats." Blood wasn't great for Eli's butter-soft leather seats seats. They weren't going to come to life, but I still had no desire to bleed on them.

If my magic wasn't fucked sideways lately, I wouldn't be bleeding. Trying to avoid the *draugr* meant I'd been careless. My temper was lousy.

"Least I got a new toy." I patted the machete in my lap. "And Beatrice owes me."

"You could have died."

I don't know if I replied. I was sleepy, the sort of sleepy that only seemed to come with massive blood loss. I closed my eyes for just a moment, but somehow my moment was almost an hour.

When I opened my eyes, Eli was driving through the city with the sort of speed that came of fae reflexes and arrogance. I was in far more danger from my average week than his driving though, so I just let myself relax as much as could.

When he scraped the undercarriage to park directly in front of the door, blocking the side walk, I didn't argue.

And I didn't argue when he half lifted me out of the car. All I knew was that we were on the sidewalk and then inside. No blood on the soil. No dead summoned to me. That was a victory.

Machete loosely in my hand, I leaned against the building while Eli rolled up the steel doors that protected the building. Mostly it was for thieves, but sometimes the newly-dead were apt to crawl into a person's home. No one liked that. Finding out that a biter was watching you was creepy. Hell, dead or not, it was creepy. I like some weird, but stalkers are another thing entirely.

My eyes were drifting closed with all these thoughts of sleep.

"Plum pudding?" Eli's voice was falsely cheery.

So, I made a rude gesture.

"I'd prefer you be awake when we consummate our love," he said.

I opened my eyes. *Our what?*

Rather than answer, he opened the door and ushered me inside the bar. We were, obviously, late enough that the bar was closed, and for that I was grateful. Eli's bar staff was alternately tense and mothering with me. No one was outright unpleasant, but I think they worried that I was about to get their boss killed.

That was how I'd first ended up cozying up to him. No human was strong enough to fight again-walkers. Eli was. I was . . . and *that* was how I ended up here. Again. Tonight was to be a simple dinner, but somehow, I was bleeding.

"My pretty dress," I said.

Eli set the locks and rolled the steel. "You look gorgeous, buttercream, even with the blood. A warrior goddess."

I grabbed a bar towel. They were clean, bleached, and absorbent. It wasn't the worst bandage ever.

"Let me get the kit so I can st—"

"Absolutely not." I dropped the new blade on a table. Now that we were secure, I could be unarmed.

I wound the bar towel around my arm. I wouldn't wake anything here, but I'd still rather contain my blood.

We were alone in the bar. Just me, Eli, and my weapons. I glanced at my dagger. It needed wiped down, and with one arm holding my cotton bar towel on the other, I was in no shape to do it.

"My stitching is excellent," Eli said, as if he was insulted. For all I knew, he was.

"Did I say otherwise?" I walked behind the bar, putting the long expanse between us.

Eli stared at me, as if his fae bullshit was going to work. It wouldn't, although that smile of his was a sort of magic.

"Geneviève Crowe, you are being unreasonable. Sit down and let me stitch--"

"Using my full name would only work if I was a faerie." I poured a drink for each of us. Shaky, but mostly in the glasses.

"Are we calling out species, delectable witch of mine? " His tone was falsely light—which meant I'd probably violated one of the eight hundred and thirty-seven rules of dealing with faeries.

Okay, admittedly, I didn't know how many rules there really were. I gave up counting somewhere around eighty. I tried, legitimately tried to have peace with Eli, but we had a complicated relationship.

"I'm not *really* yours," I muttered, stepped closer with both drinks in my working hand.

"You're dripping on the wood." He gestured to the floor.

When I looked down, he moved closer. It was the sort of speed neither of us usually used in front of the other. He hid his; I hid mine. We're complicated.

The blue-tint from humming bar lights that were still on even though the bar was closed cast an ethereal glow over him, highlighting his inhuman beauty. No human was as striking as even the least of the fae, and after our brief trip to *Elphame*, I discovered that no faery was as beautiful as Eli.

Not because he was fae.

Not because witches were susceptible to them or anything so convenient.

It was just Eli.

Or maybe I still had a lot of pent-up feelings in his general direction. Our one encounter that led to orgasms wasn't enough. Maybe we just had too much unresolved lust and it made him somehow *more* attractive—which, incidentally, was fucking horrifying because he was already stunning.

He took his drink, tossed it back, and waited for me to do the same.

"Just give it a minute," I said, peering at the gash on my arm.

"Why are you being difficult, Geneviève? Do I stitch you poorly? Have I caused undue pain?" His hand was alongside my cheek, hovering in that sliver of space where if I sighed, he'd be touching me. "You are seeping blood."

"'s not *you*. I want to know how fas' I'll heal now. This is an oppur. . . *oppurtuney*."

He gave me an incredulous stare. "Not even *you* are this brash, love."

Silently, I removed the now scarlet-red cloth from my arm. The bleeding was slowing some. Congealing. That was new. As I watched the edges of the ten-inch cut on my upper arm were straining, as if they could touch.

It was, in truth, a bit horrible to see my skin seeming to reach out. It was, well, not what human flesh did, not what witches' skin did. This was a result of my paternal heritage. Creepy arm thing? Gift from doubly-dead dad.

He was dead when he fathered me, but his status was revised to permanently dead at my hand. But as any Southern-born person knows, the sins of the father don't end at death—even two deaths. I was a freak of nature, neither dead nor alive. And after an awkward attempted murder that didn't take, I was changing.

"Geneviève?"

I looked up.

"You have lost too much blood. You are drifting." Eli gestured at me, and I could see the spectral shape seeping out of my body, as if my shadow had taken on life.

"Well, that's no good." I realized I had slid down the wall right about when Eli caught me. Propped in his arms, I took a good long drink of the bottle of white liquor he held out.

*Tequila.*

Life was always better with tequila. Eli and I were better with tequila. Hell, everything was probably better with tequila. War? Famine? Plague?

"Fucking tequila heals everything."

"Of course, it does, plum pudding. One more," Eli urged, tilting the bottle for me as my hands were feeling less than grippy.

"Is grippy a word?"

Eli shook his head, but I wasn't sure if that was disapproval or disagreement with my choice of "grippy" as a word.

"I'm stitching that cut, Geneviève."

"Pro'lly good plan after all, muffin."

He laughed. "Muffin?"

"'s what you call me. Stupid pas'ry words." I closed my eyes.

"You like it," he whispered, kissing my forehead as he settled my head gently on the bar floor. "And you like me."

I did, of course, but I wasn't dazed enough to admit *that*.

# CHAPTER 8

When we were alone, I allowed myself to nestle into Eli's arms. It was the sort of thing that I ought to avoid, a vulnerability that I seemed only able to share with him. Sometimes, I felt like it was what I needed most in the world, though, a safe place to rest. I was stitched and had consumed two bottles of liquor. I wasn't feeling my best, but I was coherent again.

Eli held me so that my cheek was on his chest, and he stroked my hair. It was soothing to be held, to be safe, and to feel cherished.

"Dating you is more stressful than I expected," Eli murmured.

I looked up at him. "This is me. What I do. Who I am."

He sighed. "Geneviève, I *know* these things, but I had hoped that dating during your seasonal lull would include more romance and fewer stitches. Is it so much to ask for some time where we can dance and avoid bleeding?"

A flash of guilt rolled over me. "I wore a pretty dress for you. Seductive, and wore gifts you bought to show my regard." I turned my head and kissed his chest. "We danced."

Eli looked at me so intently that I squirmed in embarrassment. "You read about fae customs. You wore my gifts because you *researched* my people."

"There *are* a lot of rules. I got one right, but I get a lot wrong."

"You *researched*," he repeated in a voice filled with wonder.

"Fine. Maybe I read everything I could find on fae rules over the last few years," I hedged. "I felt like I offended you often, and I just . . . you matter to me, Eli."

He held me in silence for several moments. "Enough to take no more jobs for the next three weeks?"

I thought about it. In terms of the things he asked of me over the last year, it was perhaps the easiest request so far. I nodded. "You have my word: no more jobs between Yule and Twelfth Night. We'll call it a witch bargain."

He chuckled. "Terms for this 'Witch Bargain'?"

"No talk of weddings."

"Done."

"Nothing that happens as a result of festivities is precedent-setting," I tried to sound calm, but Eli's slow smile said that he knew exactly what I was saying. Festivities often involved desserts, some of which left me as drunk as a human with a fifth of whisky.

"Of course, my crème brûlée." His voice sent welcome shivers over me. "I cannot change the law of intercourse for my people, but . . . I can touch you as often as you allow."

If I wasn't fighting to keep my eyes open, I'd be ready for that. The combination of blood loss and daylight wasn't doing great things for me. I was drifting in and out of sleep until evening came. Eli was asleep finally, so when I woke, I started to slip out of bed.

Eli, half-asleep, caught my hand. "If you need space, stay here in the guest room. I'll go to my room."

I paused. "I'm feeling better now. I could go h--"

"I want you here, Geneviève." Eli met my gaze. "Will you stay with me?"

The way he said it didn't feel like he meant just for the night, but that was all I could offer in the moment. No sharing a lover's bed. No letting them stay in mine. It was frightening to stay, but I trusted Eli with my life regularly. Surely, I could trust him with my heart for a few weeks, too.

I crawled closer to him and nestled against his side.

"So, dating you involves sleep-overs?" I asked, voice as light as I could manage.

"I'd like it to," Eli said. "I know it's not your preference, but let me have today."

"And tomorrow?" I asked.

Eli knew me well, which he proved by adding, "This is a guest bed, Geneviève. It's not *my* bed. You are simply staying in my guest room. Say the word, and I'll go to my bed. Alone."

Maybe that wasn't romantic for most people, but it made me want to swoon. Instead I kissed him. "I'll stay."

"I'll get you breakfast," he said.

Within moments, Eli held out a steaming coffee cup of vodka with a dash of grenadine and a couple cherries. Liquor was magical with my biology. Bring on the booze. It was a key part of what kept my biologically-irrational body running.

"You're smarter than anyone that attractive ought to be," I grumbled as I reached for the mug.

Eli laughed and helped me sit up. "A little fruit for the pain?"

"Yes." I reached out further, but we could both see my arm shake. Fruit, unlike liquor, made me tipsy, but after my failed experiment, I could stand a little tipsy in my—. . . I glanced at the wall clock.

He steadied the cup as I wrapped my hands around it and drank.

"Do you know how worried I was, Geneviève?" Eli asked, voice heavy. Worse yet, he was using my real name instead of whatever pastry or dessert he chose to use as a term of endearment.

I'd rather be called food stuffs than my name—especially when it sounded so ominous. "I suggested I go out without you, so—"

"Endangering yourself alone is no better." Eli walked away. He sounded increasingly calm as he added, "Beatrice sent word while you were recovering. Harold has ceased."

"Ceased?"

"Existing," Eli clarified. "She also sent a suggestion."

"A suggestion?"

"For an elixir that might aid your recovery," he said evasively. "I procured the supplies."

Then he left, and I was too damn weak to pursue him. Honestly, I hadn't intended to let some dead guy practice his subpar threshing skills on me. I hadn't meant to get injured, but was it so bad that I took advantage of my bad luck to see if my healing had changed since my semi-murder earlier that year?

It really *wasn't* my worst idea the last year.

"Eli?" I started, but it wasn't Eli in the doorway this time.

Alice Chaddock stood there. "Good morning, grumpy!"

"Alice, why are you h--"

"Oh you poor thing!" She leaned down to fluff my pillows, giving me an awkward up-close look at her cleavage. "You look even worse than normal."

"Thanks."

"I *felt* that you needed me," she continued in her cheery breathy voice. "I'm sure of it."

"Alice, you're *human*."

"We bonded, though. Witch thing." She waved her hand around.

I didn't think I could bond humans, but I'd accidentally bonded two *draugr* to me. Honestly, I really had no idea if bonding a regular human was possible, but on the off chance that Alice was my responsibility, I kept her around.

That, and the queen of the *draugr* was likely to kill her if I didn't, and I'd feel guilty. I hate feeling guilty.

"Fine. You are the best servant ever." I grinned up at Alice.

She rolled her eyes at the thought of being a servant. Alice could probably buy the whole block my building was on—and not dent her bank account too much.

"Now, *go away*," I muttered.

Alice laughed. She was growing on me, although last week she'd tried to be helpful and used steel wool on one of my knives. I'd explained that I liked the guy who sold me my last sword more than her. I certainly liked my actual friends better, but Alice waved all of those facts away.

"I'm going to do your face." She opened her bag, designer and expensive, and started pulling out her torture devices. "I was afraid you'd look terrible for the party."

"The party was last night," I admitted. Then I closed my eyes, pretended not to be able to think of all the ways my life could be better if I simply stabbed Alice. She took more energy than anyone had a right to do, but my choices were either kill her or keep an eye on her.

Only one of those was *actually* an option.

"I don't understand what Eli sees in you," Alice said, staring at me as if I had become a math problem she might could solve. "Let's at least get some eyeliner and rouge—"

"Alice, I was injured. I lost a lot of blood and—"

"That's why you look so pale!" She thrust her wrist between my lips, scraped the skin on my teeth. "Here. Top off."

I shoved her away, hard enough that she stumbled, even as my teeth descended to bite. "Stop that. I don't need the taste of your perfume in my mouth."

My so-called best friend pouted. Perfectly outlined, perfectly painted, smudge free lips jutted out like a child denied a treat.

"I'd be sad if you died, you know?" Alice flopped onto the bed beside my feet. "Tres gets impatient with me. And Beatrice is scary. And"—she darted a guilty look toward the doorway—"I don't think Eli even *likes* me."

"You belonged to a hate group opposed to *him*," I pointed out once my teeth retracted. "And you tried to kill me. He likes me."

"I said I was sorry!" Alice sounded genuinely upset. "And no one told me SAFARI was a hate group."

"It's called the Society Against Fae and Reanimated Individuals. That wasn't a clue?"

Alice patted my feet through the duvet. "I wasn't enlightened then. I am now. . . but Eli is still so grumpy with me. I like you, now."

"Alice, honey," I said, keeping my voice very level. "You tried to kill me just a few months ago. To a faery, that was yesterday."

She stared, blinked, and finally whispered, "He *time* travels?"

I opened my mouth, and then I closed it without saying a word. What was there to say? If she wasn't really as gullible as she appeared, this was the longest con ever. Her stepson, Tres, swore she'd been exactly the same since they were in school together.

Yeah. She went to the same college with him and then married his dad. Of course, my own parents were a special sort of wrong, too. My deadbeat dad wasn't even alive, much less anywhere within range of my mother's age, when I was conceived.

Alice wandered away while I was thinking. Honestly, I wasn't recovered enough to deal with her. I could hear her, presumably washing her wrist from the sounds of the bathroom sink.

"She's willing to help you," Eli said when he walked in. "I had her delivered here—"

"She's not a take-out meal."

He leaned in the doorway, giving me enough space that I figured I must be looking less like death. He was polite when I was healing, pushy when I was well or bleeding.

"Do we even know that blood would help?" I tried to stand, not quite pushing to my feet but sitting upright and swinging my feet to the floor. I was preparing.

Eli came to my side as I stood, not infantilizing me but near enough to catch me when I tumbled--which I would've if he wasn't there. He'd swept me into his arms, cradling me for a moment. "You are the least obedient patient I've met, Geneviève."

"I waited for you before trying to stand." I rested my head on his shoulder.

He said nothing, and we stayed there listening to singing from elsewhere in the house. Eli and I exchanged a surprised look. It was the sort of voice that should be immortalized, twangy enough to burn up country music charts and soulful enough to make sinners repent.

"That's *Alice*?"

"I had no idea."

We stayed there, listening. Perhaps it sounded a little better because the acoustics were so phenomenal here, but either way, she could sing. I enjoyed it. Eli obviously did, too. He began to waltz, as if we were at a ball.

"Can we *not* experiment on you? And can we avoid death, excessive bleeding, or dismemberment until the new year?"

"Yes . . .?"

Eli smiled and added, "And what if we just put a little of Alice's blood in a martini? Beatrice suggested that it might aid your health."

I scowled at him. "Fine."

"Alice?" Eli called. "Could you bring Ms. Crowe's breakfast?"

A moment later, she came into the bedroom with a beautiful glass of pink vodka. There was a lemon twist and cherry. I guessed the cherry was to hide the real source of the pink. Alice was as clever as she was bouncy.

In a chipper tone, she announced, "I made it myself!"

I held out a hand. I knew that the pink tint to my martini was a result of additives she took from her vein.

Truth be told, I'd considered trying blood, but it felt wrong. I had moral qualms about drinking from anyone, and I was fairly sure I shouldn't have to do so. I'd existed for most of my twenty-nine years with a mix of vodka, green smoothies, and assorted herbs. Never sick. Rarely tired. Since the venom injections, I was always tired, and no amount of liquor made me feel satisfied.

I took a tentative sip of my blood-tini. "This tastes different."

Alice looked at Eli. "I made it *just* the way he said to."

"Hmmm." I drank half of it. "It's good. Spicy, though."

She folded her arms and looked at Eli before blurting, "That's the blood. He made me. I wasn't going to lie, but--"

"Okay." I drank the rest.

Eli rolled his eyes at me, and Alice stared at me in surprise. It was sweet that her loyalty to me made her unable to lie.

Honestly, it didn't have much taste. Vodka. Touch of spice. My blood martini was surprisingly unexciting, despite the anxiety that I'd felt even considering it. The reality was far less exciting than my fears, and I felt like my stress was washing away—or maybe that was my hunger fading.

I wanted to be normal, whatever *that* was. I wouldn't ever be human, so *my* normal was a little different. I didn't mind the witch part, mostly didn't even mind necromancy. I minded my paternal DNA. A lot. I was terrified of being a *draugr.* I grew up as the equivalent of a rose garden to every bee in range—but instead of bees, I attracted the dead. They were drawn to me, and I responded as well as anyone would when dead things popped up everywhere.

I killed them.

What did it mean if I was *like* them? If my genetic soup was more dead than witch? Necromancy worked by pressing life into the dead, and apparently, it worked on *draugr,* too. I shoved life into them, and suddenly, they functioned as if they were a century old. Coherent. No longer slavering toddlers. What would happen if I was changing? Would I be unable to kill them? Would I be unable to heal? To summon the natural dead? Maybe it wasn't that I wanted normal. Maybe I wanted to control who I was, what I was. Define myself.

"How do you feel?" Eli took the glass, unfolding my fingers from the stem, and I realized I'd licked up the last drops of my blood martini.

"Embarrassed." I paused. "Better though. Energized."

Alice tossed herself at me. "You do need me! I knew it. Like it's our *destiny*!"

"I . . . umm . . ."

She straightened up. "It has to be fresh, but I'll be *right here* whenever you need me."

It had to be fresh? That was news, and not the good sort. Questions popped around like manic bunnies in my brain. How fresh? How often? How much? Was it all the same? Should we test the theory?

But Alice was already gone, and I doubted she had the answers I needed. I glanced at Eli.

"We'll figure it out," he said, undoubtedly seeing my worries and questions. Obviously, the answers weren't ones he knew or he'd tell me.

I swallowed my panic and nodded. One crisis at a time.

When Alice returned, she had a cocktail shaker in her hand. "I made more. Just in case."

Eli held out my glass, and Alice filled it. "I'll mix up another batch before I go."

She gave me a little finger wave like she was in a parade, and then she was gone again.

"Hey, Alice?" I called after her. "I like your singing."

Her squeal, presumably a happy noise, was all the answer I got. Okay, maybe she *was* growing on me. The whole attempted murder thing was still a factor, but she was so damnably cheerful that I couldn't entirely resist.

"We're friends, aren't we? Alice and I are friends," I whispered to Eli. "I . . . *like* Alice."

"You were too hungry to think clearly," he offered. "Like a duckling imprinting on a food provider . . ."

Alice's voice rang out, louder this time, as she presumably was mixing up another batch of blood and vodka for me. She was singing an old blues song, again managing to make it sound like it ought to be on a stage.

"I'm doomed if she keeps feeding me *and* singing."

Eli laughed. "Drink up, butter cream. You sound more like yourself already."

I hated how right he was, but I felt alert. I felt focused. Alice had just rescued me.

Although Eli didn't point out that I'd been off since my attempted-murder, we both knew it. And it wasn't just the appearance of fangs now and then or the weird energy. My necromancy had been erratic before I was injected with *draugr* venom. Since then, it was all over. Some days, my blood was calm. Other days, I could feel it thrumming inside me like war drums. I could summon anything. I felt sure of it.

But energy required balance. Magic always had a cost. And I wasn't sure what the fee was—or if I was ready to pay it.

# CHAPTER 9

**B**y evening, I was feeling more alive than I had since my attempted murder in the fall. I vacillated between thinking that there was something energizing about blood and that my heritage had finally caught up with me. Either way, my cocktail hours throughout the day were revitalizing.

By the end of the week, though, blood martinis, murdering "best" friends, and machete-wielding dead men were the least of my troubles. I'd started to suspect that without regular blood I was going to flag. Eli and I set out to see Mama Lauren, closely followed by Jesse, Christy, Sera, and for reasons I'd never admit, Alice. Chanukah wasn't a *major* holiday for Jews, not a high holy day despite the fact that it was one of the only ones Christians knew we had. Still, my mother was keen on any excuse to cook for my friends.

It was a topic we rarely addressed, but my peculiar diet was a challenge for her. I was fairly liquid based, and the few solid things I ate were a choice not a need. Honestly, it was a testament to her cleverness that she discovered that I needed alcohol of all things. To her, I was a hummingbird, existing on some sort of water with additives.

Technically, we were there for the holiday, lighting a candle and sharing prayers and food, but in truth, I also needed maternal insight on what was wrong with me. She could tell. She had always been able to tell what I needed, as far as I knew, so if anyone in the world had answers, it would be Mama Lauren.

In some ways, driving into the Outs for this was not that different than driving to see Beatrice. The primary distinction was that I rarely had the chance to do this of late.

The Outs were dangerous for me in a way that they weren't for most people. I was tempting to the dead, and my childhood included waking too often to desperate monsters trying to peel off the rolldowns.

Mama Lauren coped, but she always just shrugged and asked what else was she to do? The sort of people who lived here were peculiar. The cities were where folks clustered, and the immediate space outside that—the ghost zones—were where *draugr* gathered. The Outs were their own thing. No utility services. No sheriff. No law. A special sort of madness drew folks to live out in nature.

Your energy was via solar or wind power, and your liquids were well water, septic, and leach fields. Law? Well, that was a combination of firepower and the judicious use of roll-downs for every window, door, chicken coop, and greenhouse on her farm. In the Outs, you didn't go outside once the sun set—which made the sunset candle lighting a challenge.

We'd always made do. Our "sunset" was noon for the purposes of holidays with friends. The alternative was staying over, and that was complicated sometimes with the way I beckoned to dead things. Mama Lauren could cope, but I didn't want my friends to wake up to *draugr* clawing at the walls to get in.

We crawled down the pitted lane, and Eli's steering managed to avoid pits that seemed likely to swallow his car whole. Maybe it was nerves, but I wasn't feeling like talking. I clung to the "oh shit" handle on the door as we bounced along.

Mama Lauren was expecting me, so she stood outside watching

for us. Her hair was starting to gray, and she'd pulled it back into a long braid for a change. It was almost always tied up in a knot, but today it was bound in a braid that reached past her hips. My tresses might be blue-dyed, but the thick coils were obviously from her genes.

She had on her usual tall boots, dress, and a pair of pistols holstered at her hips. Today an apron covered the dress. Her hand rested on the butt of one of those guns until she saw me step out of Eli's car.

I *flowed* toward her before anyone else was out of the cars.

"Eli's here," I said. "Alice, too. Please, don't hex either of them."

Mama Lauren laughed and swept me into a hug that reminded me that she was strong for her age. Honestly, she was strong for *my* age. "You worry too much, bubeleh. "

Then she was off to greet my friends. "No Yule log, my darlings! I do have the menorah in the window, but . . ."

I tuned her out and watched Eli.

I think she enjoyed the confusion her mix of Yiddish, Hebrew, and pagan terms caused a lot of people, but honestly, none of my friends blinked at it today. I'm not sure they ever did.

I wondered, though, what Eli would think.

He waited until everyone had greeted her, and then he bowed so deeply you'd think she was royalty. "It is my honor to meet you. I am not nor will I be worthy of the gift that is your daughter's attention."

"True." Mama Lauren nodded at him. "Not even a prince is worthy of Geneviève. She says you are helpful, though."

Jesse snorted in laughter.

"I do attempt to be of use," Eli said with not a hint of laughter in his voice.

Then, my mother patted his cheeks. "That's all any of us can do." She looked over at Jesse and swatted him. "You! You haven't visited your family."

"Yes, Mama Lauren," he said, laughter vanishing. Jesse had been my childhood bestie, so he was well aware of my mother's temper —and her stinging hexes.

But then my mother looked down at Jesse's hand, holding on to Christy's. "At least you figured that out."

She shooed us into the house, where she'd set a table that no city restaurant could match. That was the not-so-secret truth of life in the Outs: there were things aplenty that might kill you, but there were also benefits. For someone so bound to the soil, someone who grew her own food and herbs, there was no contest.

Later, when I had fewer witnesses I'd ask my mother about the blood. For now, I simply asked for a "pick-me-up" and downed whatever concoctions she handed me during our visit. I wasn't typically this compliant, but I wasn't ready for my mother or friends to discover how much I needed the blood martinis that Alice made me.

And Alice was, for all her cheery remarks, looking tired. So, I was without my martinis for a few days. Maybe I lied to her that I was fine, but I wasn't going to leech away her energy when she was clearly donating too much.

We all tucked into our odd version of a holiday, knowing that I would much rather stay for several days, and no one remarked on the way that Sera and Christy both kept track of the time. Holiday or not, the *draugr* would come if I was out here after hours—and after my run-in with Harold, I'd really rather have a *draugr* free event.

# CHAPTER 10

Sometimes I thought that every single time I believed things might go well, there ought to be a laugh track in my life to remind me that was never the case. I'd been shot at for being a witch, had my arm flayed open by a pissy *draugr*, discovered a need for blood, and accidentally entered a courtship that was supposed to result in marriage in a matter of weeks.

I might have managed to avoid the conversation, and loudly argued that we weren't actually getting married, but fae customs were better understood as laws than traditions.

The only thing that had gone well was introducing Eli to my mother. Our trip to the Outs was good, and it drew me closer to him.

Okay and dating Eli as a whole. That was going really well.

And so was my resolve at the not-having-intercourse with Eli.

Honestly I tried not to think about it, but Eli was as damnably perfect for me. I felt treasured, but also satisfied. It was enough to make a rational woman beg to marry him. A lifetime of that? *Yes, please.*

Unfortunately for both of us, I like Eli far too much to marry him.

I spent a few hours resisting the urge to see him, but I failed over and over—which is why I was sitting at the bar watching Christy free a tourist of the burden of his bank roll. Honestly, if he hadn't been flashing it around, she would've gone easy on him, but flash a thick roll of twenties, and someone will have it by the end of the night. At least Christy's method wouldn't involve bloodshed.

When I received a festively-decorated package that was delivered to the bar on ice, I had the good sense to carry it into the back room. Maybe it was fine. Maybe it was edible. But it was delivered by a *draugr*.

When I saw that it was from Beatrice, I had my doubts that anything good would come of it.

"Butterdrop?" Eli asked.

"*Draugr* delivery."

We closed the door and exchanged a look. I held up an envelope. That was easier to make sense of: cash. Beatrice paid me well for my services. I set it aside. I knew it was more than I'd charge, but I wasn't too proud to accept it. No one else could do the things I did. Sometimes people who realized that paid extra—which meant that when they needed me again, I'd make time for them.

I plopped the silver foil-wrapped box on the counter and untied the bold blue ribbons. "Maybe it's a toaster or pressure cooker? Rare liquor?"

Eli gave me a look. "And maybe you'll take up macramé."

"It could happen. I have hidden depths." I loosened the lid, not quite ready to face the contents. Nothing involving Beatrice was ever simple.

"You're stalling." Eli pointed at the box on the wooden table beside us. It looked festive, and whatever it was, I doubted that it would explode or injure us.

Tentatively, I opened the box. To exactly no one's surprise, there was no pressure cooker, salad bowls, or even macramé supplies.

There, surrounded by ice packs, was the head of Weasel Nuts, the man who'd shot at me at the Cormier job. On top of his severed head, jabbed into the meat of his forehead, was Harold's ornate broach.

"There's a letter." Eli unfolded the paper that had been in the envelope and read: "'Hunters ought to be rewarded. Harold employed miscreants to discover your abilities. This human expired before sharing further knowledge.'"

"Is it me or are there a lot more brushes with death lately?"

"It is far more frequent than I'd like." Eli tucked the cash and letter in a pocket.

We'd long ago realized that I'd misplaced far too many things for me to be the one handling deposits. Eli, along with being my partner in the field, had begun to handle my accounting. I trusted him more than myself on this.

"Do you know what to *do* with that?" I nodded at the garish jewels jabbed in Weasel Nuts' forehead.

"Sell or store it." Eli shrugged. "Antique, obviously."

I wasn't squeamish often, but unpinning the broach from the dead man's head was not terribly appealing. I put the lid back on it for now.

"I have a woman who handles gems. I brought a cache with me when I moved here," Eli said in that uniquely Eli way that was somehow downplaying his connections and wealth. "They covered the bills of a life here—until I established the tavern—and then I sell one now and again."

He looked at me and stressed, "Bonbon, I would suspect the ruby alone will be between six and thirty thousand, simply due to size and clarity."

I swallowed. Who in their right mind wore jewels like that? And who pinned them to the head of dead men?

Obviously, Beatrice was not wanting for funds, but her proclamation of familial ties was said so carelessly. I was starting to think my dear, dead, many-times-great-gran truly liked me. It was, in truth, a bit disconcerting.

I shuddered. "Do whatever you think best with it."

"Shall I dispose of . . . the contents as well?"

"I have no use for the head of Weasel Nuts, and re-gifting that would probably lead to awkward questions." I shoved the box slightly toward him.

"You never bore me, my dear plum pudding. For someone with eternity ahead, that is a treasure."

~

I THOUGHT MORE than a little about Eternity as I prepared for the trip to *Elphame.* Unlike my visits to Beatrice or my mother, this trip was a multi-day affair. Oddly, perhaps, time between the worlds was uneven. My first stay there had been a month, but in New Orleans a mere three hours passed.

Going there did not mean I missed anything at home. My city was not left unpatrolled, and it wasn't as if the police did nothing. New Orleans had reconfigured their entire force. They protected the city, watched for the *draugr* and aided the citizens.

Still I was, for reasons that I was not pleased to admit, anxious.

Witches from the Outs were not a good fit for royal courts. I mean, sure I coped with the *draugr* queen's soiree but that was because I figured I'd get to threaten or stab someone. Eli repeatedly stressed that neither of those were advisable at the Yule celebration with his uncle, the king of the fae.

Tonight, though, Eli and I were having a "date-night." A few hours locked away in my home, surrounded by fight dummies and weapons. It wasn't as romantic as his place, but it was my home. It was important to both of us that we spend time here, too.

I wasn't the world's best date, though, much to my frustration. My nerves were frayed, and it was making me filter-free. "What if I glare at him? Is that—"

"A terrible idea?" Eli said. "Yes, it is."

"Can I hex him?"

"No."

"Make a bargain?"

"No!" Eli gave me a look that everyone in my life did from time to time. It usually meant I was a lousy patient, but . . .

"I'm *hungry.*" I was both pleased to realize why I felt surlier than usual and surlier because I had the distinct feeling that a good bottle of gin wasn't going to fix this.

Alice wasn't there, and the martini shaker was still empty. Draining her energy had me on restriction, and I still couldn't bring myself to ask anyone else. I knew my friends would tap a vein for me, but I just . . . couldn't.

"I swore I'd die before I become like a *draugr,*" I said, admitting the thing that had been plaguing me more and more. I'd survived an attempt on my life a few times, bad luck, pretending to be more human than I was, but the injection of venom a few months ago was life-changing.

Eli walked out of my apartment without a word.

When he returned, he had a bag with the top of a dusty bottle of whisky sticking out.

He pulled the bottle out and put it on my coffee table with more force than he would've if he were calm. Then, he looked at me.

"What?"

"If I didn't know how hard this was for you, I'd accuse you of trying to avoid my home country," he started. He opened a bag again and pulled out two glasses.

When I opened my mouth to object, he caught my hand. "You are impossible, Geneviève Crowe. Difficult to get to know. Fierce to the point of recklessness. But you are not a *draugr.* You are not monstrous, by any definition."

I nodded because what could I say? I knew he believed it, but sometimes I felt monstrous. I had *draugr* eyes, and I could *flow.* I was the only one of my kind, and the dead came to me at my will. The faery king called me things like "death" or "dead witch," and more than a few people thought I ought to be dead *because* of being a witch.

I didn't exactly *feel* loveable.

He poured whisky into both glasses.

Then Eli reached in the bag again, and when I saw what he held I was standing on the other side of the room. A small, gleaming knife. Mother of pearl handle. Thin blade. Watching me the whole time, he pushed up his sleeve and slid the blade over his forearm.

He turned his arm so the cut was over a glass. Still holding my gaze, he said, "Given freely."

"Eli . . ." My mind said no, but my teeth were there to remind me that I was less witch than I used to be.

I shook my head no even as I stepped closer, watching blood--*his* blood, fae blood—drip into my glass.

"My life is yours, Geneviève Crowe." He took a bandage from the bag and pressed it to his arm. "I would shed every drop for your safety, your health, your happiness."

"Eli . . ."

He held out the glass of blood and whisky. "The fae date with eternity in our minds, dearest. Everything I am is yours, including my body inside and out."

I took the glass with a shaking hand, and he lifted his blood-free drink.

"To eternity," he said.

I clinked my glass to his and echoed, "To eternity."

# CHAPTER 11

After Eli's blood gift, there was nothing to do but behave as I hoped would win the favor of the fae. His blood and his words made his seriousness exceptionally clear. No person could ask for a better partner than Eli. I didn't deserve him, and I never would. Of that, I was sure—but I was damn sure that I would do my absolute best to try to be an asset as we stepped into *Elphame* a few days later.

We were arriving an hour before the Yule Ball. He was no more interested in a longer stay than I was. Eli was subtle about it, but he'd made clear when we were here the first time that he had no desire to assume the throne. Eli liked my world, *our* world. Maybe he wouldn't always feel that way, but right now, he was opposed to becoming a king.

Luckily, the king was young enough that we weren't yet at that crossroads.

When we arrived, we were greeted by a contingent of royals and the king himself. I still didn't know what to call him. The fae were not free with their names. Maiden, lady, lord, or a false name were often used. I knew that.

They, of course, knew my name. I'd given it freely as a sign of trust.

The royals that met us, exactly six lords and six ladies as well as five guards, were spanned out from the king in a formation that would allow weapons. I smiled at that. The thought of training with fae warriors was more tempting than any ball could be.

"Welcome, Geneviève of Crowe." The king looked at me with an implacable expression.

But I felt the others judge me, eyes lingering on the Renaissance-meets-function dress I wore. Soft blue with silver-shot designs, it was as festive as I ever was.

The king, to his credit, made note of the colors and knew enough about me to say, "We are honored that you would join us during the festival of Chanukah. *Chag Urim Sameach.*"

I could tell that he'd practiced his words, and it made me feel a little warmer.

"Blessed Yule, and *Chag Urim Sameach,*" I said with a deep curtsey.

And yes, I'd practiced *that.* I had never in my life curtsied before, but if I bowed, the faery king and his entourage were going to be staring into my cleavage. That seemed a bit awkward, so curtsey it was.

The king, to his credit, didn't comment on my willingness to observe protocol. I gave him a genuine smile when I straightened. The ruler of *Elphame* was striking and raw in his beauty, more warrior in appearance than nobility. He was draped in a white-fur-lined cloak, and a simple circlet of silver with green gems sat atop his hair. He did not look any older than Eli, but that could mean he was anywhere from forty to four hundred.

There was no queen at his side.

I realized then that he'd never wed. Faeries' lifelines were bound together, so by staying unwed, the king had not risked dying because his partner did. It said something about his priorities and independence. In this, he and his brother—Eli's father—were very dissimilar. It was also a thing *I* understood.

Eli offered me his arm, and we walked to the king's side, and without a word, we walked in a procession from the gateway to an open field. There under the boughs of a beautiful oak tree, the fae king went to his throne. It looked as if the earth herself had crafted the chair.

Beside the throne was a silver menorah. There, in Elphame, the king of the fae motioned me forward.

"I do not find it is my place to say the words you'd need," he said. "Light your candles, and know that you are welcome here, Geneviève of Crowe."

I whispered my prayers, and I lit the candles.

Then, the king walked to that stone and wood throne.

Eli took my hand. He led me to the exact center of the field, knelt to remove my shoes and whispered, "I would offer you everything I possess in both worlds if you were here willingly."

When he stood, I sighed and slid my hand into his as we prepared to dance. "I am willing, Eli, more so than is good for either of us."

Maybe it was the amount of Eli's blood that still rolling through my veins, or maybe it was the holiday. Or perhaps, despite every ounce of willpower, the act of dating this man had been wearing down my defenses. I still was not going to doom him by marrying him, but more and more I was wishing I could.

We danced, feet bare on the earth, and when the first song ended, the field filled with fae couples. Fireflies and stars lit the night, and candles and bonfires burned. There was peace here, among the people of the wood and air. There was acceptance here, more than I allowed myself.

And when the king greeted the dawn's light with a deep bow to me, I barely flinched.

"I present to you Geneviève of Crowe. Betrothed of my nephew. Born of magic. Giver of life and death. Future queen of *Elphame*."

The faeries bowed, curtsied, or knelt. Swords and gowns were brought before me. I winced at the whole thing, but on the outside, I smiled and replied, "It is an honor to be made welcome by the people of earth and air."

It was not an acceptance, but it was more than I thought I'd be able to muster. Eli kissed me soundly, and for a flicker of a moment, I let myself imagine a future here with him. Nature unbound. Acceptance. Love. There was much to treasure.

But I was not made for ruling. I was a warrior first, a creature that summoned the dead, and a woman utterly unsuited to motherhood. No amount of wishing would change that. My womb would not create life, not even for Eli.

THE FOLLOWING AFTERNOON, I was sleeping outside on a mossy hill with Eli beside me. Well, half under me. I was held against his side, my head resting on his chest, and we were both pillowed by thick moss.

He may not have napped; I wasn't sure. What I did know was that we needed to address matters.

"We have a bargain, and I do not seek to break that," I said, treading carefully. "I fear that it was entirely to my benefit, and for that I am grateful, but nonetheless . . . I need to ask you to let me speak of the future in general."

He sighed. "I know."

"I won't speak of our future," I hedged. I'd been thinking of ways around the rules because, well, *of course I had*. I was not as clever as the fae, but I had spent a lot of time researching faery bargains.

Eli smiled, although it looked sad when he did.

"Courtship . . . dating . . ." I started, awkwardly fumbling forward despite knowing that danger was ahead. "I need to understand this, Eli. It's not fair to expect me to know things when this is not my culture."

"Do you think of the fae as fair, Geneviève?" His hand trailed over my back, fingertips tracing my spine.

"Eli . . ."

He sighed. "At the end of the courtship, one must accept the betrothal with an exchange of vows, or one must forsake the betrothed."

My heart thudded at that.

"That is traditional." Eli paused, and I knew he was trying to impart some wisdom to me. "There are no other options, traditionally. Matrimony or division. A date was set, and without an extenuating event, there are only no further options."

I weighed the things he admitted, pondering options. "So, that means that on Twelfth Night I have to commit or quit."

He looked at me. "We may not discuss our future, Geneviève. There are laws. The *terms of a bargain* overrule every other tradition for my people."

"If I quit?"

"Then I will never speak to you again," he said, voice tight. "Not as friends or partners. Nothing."

"But I'm not ready to marry anyone," I exclaimed. I sat up, glaring down at him. "And I can't lose you. I . . . have *feelings* for you."

Eli took my hand. "I am aware of all of this."

"But I can ask for anything?"

"That is our deal." Eli stared at me, and I let myself read the images he was trying to will to me.

*"I would wait,"* he said. *"I am in no rush, Geneviève. I have no desire for a wife unless you are that wife."*

"If I ask for our engagement to end? As my request?" I prompted. "End but you not forsake me as a . . . friend and partner?"

"I could never touch you intimately."

I realized then what options he'd offered me with this bargain. I could not end it without losing him, and he could not end it at all.

So, my options were marriage in about two weeks, or to ask for a request that was so carefully worded that I would have time. We would still court, but with no intent—on my part—to marry.

"It's exhausting, dealing with the nuances of the fae," I muttered before pushing him down and snuggling into his arms. "I like dating you, though."

Eli laughed. "There is much to be said for dating."

"I could do it for a very, *very* long time," I whispered.

"Indeed." He kissed my forehead. "I do enjoy our dates." He paused and in a low voice asked, "Where do witches stand on orgasms outside?"

"Pro. Some witches, in fact, are distinctively in favor of this. Was there one in particular witch you were asking about?"

He rolled me onto my back as he moved over me. "Mine."

I'm not sure I'd have objected to the possessive tone in his voice, but it didn't matter because he covered my mouth with his and kissed away any words I might have had.

# CHAPTER 12

When I returned to New Orleans, I was worn out, weary, and ready to ask for a time-out on my life—as much as I was ready for the next week to pass so I could test my plan on my faery bargain.

I'm pretty used to drama, and the holidays are full of it for most folks. Between the three types of beings in my life—human, *draugr*, and fae—I was ready to propose a time share for future holidays. One species per year. Of course, *my* humans included my witchy mother and friends, so given my wish, I'd stick with just them.

Still the money, wisdom, and favor from Beatrice were useful.

And maybe the swords from the faery king were nice.

But I was ready for a nap after dealing with everyone's agendas —which was why I was anything but charming when Beatrice *flowed* to my table at Bill's Tavern.

"Really? Don't you have a daytime nap or something to attend? Beauty sleep? Minions to frighten?"

"Invite me to be seated."

"You need an invitation?" I perked up. *Draugr* rules were as hard to find as rooster's teeth.

"No, Geneviève." Beatrice's pale lips curved in a mimicry of a smile. "I simply have manners."

I sighed and gestured to a chair across from me. Beatrice, ever the cooperative dead lady, sat next to me.

"There are those who would wish you dead no matter what," she started.

"You must be a riot at parties."

"The last party included beheading vermin." She met my gaze. "Did you receive my gifts?"

I nodded. What exactly was the protocol for a box with the head of man? Or the antique jewels from a man who undoubtedly became dust and ash? I figured I'd go for subtle and said, "It was a very you"—I made air quotes—"gift."

Beatrice smiled. "I have another gift, Geneviève."

She slid a book to me. It felt heavy with magic, and I knew that it was a grimoire of some sort.

"I understand from your friend's shop that the buyer for this would be you," she said. "I've supplied others you or Lauren sought, but this is not one you could afford even with Harold's jewelry."

I couldn't even joke that I had nothing to give her. There were gifts, and then there were *gifts*.

"Why?" I managed to ask.

For a moment, Beatrice appeared centuries old; not that she suddenly amassed wrinkles, but that she looked weary in a way that reminded me that bitch though she could be, she was a woman in a man's world—and had been for centuries.

"I have removed threats, but there are those vile men or *draugr* every generation that seek my descendants out. You, Geneviève, are more of a target than most. You are witch and mine, but you carry other traits."

I swallowed.

"Threats will come. They are a storm, waves pounding as if they will wear us down in time." Her eyes were glimmering with a light that was eerie to behold. "I do not lose. I will not. And you, daughter of my daughters' daughter, are the last of my line. They will come, and you will be able to win." She tapped the book with a finger. "Learn."

Then the *draugr* queen stood to go.

Before I could think too long on it, I asked, "Would you want to have dinner with Mama Lauren and me? I mean sometime . . . maybe not dinner, but—"

"I will"—she smiled wickedly—"BYOB, as they say. Bring my own blood."

I laughed, more at her delivery than her bad sense of humor. "And we could talk. I think my mother would like that. I would, too."

I WAS STILL SITTING THERE with my book in silence several hours later when Eli joined me. "Frosting?"

I looked up.

"Are you well?"

"Beatrice brought me a book." I stroked the cover again. I wasn't prepared to open it yet, and certainly not here.

"I see . . ." He sat beside me. "Alice had this sent by courier."

The hot pink canteen he handed me looked more practical than I would typically have thought of when thinking of Alice, but when I opened it, I recognized the scent. I'd already begun to be able to tell the owner of cocktail by the scent. My body had changed.

A server brought us both mugs of what appeared to be tea for Eli and vodka for me. It made a weird sense. Alice's blood worked well with clear liquor; Eli's was more suited to whisky.

I poured a generous shot from my hot pink canteen into my mug of vodka. I tossed the whole thing back and looked at him. "I am ready to claim the request at the end of our bargain."

"It's still December and—"

"I know." I stared at him, and I saw the anxiety there. Did he doubt me so much that he thought I would give up what we shared? I wasn't easy to love, but I suspected he loved me. I wasn't going to lose that.

Carefully, I explained, "I'm already exhausted. I feel like there are disasters at every turn, and faery bargains are hard, so I want to do this while I *think* I can say it right."

"Geneviève, please, don't—"

"I do not forsake you," I said. "I do not agree to enter a marriage *on that date.* By the terms of this bargain, I can make a request. Eli of Stonehaven, my request of you is that the courtship we have begun here continue until such time as we both agree that marriage must and should happen. To each other or you to another."

He was smiling as he took my hand. "At this time, I understand that you will not release me from my pledge to you, but neither will you enter marriage."

"This is my request."

"And so the rules of courtship shall continue between us, and you have willingly entered this courtship with me," Eli added.

"I have."

"Your request is granted, Geneviève Crowe," Eli whispered. "My betrothed."

"So, mote it be."

Somehow, it felt as if nothing and everything had changed. We were still engaged, and I was still masquerading as a viable partner, but by way of a faery bargain we had secured a modification to that betrothal that not even the king could overrule.

It wasn't perfect, but the holiday season had turned out far better than ever I had hoped. Sure, there were more gatherings, bleeding out, and the addition of blood martinis to my diet, but all said, it wasn't terrible.

"I'm fairly sure that courtship includes kissing," I teased. "There's even mistletoe over the doorway."

"We're nowhere near that doorway." Eli was smiling when he

leaned in to kiss me, though, and everything felt just about perfect in that moment.

Death threats, *draugr*, and drama with relatives were undoubtedly in our future, but for today, I'd enjoy my blood martini and mistletoe kisses.

The End

QUALITY CONTROL:

This work has been professionally edited and proofread. However, if you encounter any typos or formatting issues, please do contact us, so it can be corrected: assist@melissamarrbooks.com .

# DAIQUIRIS & DAGGERS

A Faery Bargains Novella

Set after BOOK 2

# CHAPTER 1

"Come down here!" I stalked around the edges of the mausoleum. Some enterprising soul had festooned the edges of the mausoleum roof with concertina wire. The deadly décor glittered right now thanks to the mix of torrential rain and the glowing streetlights.

Millicent Johnson, eighteen and dead, was supposed to be in her grave, but Millie had crawled out of the earth, infected with *draugr* venom. That or necromancy were the only ways to walk after death.

With much wailing and angst, the Johnsons hired me to retrieve her and deliver her to a T-Cell House. After a number of years in containment, Millie would be as rational as any teen. She'd need blood, and never physically age, but short of beheading, nothing would end Millie's un-life.

For that un-life to progress, I had to capture Millie tonight. I'm a necromancer, sometimes freelancer for NOPD, and I do the occasional job for the queen of the *draugr* in this region of the world. All that considered, capturing one dead teenager ought to be easy.

It wasn't.

"Come on, Millie." I held out my arm, not beckoning her exactly, but extending my arm as if I were holding kibble out toward a cat in a tree.

As rain continued to soak me, I was willing to pretend to be kibble if it meant she came down easily. This was to be a simple bag and tag, the sort of recovery that I'd been able to pull off even as a teenager still trying to get comfortable with a sword.

"So help me, if I have to crawl up there . . ." I circled again, not entirely sure how to manage this. "Get *down* here, Millie!"

Millie growled at me, glaring at the sword in my hand. She was hunched over, balancing on her hands and feet like she was imitating a less verbal primate. I'd nudge her ass-over-tea-kettle if I could, but the height of the mausoleum meant she was out of reach. And the concertina wire meant that I couldn't vault up there without spilling my blood—which, as a necromancer, I wasn't keen to do in a cemetery.

"If I can't contain you, I *will* chop that pretty head off," I threatened, stalking her from the sopping wet ground. At least if she leaped down, I could catch her. "I mean it, Millicent, pop goes the weasel! Off with your head!"

Millie paused, but unfortunately, she couldn't actually be threatened into clarity. *Draugr* didn't start their "second lives" terribly coherent. They were akin to toddlers, all instinct and drool.

My job was stopping them before they went around New Orleans ripping throats out. Or, in cases like this, I was hired for bagging and tagging so they could be warehoused.

I pointed at the muddy wet ground. "Down, Millie!"

She plopped down on the roof of the mausoleum--looking like a dripping-wet, dead princess--and stared at me.

"Not what I meant!" I swiped at the water sluicing down my face.

Millicent was very obviously *not* coming down. I wasn't an archer, so I had no projectiles other than bullets. That left me with the choice of either waiting until she eventually came down or leaving a confused *draugr* perched on top of a grave. Both options sucked.

I shoved my hair out of my face, flinging water. "Damn it."

I hated bag and tag jobs. Killing was easier than capturing, but that wasn't my objective tonight.

"Millie?" I beckoned. *"Please?"*

I was a witch, born and raised as one. It was a part of my maternal lineage, along with Jewish faith. My paternal genes were more complicated. The sperm-donor was already a walking corpse when he impregnated my mother, so I was the world only living dead woman. Half dead. Half witch. Between the two sides of my heritage, capturing Millie ought to be easy.

Until recently, it *was*. In fact, I was the only human *draugr* in existence as far as I knew. I had counted on that aspect of my heritage to be enough to handle a simple job. For most of my life, I could summon the dead from their graves to help me in whatever I needed. It made for an awkward childhood, but it was the basis of my career. I was the witch to call for beheadings, summoning the dead, or capturing the walking dead.

However, a few weeks ago, I'd summoned so very many corpses that I'd accidentally restored a dead man to life. Since then, my necromancy was . . . sluggish. Apparently, if I drained my magical reserves, I needed time to recharge.

Who knew?

"Damn it, Millicent. Get your dead ass down here. Right this moment . . . or else!"

"Bonbon?" Eli's laughing voice behind me had me spinning around too quickly.

My feet went out from under me, and I landed flat on my back. Now I was not just soaked but muddy, too. Slimy ooze coated my back, squishing into the neck of my jacket. "Ugh."

My husband held out a hand, as if to help me from a carriage not a muddy mess. I accepted, letting him tug me to my feet, but I dug my feet into the ground, stopping him from embracing me. "What are you doing here?"

"You were late, so . . ." Eli gave an elegant half-shrug that pretended the act was nonchalant. It wasn't. He worried since my magical depletion, balancing on a line between infuriating me by hovering and happening to be near when I needed help. It was graceful enough, explainable enough, that I couldn't even yell at him for being smothering.

And truth was that I *needed* the help more than I'd like. The past three months had been rough. My magic was absentee, and I was restless.

"Plus, I missed looking at you," Eli added lightly. The look in his eyes—and the fact that the fae can't lie—made it clear that he somehow found me appealing even spattered in muck.

I tilted my head up, letting the still-pouring rain wash away some of the mud. My hair, more brown than its usual blue thanks to my impromptu mud bath, hung in clumps, and I was doing a great impression of a wet cat. "You, Eli, are a lunatic."

"Perhaps." He shrugged again. Sometimes, I wished he was a little less breathtaking. The combination of the way he looked at me and the way he looked was distracting. From cut glass cheeks to courtesan's lips, Eli was much too beautiful to be in the rain with my muddy self. Even dripping wet, his darker-than-black hair hid glimmers of stars. Entire universes blinked out at me.

"You shouldn't look at me that way when I'm . . ." I gestured at my muddy self.

Eli shrugged in a way that only a man like him could pull off: elegant, careless, and utterly telling all at once. "You would need to pluck my eyes out for me to look at you any other way."

"Fine. You're pretty, too," I muttered.

Eli chuckled before looking up at the dead girl who was watching us with a keen interest. "How's work?"

"Obstinate. Work is obstinate." I swiped mud out of my hair. "Princess Squirrel here won't—"

"I see," he interrupted before I could rant. "Could you summon her? As with proper corpses?"

I sighed and admitted, "If someone gave me an energy boost . . ."

"My damsel in distress," Eli murmured, stepping closer.

I had a sword raised before he could touch me. "Not a fucking damsel."

"*My* damsel." He pushed my sword away. "As you are, undoubtedly, also my knight."

"Sweet talker." I pulled him closer with a muddy hand fisted in his shirt and kissed him. The moment my lips touched his, I felt the wave of faery magic. His magic. I should have been able to draw on it at will since we were wed, but that, too, was beyond me currently.

Eli poured his energy into me, and I could taste fresh water and blossoming trees.

When he pulled away, I had only moments before that surge would resettle itself in me, feed my depleted reserves, and vanish. I needed my magic to return to me.

I stared up at the dead girl. "Get down here, Millicent Leigh Johnson."

This time, my words held a compulsion, a magical command wrought by my necromancy.

The *draugr* girl stood and cartwheeled to the ground. Millie landed with a sploosh of mud, but as I was already filthy, I couldn't object. Quickly, I bound her hands and feet, smacked a bite-proof gag over her mouth, and dropped my magical hold.

Eli waited, not touching me while I did what I must.

"I free you, Millicent Leigh Johnson. Not mine. Not yours." I stepped back just as the light was returning to her eyes.

As soon as I dropped my compulsion over Millie, she flopped around like an angry caterpillar trying to bite me through the gag. No longer calm, she wanted my blood or at least to strike out at her captor.

"Cutting it close, bonbon," Eli murmured.

I nodded. If I was connected to any *draugr* when Eli's magic stopped working for me, the dead would become my responsibility. I was a human, a witch, so it ought not work that way. Unfortunately, the secret that only my closest friends and family knew was that being a witch-*draugr* hybrid meant that my particular magical affinity—necromancy—had combined with my *draugr* genetics. In sum, I could do things that only the oldest *draugr* could do: bind and control. Any *draugr* I bound to me would be coherent as long as she stayed near me, and if that particular information were to be revealed, I would be both a threat to existing *draugr* hierarchy—and sought after by those who wanted to be brought back to a second life.

However, I had no interest in collecting minions. I'd already accidentally bound two *draugr*, and I was fairly sure I'd bound my human assistant, too. I felt responsible for them, which I hated. I was not interested in adding to that list. Some people wanted an army, or a flock to mother, or didn't feel responsible for those who served them. Me? I didn't even want to have houseplants.

Eli called for transport while I hauled Millie to her feet. "Come on. Up you go."

My hand on her bound wrists wasn't enough to keep her standing. Millie jerked out of my hold and fell to the ground. We repeated the process several times, mostly because I was too stubborn to ask Eli to help, and he was adamant that he would not "overstep" unless my life depended on it.

So, I hauled a trussed up dead girl to the gate where a bright purple van with T-CELL TRANSITION HOMES emblazoned on the side waited.

Once they took the growling girl away, I stood there, wet and muddy but victorious.

"Shall I tell Alice to invoice the Johnsons?" Eli's voice was calm enough to make clear that he wasn't sure of my mood.

"Yep. And add ten percent for complications." I met his gaze. "Dead folk are not supposed to perch on any roof."

Eli nodded, his expression unreadable.

"What?"

"Would you object to walking to the bar, Geneviève?" He offered me his arm, chivalrous as always.

"What? No chariot?" I looked around for his little blue convertible.

Eli was silent for a long moment before saying, "You smell rather atrocious, love."

I sniffed. Obviously, someone had been taking Fido on walkies in among the graves and not scooping. The slimy mud in my jacket was not *just* mud from the smell of it. "Ugh. I stink. I need a shower and a vacation."

"As you wish, bonbon."

And then my patient spouse escorted my mud and poo-coated self to Bill's Tavern, where we walked through the bar and into the back. I all but ran to the shower while Eli was still peeling off his soaking clothes. He was polite enough to give me space to get clean before joining me.

# CHAPTER 2

I sat at the breakfast table as the sun started to dim the next evening. Eli was out somewhere, so I woke alone and filled with nervous energy. I couldn't say that anything specific was wrong. No open cases. No recent attacks or threats on my life. No question or doubt in my relationship. I ought to be more relaxed than I felt. Maybe I was simply accustomed to anxiety and worry.

Eli and I were bonded. Together until one of us died. We'd had a month-long honeymoon after our bonding, and although everyone else was nagging me to get on with dress shopping and venue booking, Eli was being absurdly patient about planning wedding ceremonies. *Plural.* I'd have to endure a wedding in *Elphame* as well as in New Orleans—well, in The Outs where I was raised. We were having a wedding on the land where my mother homesteaded not in the city proper.

Wedding talk was as overwhelming as my magical depletion and my newly married status.

My life was out of *my* control lately, and the details of the weddings were more than I could manage. I'd gotten as far as agreeing to two ceremonies. It was either that or only have the fussy future-queen ceremony in *Elphame.* That was a hard pass. Not everyone was able to travel there. The realm of the fae was separate from the human world, and *most* faeries stayed there. The man who'd once been my friend, fight partner, and was now my spouse had failed to mention that he was not only fully fae, but the self-exiled prince. I had no interest in thrones, but if that's what I had to do to be with Eli . . . well, love makes a person do weird things sometimes. In my case, it meant politics, fussy dresses, and several weddings.

I'd decided that if there was going to be a wedding at all, I'd have at least one wedding that was to *my* taste. We started out discussing the two "suitable" places for formal weddings in the city: the Touro Synagogue, one of the oldest synagogues in the nation, and Saint Louis Cathedral in Jackson Square, the oldest church in the nation. They both held the gravitas appropriate for the wedding of the heir to *Elphame* and his bride, but the thought of being a spectacle, of having strangers gawk at us, of the sheer pageantry of it all made me cringe.

And so, I'd been delaying. Avoiding. Eli and I were already married, so who needed a big fancy mess? "Avoid and procrastinate" was still my default setting for emotional things. Weddings, much like funerals, were for the attendees, and so I wanted nothing to do with either. Call me selfish, but I thought that some things, some moments, ought to be reserved for the guest-of-honor.

Eli was simply content to do whatever made me happiest.

So, I stalled.

I pondered it constantly, though.

The door downstairs opened, which meant Eli was here. No one else could enter. Not surprisingly, the home of the one and only fae prince was fairly secure.

I topped off my drink, pouring mead and blood into my glass in equal measures. Think alcohol smoothie. Add a generous splash of blood, and that was my diet. My metabolism was high—and weird. Alcohol fueled me, but I wasn't intoxicated by it. I was basically a fanged hummingbird.

"Bonbon?" Eli paused, frowning at me. "Has something happened?"

"Nope."

"Are you unwell?"

"Nope."

"Are you planning on explaining or saying 'nope' at me until I guess?" He came to the table, took my hand and pulled me to my feet. "Maudlin?"

"I'm sick of my magical depletion," I admitted as I stared at the only person not yet frustrated with my moods lately. "I want to *do* things. I can't raise the dead, and—"

"You brought a man back to life, Geneviève."

"A bad man."

"Iggy hasn't done anything troubling." Eli wrapped his arms around me.

"Yet," I muttered.

"Perhaps you need a get-away. Something to let you relax so your magic can resettle."

"I feel useless. To do basic things, I need to borrow your—"

"Our," he corrected. "*Our* magic."

"Our magic," I repeated, after a scowl. "Fine. Fine. I can work, but . . ." I glanced up at my husband's very emotionless expression.

"You *are* working, then?" he prompted.

"Yes." I moved out of his embrace.

"But you must rely on me to do so, and that is frustrating after being self-reliant since as long as you can recall," Eli explained my work anxiety calmly and succinctly.

I smacked his chest lightly. "Yes, damn it. I feel weak."

"You have faced Death more times than anyone I know, and each time Death runs away like a frightened dog." He caught my chin in his hand and tipped my face up so I was looking at him before continuing, "You are not weak, Geneviève. You are trying to refill your magical core after managing a god-like feat. You ought to relax rather than trying to force it."

I was about to agree that he had a point.

Then he added, "But you are an absolutely horrible patient, with the serenity of a child who ate a bowl of straight sugar."

"Hey!"

"Am I wrong?"

I deflated. "No."

"So, let us ponder options." Eli walked away, heading into his —*our*—living area. I could ignore the invitation or follow. He'd offered me the control.

And I was reminded for the two million six hundred and eighth time that Eli really was perfect for me. It apparently took the patience of a faery to worm his way into my heart *and* to live with me.

I followed him, marveling over the wonder that he wanted me despite my catalogable list of complications. Not that he was without difficulty. He came with a damned throne, longevity, and traditions I barely understood most of the time.

We compromised *a lot*.

He'd added a fight dummy to the far side of the living room when we got married. To most people, it probably wouldn't seem like a romantic gesture, but I like hitting things. My own apartment had most of the space dedicated to fighting, but now that we were bonded, I preferred to sleep here at least half of the time.

I touched the dummy, Harper, on the way past. Yes, I name all my fight dummies. Elvis, Bruce, and Doris were my first three, and I'd considered each of their names at length. I liked Doris the best for punching. She was on a wheeled mount so she "flinched."

"I have taken the liberty of giving Christy a long weekend off either this week or next," Eli said as I sat next to him on the sofa. It sounded like a non sequitur.

"Okaaaay . . ." I wasn't sure why he'd given his bar manager, who was one of my closest friends, the weekend off.

"I have *also* taken the liberty of asking Sera if she would be free. Her schedule is more complicated, but—"

"I'm going to need more details, Eli. What does any of this have to do with *anything*?" I interrupted.

He held out a shiny laminated card proclaiming me fae royalty. I'd seen his diplomatic card, but this one was mine. My name. My passport.

"You are the future queen of Elphame, Geneviève. You have a diplomatic passport. No questions. No temperature checks."

"I . . ." I blinked at him, too stunned to process. I'd never really been able to travel far or often. Sure, there were cities that were exceptions, but there were a lot more cities that were forbidden to *draugr*. Those were where I wanted to be, cities where I could truly relax. No dead folk to behead. No pressure to patrol. Any gate checks for such cities could expose me, and after my recent injection of draugr venom I was sure I'd fail. I had failed when we tried to go to Houston. If not for Eli pulling his own diplomatic passport, we would've been turned away.

And the fact that there was a *draugr* with a heartbeat? That was the sort of thing that made international news. The reality was that being one of a kind was dangerous.

"There were not insignificant delays." Eli's voice hid an edge that made me realize that he'd been angrier about those delays than he typically got about anything. "But the matter has been resolved."

I clutched the card, staring at it and marveling. I stared at him. "I can travel."

He nodded.

"Holy goat milk! I can *travel*." I hugged Eli. "For real, travel to places."

"Yes." He smiled possibly because it had been a minute since he'd seen me quite this excited about anything that involved both of us wearing clothes.

Eli lifted a thick manilla folder from the side table. "Alice has been researching, and she will be available this weekend."

He slid the folder toward me.

The last time my assistant had researched a trip, I ended up owning far too much frilly lingerie and accidentally marrying Eli. I had no regrets, but sometimes I thought Alice Chaddock had a magical chaos magnet in her body somewhere.

Tentatively, I opened the folder. "HOUSTON?" was written in Allie's handwriting across the top of a print-out of stapled pages. I lifted the sheath of pages. Underneath was "PRAGUE? PROBABLY TOO FAR." A fanged frownie face was drawn there. Several other packets were under those two.

"Alice researched options for a 'Girls Weekend,'" Eli said, wincing a bit at the term.

I was across the slight distance between us and in his arms in the next moment. My husband, my perfect faery prince of a spouse, had put the wheels in motion so I could go away with my friends.

"You are the absolute best," I announced before setting out to prove that truth.

# CHAPTER 3

Later that evening I curled up with the travel options. Prague was, regrettably, too far. I'd seen so many pictures and videos of the Czech Republic that I desperately wanted to visit. And Edinburgh. And Amsterdam. And Berlin. So many places, and suddenly I was allowed to go to places that my genetics had forbidden for my whole life.

After narrowing in on three options—beach, beach, or beach—I decided it was time to get outside opinions. I called Allie, Sera, and Christy for a meeting.

Since Christy was visiting her boyfriend Jesse at work at Tomes and Tea, the bookstore I part-owned despite refusing to cash any of my checks, we agreed to meet there. Since the bookshop was in Gentilly, a good five miles away, I texted Allie and asked her to pick up Sera. Jesse was my oldest, dearest friend, but this was a designated *Girls'* Weekend, so we'd be leaving him behind.

I set out on a jog through the city--not that I *wanted* to jog but I was developing a fear that my *draugr* speed would vanish, too.

Maybe it was silly, but then again, my necromancy's absence had seemed impossible before now, too, and yet here I was, unable to raise even a dead rat.

I fucking hated running, but the part that no one talks about with physical jobs—and beheading the dead was often an exceedingly physical job—was that you had to keep in shape. Not like boxing movie training montages, but everything from push-ups to jogging, yoga to canoeing. Lots of muscles meant that a varied workout was important.

With my magic on the fritz, I was pouring that frustration into exercise.

I paused along the sidewalk for a long pull of vodka with frozen blood cubes from my water bottle. Hydration was *extra* essential. My diet was almost fully liquid. I could—and did—eat solid food, but it wasn't, strictly speaking, necessary. I used to live on liquor and smoothies, but lately my liquid diet included blood, too. It made me feel gross if I thought about it, but if I ignored that element of my nutritional needs, my stomach cramped, my reflexes slowed, and my general well-being suffered. *Draugr*, although once thought to be nothing more than Icelandic folklore, were blood-drinkers. They sustained their organs with the blood of the living, which meant that I, despite being alive, had started to need fresh blood. It was as gross as it sounded, but I had no choice.

So, there were little heart-shaped, frozen blood cubes in my vodka.

Thankfully, I hadn't started sweating or weeping blood like some bad film. However, I did sweat enough tonight that I smelled like I'd been on a bender, but this was New Orleans. Even after the *draugr* were revealed, we were clutching our Sazeracs and Hurricanes on Bourbon Street. Nothing stopped the party that was life in the Crescent City, not even the appearance of the again-walkers. Booze might not literally be the lifeblood of the city, but it was as essential to our locals and our tourists as the history and music that made New Orleans a glimmering light in the world.

Inside Tomes and Tea, business was still hopping. I was pleased to see little group of readers, including the new start-up "book club with car service" I'd proposed last month. People, locals mostly, were less inclined to go out after hours because of the *draugr*, but Jesse's bar was a "no *draugr* territory"—under penalty of death—thanks to a little discussion with my dear dead grandmother, Beatrice. We'd sort of reconnected. Although she was one of the dead creatures I hunted, she was also my ancestor, and she was eager to make me happy.

Ergo, my bestie's bookstore was a secure place for humans.

Once I knew the shop was a safe space, I'd proposed that Jesse start a night owl's bookclub. It was an opportunity for New Orleanians who were pretty much locked in from dusk till dawn to go out somewhere that was guaranteed safe. From the looks of it, the club was already larger than we'd initially dreamed.

When I walked toward the stairs to go up to Jesse's private space, I paused.

Jesse had the frustrated expression everyone who has ever worked in a shop has worn at least a few times. Next to him was an older man pointing at one of the books in the containment boxes.

Jesse had a tight expression. "As I said, that isn't currently available for sale. They're more decorative—"

"Do you have any idea what that *decoration* is worth?" the older man interrupted.

"Since I'm the one who purchased it, I do, in fact," Jesse said.

"Name a price."

"It's not for sale." Jesse stressed each word, attempting to sound more intimidating that he was. Although Jesse was the sort of man who looked like he wasn't afraid of much—muscles, deep eyes, dark skin, assorted tattoos—he was kind to a fault.

I strolled up with the confidence that came of too much comfort with weapons and magic. A quick glance at the book clarified exactly what I needed to know. The tome in question was one darker than Jesse ought to ever touch, so I'd paid for it when it arrived at the store. I didn't use it, but it was, technically, mine. Being mine didn't mean I wanted the book in my house. Some books ought to be kept in magic-proof cases. This was one of them.

"Mr. Woods is trying to buy a book that's not for sale, sis," Jesse said as he moved back.

Calling me "sis" casually was our way of saying "step in." I'd started it, calling him "little brother" when I wanted him to get out of the way, and "big brother" when I wanted him to chase off a guy who was obnoxious. Jesse was family in all ways but blood.

"I believe my brother has already answered you." I smiled at Jesse as he walked away. Then, I turned to the man. "We aren't interested in selling this book."

"We?"

"It's my store, too." I smiled again, colder now as I was feeling both irritated at the reality that the customer was, in fact, not always right and because this one was screwing up my good mood.

"Perhaps you'll see reason, Miss . . ." The man extended his hand like we should shake.

"Crowe." I ignored the outstretched hand. Magic sometimes required touch, and I wasn't in the habit of making that easier for any potential enemies.

I felt tendrils of inquiry, magical questions brush against me, and it irritated me. My own magic was still sleepy, but I felt it stirring in defense. To him, though, I seemed weak.

Slowly and purposefully, I drew a dagger that was almost long enough to be a single-handed sword. At the same time, I used my absolute best customer service voice and said, "Mr. Woods, I am a necromancer. I freelance for NOPD and the queen of the *draugr* in this region. Do you really want to provoke me?"

He pivoted and left without a word.

From behind me, I heard, "You're sort of scary, boss."

Alice Chaddock—thirty, beautiful, and dressed to stun--stood there with a flat of coffee cups from Sera's place. Next to her was Sera. Both were curvy redheads, although Sera was deep rich red and Allie had that just-set-fire red. Honestly, they looked like they could be related. The difference was that Allie was always ready to pull up a chair and have popcorn when I was in a situation, and

Sera gave me that look that said she'd seriously been pondering shoving my ass into a tower in a remote forest because she just wanted a break from worrying about me. My near-death event before the holidays had rattled my friends a lot. Okay. So had my brush with death during the holidays.

And it was quite possible that I'd caused a bit of anxiety with my recent necromantic event where I raised an ancient cemetery and brought a dead Hexen back to life. Sera was eying me in ways that made me want to scream. This was me. Who I am. What I chose. It wasn't like I wanted to die, but I was gifted with skills that made me suited for conflict. I felt obliged to do the proverbial "right thing" even though it stressed out my friends.

In my defense, none of the near-death things had been planned. I didn't really *like* being attacked, stabbed, shot, or other things either. It was just a hazard of being me, and for all that my friends loved me, I think my job was exhaustive to them, too.

"Christy's upstairs," Sera said in that tense "not this again" voice. She nudged us that way. "Time for vacation planning."

"Should we relocate that book first?" Allie asked. "He doesn't seem the giving up sort. Should I call Bea—"

"Not tonight." I folded my arms and beamed at Sera, trying to non-verbally let her know everything was just fine. Cheerily, I added, "*We* are planning a trip. The book can wait for tonight. It's been here three months. Three more days will be fine."

"Are you sure?" Allie prompted.

I looked at Sera, and decided that whatever else was going on, we all needed that holiday weekend. "Positive. Let's go."

Jesse waved cheerily as the man stomped out the front door, and then he flipped the sign to closed, locked the door, and went back to his night owls book club.

"Juice in the fridge, Gen!" he called.

"I really have the *best* brother." I flashed him a smile and left him to debate the merits of the latest read.

As I headed up to the apartment with Sera and Allie in tow, Allie quietly murmured, "I think we ought to tell Beatrice."

I sighed. "Agreed. Just . . . not today."

My assistant was a *lot* on her best of days, but I trusted her instincts. Actually, I trusted all of my friends' instincts. That was sort of the point, though. True friends, we'll move-a-body-for-you friends, were the people who filled in the gaps for one another. We were a family of sorts, a misfit-band who might not look like we were all one unit, but when things were stressful, we were a team.

"Seriously?" Christy's voice came from the kitchen where she was watching one of the security cameras. "I swear that man could be nice to Satan herself—"

"Do you mean Beatrice or real Satan?" Allie paused in her texting to ask. "Ohh, is real Satan like *real*?"

No one answered in the three seconds that followed so Allie kept going: "Can I get a screen shot from the security cams? I took a few pictures, but Lady B's assistant . . . I wonder if there's an official assistant group that--"

"Allie. Focus."

Allie walked up to the monitor in front of Christy and pointed. "Right! So, can I?"

Christy Zehr was both one of the smartest people I knew, and one of those stunning women that pulled off either intimidating or fade into the background depending on which was needed. The towering Black woman looked down at the diminutive chatterbox in front of her and asked, "Gen?"

One syllable was all I needed.

"Alice is coordinating info in case the guy downstairs was a magic worker," I clarified. Then I looked at Allie. "Please, Allie, do not ask my grandmother if she's Satan. She might be a dead woman, but she's a *Jew*."

"So . . . Satan can only torment Christians?" Allie asked in an increasingly twangy voice. In public, she contained her rural roots, but I swore she sounded like this just because it got a rise out of Christy.

Like I said, we were family, and this family's shit-stirrer was Alice. She'd tried to murder me last year, and Christy and Jesse were the hold-outs on the forgiveness front. I understood why. Allie had been in a bad situation, and back then, I was just a stranger. Alice was a lot of things, but she was loyal to a fault. That loyalty was mine now, and honestly, I understood *why* she tried to kill me then. My friends were a lot less accepting.

Silently, I held out my back-up water bottle to Christy. "Vodka, no blood."

Christy took it and walked into the living room. Sera followed.

"Behave or I'll leave you home to babysit the fight dummies," I warned Allie.

She offered a semi-penitent smile. "Yes, boss."

"I mean it."

This time, she straightened up. "Let me send this to Lady B and then I'll be good. Scout's Honor!" She crossed her heart, which even I knew was not the right gesture, but really there was a limit to what was possible where Allie was concerned.

# CHAPTER 4

"So South Beach? Myrtle Beach? San Diego? Savannah?" Sera knew me well enough that she didn't bother asking about inland options. I'd had dreams of beaches as long as I could recall. New Orleans offered the banks of the Mississippi and a gator-filled bayou. It was lovely in its own way, but not quite the beach of my dreams.

I was trying to be considerate, though, so I said, "I thought maybe some of you might have opinions . . ."

Christy shook her head. "As long as there's liquor, I'm flexible."

I frowned. Christy wasn't a big drinker. She ran Eli's bar, and she'd hustled pool in it for years. Both required sobriety.

"Liquor? *That's* the criteria. Why?" I asked.

"*Hangry* Gen? No thanks." Christy grinned at me, and then she pointed at Alice. "And dealing with *her* while we're sober?"

Allie, thankfully, had taken my warning seriously. "I swear to be good. If you say 'shut up,' I'll—"

"Shut up," Sera interrupted.

Allie stared at her, but she closed her mouth. After a few moments, she raised her hand like we were in a classroom.

"Yes?" Sera prompted.

"I have a place down on the North Carolina coast, or there's a great spa in San Diego. Either one would be super cheap." Allie plopped down on the sofa, folding her legs up in some sort of yoga-ish way.

We exchanged looks.

"How is the spa cheap? Spas are usually expensive, aren't they?" Christy finally asked.

"Sure, but . . . I sort of bought it when Prince Eli said you wanted to get away," Allie muttered.

"You bought a spa when . . . we . . . seriously? Who *does* that?" I stared at her. My assistant was wealthier than anyone I knew-- other than my husband--but sometimes it still made my head hurt that she was so impulsive.

"I didn't buy it *for* you." Allie pouted like the trophy wife she'd been when I met her. "I just thought that it was a way to atone for the SAFARI days. I would run fae specials, witch specials, and maybe *draugr* specials, but only for those Lady B approved."

Alice gave me a look that shouldn't work on me, but still did. I knew she was sincere, trying to atone for her prior hate-group affiliation, and she honestly had the excess money. I just didn't know what to say. "But . . . you *bought* it?"

"Lady Beatrice looked over the investment papers. I even ran it by Prince Eli." Allie looked proud. "We don't need to go there, but at some point, I do. I mean, I bought it. So, I ought to visit and see it."

I exchanged a look with Christy and Sera.

"I'll give you a good discount," Allie added. "Like a package rate! And maybe you can give me business owner tips?" She looked first at Sera and then at Christy. "Or management tips?"

"San Diego, then?" Sera asked.

"San Diego," Christy agreed.

As much as I didn't know how I felt about the spa part, I couldn't contain the smile on my face. "I'm going to see the Pacific fucking *Ocean*."

. . .

WITHIN MOMENTS of deciding where we were going, Allie had whipped out her laptop to book flights.

"We can charter a flight to go direct," Allie suggested. "Or there's coach class with a layover."

"Charter," Christy said. "The boss is covering the flight." She shot me a sympathetic look. "Sorry, Gen. He's worried about too much publicity because of the you're-the-co-heir-to-the faery-throne thing."

I nodded. I was only the heir at all because of marrying Eli. I had zero interest in being royalty—although I was pretty damn stoked by my diplomatic passport.

The reality, however, was that I was remarkably unsuited to any throne. I couldn't quite wrap my head around the idea that anyone would give two shakes of a duck's butt about me. I guess blue-haired necromancers were rare enough, and the thought of a human—and witches were, in fact, considered human--marrying into fae royalty was supremely news-worthy.

*Draugr*-human, on the other hand, might create a different sort of news. I'd lived most of my entire twenty-nine years so far with a vague fear that I'd end up in a lab, dissected by zealous scientists. Don't get me wrong: I'm very pro-science. I'm also very pro-not-dying. And the fear—the *rightful* fear--humanity had of *draugr* meant that I wasn't sure science would care too much about my death if it resulted in answers that would assuage fears. I was genetically linked to the monsters. I couldn't blame scientists for seeking answers.

But I was hoping to never get exposed for what I was. That meant no travel. My weird genetics would set off alarms. Now, though, my first flight was going to be on a small, chartered plane.

". . . and they specialize in unique clientele," Allie was saying. Obviously, she'd been talking while I was still pondering, so I nodded as if I'd been listening.

"So, you're saying 10 in the *morning* actually works for you?" Christy prompted.

I guess I'd missed that detail.

"Sure!" I said in forced cheer.

"The boss can nap in flight." Allie clicked a few more keys on her laptop with a flourish. "Tomorrow, we head west!"

THE NEXT DAY, hours after our meeting, the four of us were picked up in an extended-length, black SUV. When I climbed in, I had to suppress a wide smile.

"Excited?" Christy prompted.

My attempt to look calm faltered. "You have no idea."

I'd packed light on clothes and modestly on weapons. My sword-and-bikini bag clattered as it was loaded into the rear of the SUV.

"Are you still going to sleep in flight?" Sera shot me a concerned look.

"Cat naps are all I really need since my, err"--I lowered my voice--"accidental marriage."

"Accidental?" Christy scoffed. "Did you trip and land on his dick? While naked? And professing love?"

Allie and Sera both smothered laughs, and I couldn't help but smile, too.

"Tripping over Eli and being naked is not as uncommon in my life as you might think," I faux protested.

"You're so lucky." Allie made a swooning, sighing sound.

"True," I admitted with a smile. I really really was. *Anyone* finding love was lucky.

I had never expected to be married, but Eli was everything I could want. He understood me. He saw me as an equal. And he never tried to change me. Plus, to be fair, he was the single most beautiful person I'd ever met.

Calling my marriage accidental was unfair. True love and sex created an unbreakable marriage bond with the fae, and my suspicions that what Eli and I shared was true love had been confirmed when a moment of perfect unity—a naked and sweaty moment—had resulted in an eternal bond.

I didn't regret it.

Before that, there were loopholes we'd tried to exploit initially —or rather, loopholes I'd tried to exploit. By the time of our naked, only-two-person-in-attendance wedding, I had been ready to try marriage. Magic involved intent, and my magic knew what I wanted before I truly admitted it.

While I was pondering my newly married state, my friends and I were driven to the little airstrip reserved for charter flights and private planes. Our ride was all tinted glass and driven by a man in an expensive suit and shades. When he parked, he began opening doors.

"Ma'am," he said opening the door for Christy. He repeated the word as Sera stepped out. Allie got the same gentlemanly hand and "Ma'am."

I was last.

He bowed before extending his hand. "Your Royal Highness."

I bit back my grumble. In the short time between marrying Eli and now, I'd been letting Eli handle all the etiquette stuff I didn't know. I didn't have that luxury today. I accepted the driver's hand, stepped out of the car, and tried not to trip.

Four similarly suit-and-shades clad people--a man, one nonbinary person, and two women—surrounded us in obvious formation. Guards. It appeared that my car service was not simple luxury.

"Are the windows bullet-proof?" I asked quietly.

"The entire vehicle is," one answered.

"And you are . . .?"

The one woman, who had undeniable fae features, met my gaze unflinchingly. "Fae Royal Service. When His Royal Highness, Prince Eli of Stonecroft said you would be traveling, His Majesty deployed us."

Maybe it was the early hour, but my temper sparked enough that my hair seemed to be lashing around me like silent, blue serpents. I had my phone in hand with the speed usually reserved for weapons.

Eli answered on the first ring. "Are you bleeding?"

"I only left thirty minutes ago. Why do you always think there's trouble?" I teased, but I grinned despite myself.

The sound of his chuckle drew my sour mood closer to level. "Because you are never predictable, bonbon."

"Did you know the car was bulletproof, Eli?"

"Of course. Aren't all car services?" He sounded perplexed.

I watched as one of the Fae Guard went onto the plane, checking for whatever he felt necessary. The others stood around us as our luggage was loaded.

"I don't want guards," I grumbled into the plane. "I'll accept an armored car, and I'm thrilled by the chartered plane and diplomatic passport, but what sort of fun is a spa weekend with a host of armed guards?"

"Guards?" Eli echoed. "What am I missing, Geneviève?"

"Are they not your guards?" My hand went to my gun. All I'd had was a stranger's word. I was getting sloppy.

"Royal Decree 312," one of the guards said loudly.

I flicked the phone to speaker and slid into the holster that had been holding my preferred revolver. Two birds. One holster.

The Fae Guard continued, "In the interim between bonding and anchoring, the non-fae spouse shall be kept secure and uninjured if said spouse separates from the fae spouse for any length of time longer than thirty-three minutes."

"Legit?" I asked Eli over the phone. My gun was still loose in my hand.

To my left I saw Allie pull her far-too-large .45 from her purse.

Christy pulled out one slick 9mm and one near machete-sized knife.

Sera simply stepped behind Allie, but she accepted the knife from Christy. She wasn't a weapons person, but she could be as fierce as an angry raccoon if necessary.

The Fae Guards eyed us all curiously.

Eli's sigh was loud. The word he said sounded like "row sheen," but I realized it was a name when one of the female guards said, "This is Roisin, Your Royal Highness."

"I assume my uncle sent you," Eli said.

"He did." Roisin watched us, looking almost fascinated. Her gaze lingered on Sera, and I hoped it was only a flicker of interest as opposed to not selecting a target.

"Stand down, Roisin." Eli's voice was deep with anger, and I knew that if I could see him right now, his normally calm façade would have slipped.

The Fae Guard grinned. "You're not king yet, Prince Eli, and I'm no longer your training mate. Unless my king orders me to do so, my squad will be with Her Royal Highness."

"Can I shoot them?" Allie loudly whispered. "I bet we could stop them from getting on the plane."

Roisin and the other guards all flinched, but Roisin was the one who replied, "We don't ride in metal tubes. We will meet you upon arrival."

"How . . ." Sera started.

"Plane. Now." Christy motioned Sera forward, and Allie followed.

"I'll speak to my uncle," Eli said before the phone went silent.

Once I boarded the plane, the steps were raised. The Fae Guard watched. Once we started taxiing, I looked through the window again.

I could see one of the guards rip a slice in the air. In a moment, they'd all stepped through the shimmering veil. They'd travel into *Elphame* and then re-appear in San Diego. The land of the fae was not beholden to normal laws of science; time, distance, and space were different there. The fae could hop anywhere in the world of humans by crossing through their homeland. My mind boggled at the possibilities—and the speed. It was the next best thing to the *draugr* ability to *flow*—their travel was faster than mortal sight could follow.

Despite the other options available to the fae and the *draugr*—options I could use, too--I was excited to be in the air. The other ways might be faster, but flying felt like a magic all its own. No feathers, no hollow bones, and yet humanity had found a way to hurtle themselves into the sky.

I watched the ground seem to drop from under us as the plane launched into the air. Every bit of logic I had said it ought not work, but there we were, escaping gravity, escaping the very ground, and racing through air. It might not be the sort of magic witches knew, but it left me exhilarated all the same.

# CHAPTER 5

"We could land in Long Beach," Allie said, jarring me into wakefulness.

I blinked up at her. Apparently, I had dozed off in the comforting fluttering movements of the plane. The pilot had called it turbulence, but it felt a bit like the few times I'd been on a small boat in the Mississippi River, rolling and jolting. It had lulled me to sleep the same as the river's waves had done.

"Context?" I asked.

Allie held out a cocktail with a proud flourish. "Spicy breakfast."

My assistant had a fondness for naming the blood concoctions that she procured. I sipped, paused, and sipped again. "Not Allie juice. Whose blood is this?"

She sighed. "I told her you'd know!"

I sipped again. "Not my grandmother either. Not Eli . . . not human, though."

"Lady B's assistant." Alice patted her purse, where I knew a large handgun and lipstick and itinerary were stored. "I added cayenne, cumin, tomato juice, vodka, probiotics, garlic; it's, sort of like a Tex-Mex Bloody Mary, heavy on the blood. I *told* them you'd know it wasn't my blood."

"Why?" I sipped. Tomato, contrary to many opinions, was a kind of fruit. I knew that with certainty because I was getting a break-fast-drink buzz.

"Oh, well, in case you needed more blood than I have." Allie was chipper as she announced this as if my leechlike appetite wasn't exhausting. Before I could object, apologize, or lament, she patted her giant handbag. "It's like preparation for if I ever need to carry baby formula. I mean, except for the vodka . . . and the blood . . . and—"

"Long Beach?" Sera did not look like she'd slept, more like she'd developed a distinct case of air sickness.

"So, the guards will be at San Diego Airport, but *we* could land at Long Beach—like an hour on the freeway this time of day—and drive there. No guards. No armored cars. Just us." Allie grinned.

"Do it." I didn't even pause. Maybe Eli could call off the guards, but if not, the fact was that an armed entourage drew attention, and I was not interested in that. I wanted to lose myself with my friends and sit on a beach.

"They'll still meet us at the spa," Sera pointed out.

"*My* spa." Allie rummaged in her purse and held up a little packet. "Electrolytes. Great for hangovers and flights."

Sera gratefully accepted, and then Allie went off to talk to captain.

"She's terrifying," Sera muttered.

"You're not wrong." I sipped my breakfast. The fruit would leave me vaguely tipsy, but wasn't that the point of the weekend? Girls' Weekend. Fun, freedom, and frolicking.

By the time we'd landed, I was both excited and tipsy. Sera was even more motion sick. That left Christy and Allie in charge of decisions for car rental, luggage gathering, and navigating. We all showed travel cards—and everyone except me had a temperature and pulse check.

"Would you like to *volunteer* to have yours recorded?" the man asked.

I laughed. "Witch melded with a faery. My readings would be too weird. Plus, I have this." I shook my diplomatic passport. "Wouldn't want to anger the faeries, would we?"

He walked away quickly, much to our relief. I had no idea what readings I'd get. I was not just witch and fae, so I'd register in potentially dangerous ways.

Allie swept away to get a car, and Christy stared after her, frowning.

"What's wrong?" I prompted.

"I may like Alice if she keeps being so . . ." Christy waved her hand in the direction of my cheerful assistant who was clapping her hands at something the rental car agent said.

I nodded. "That's what happens. You're going along minding your business, used to finding chirpy women irritating, and then she pulls out a gun or stocks your drawers with really useful lingerie, or runs over a *draugr* with her car. Then you realize you actually like her."

"Lingerie?" Christy echoed.

"Or she sings," Sera said. "Honestly, if she sang all her prattling answers, I'd listen to whatever she was going on about."

I patted Christy's shoulder and offered her my drink, forgetting the blood part until Christy winced. "Strictly non-blood, Gen."

"Sorry." I fired off a quick text to Eli, letting him know our changed plans.

When Allie returned, she refused to tell us what she'd rented until we rolled our bags to the car. There, gleaming like a bright, beautiful bad idea was a cherry-red Mustang convertible.

"Seriously?" Christy looked at Allie.

"Yep." Allie popped her "p" like it was bubble gum. Then she tossed the keys to Christy. "You said you loved convertibles, and"— she motioned around us—"ocean."

"Damn it." Christy looked at me. "I'm done for."

Sera and I laughed, and we all stowed the luggage and clambered into the car. No guards. No work. Four women in a convertible at the beach.

What could possibly go wrong?


BY THE TIME we reached the spa, things were so ideal that I expected the spa itself to be a dump. However, it was anything but low-brow. Christy pulled the car up to the lobby area, and bellmen swooped out to collect our bags and open our doors.

"I didn't tell them I was coming," Allie whispered quickly. "It's like a stealth inspection." Then she raised her voice and said, "Reservation for Zehr, party of four. Full deluxe package."

"Of course. Right this way."

We were ushered to the front desk, and I was glad I was sober enough to take in the lobby. A massive pedestal fountain, surrounded by tiers of flowers, dominated the high-ceilinged space. Some sort of soothing music, acoustic and earthy, filtered into the room. And the entire space was perfumed with some sort of— lavender? vanilla?-- earthy fragrance. I couldn't identify it, but it was very relaxing.

A uniformed man approached with glasses of what looked like pink champagne, despite the early hour. Apparently, they took relaxation very seriously here.

I accepted a glass and glanced at my phone.

"We have no cell signal on the main grounds," the man said in a low soothing voice. "Jarring things are not permitted, out of respect for the other guests. Phones will not work here."

I expected a reply from Eli, but nothing came up. I frowned and tapped off another text to Eli. Sooner or later, he'd get the message when we hit a hotspot or I caught the wifi in the room.

At the desk, Christy was filling out paperwork. She paused, glanced at me, and slid a black credit card over to the woman. "For all expenses."

The young woman took the card, ran it, and in short order, we were being whisked away through a maze of halls and across court-yards, each with burbling fountains and flowers. A young man with the sort of timeless beauty that spoke well of the spa's service strolled through the grounds, leading us. It felt a bit like we were walking in circles, a labyrinth of landscaped beauty that I presumed he was showing off.

The group of us exchanged a few looks, pointing at flowers—especially the sheer number of Birds of Paradise. They could grow in New Orleans, but here they were seemingly cropping up like bright flocks around fountains.

"Through the statuary garden, you will find trails." Our bell-man--staff guide, whatever he was--motioned. "Beyond the spa rooms you can reach the ocean. Our facilities offer the best of Southern California without the inconvenience of driving or ever leaving the estate grounds."

"It's beautiful," Allie said with a grin.

The bellman finally stopped beside a building. "Your casita."

Sera stepped forward, but he put his hand up.

He slipped off his shoes, standing barefoot inside the door. No, at closer look, he had on what looked like thick gauze socks. "We want nothing outside to contaminate the cleansing energy of the casita."

When none of us reacted, he added, "We don't wear shoes inside."

Once we all took off our shoes, he opened the door for us to walk inside. It felt a bit like the home I shared with Eli, as if nature had come inside. Another fountain. More scented air. This time, the earthy fragrance reminded me of jasmine.

Our guide walked to a large dinning table. On it were several carafes of chilled water with condensation trickling down the bottles. And at the head of the table were four folders.

"Each client has a spa rejuvenation and detoxification schedule," he explained. "This schedule will enable you to purify your body and soul."

He pointed to wall where a color-coded "group schedule" was written out in lovely penmanship. "As you can see, meals are also scheduled. Your optimal nutrition for your age and fitness will be provided. No sharing of entrees, please, as it complicates the chef's creative process."

At that, Sera snorted.

"Can anyone enter the facility who isn't a registered guest?" Allie prompted.

"Absolutely not," he said, sounding aghast at the thought. "We are an *exclusive, private* spa."

"Excellent." I wandered toward the kitchen, and then the living room, and finding nothing, paused. "Where is the bar here?"

"The casita is not stocked with alcohol." Again with the appalled tone. "It's dulling."

Allie scowled. "So, it's only served at the restaurant?"

"Restaurant?" The man pressed his lips together briefly. "Each guest will have a personally selected meal. We do not burden our guests with making decisions on meals that they may not enjoy."

I exchanged a tense look with Allie. Somehow, I doubted that they'd have my preferred meals available, but we could always go out into San Diego and shop.

Christy shooed the man out. Once he was gone, she met my gaze, "Plan?"

I shrugged, determined not to let a teetotaling stance at the spa ruin my weekend. It was a minor inconvenience, but the resort was lovely, and the spa experience sounded destressing. "Spa visits, and then we can go out in the morning to grab my food."

# CHAPTER 6

Lunch arrived a while later. The waiter placed each tray in front of a seat. Our napkins were color-coordinated with our spa charts.

"Your needs are specific to your person," the waiter said. "Your meals fulfill your particular needs in the best way. You will eat the meal provided."

It felt like a threat, which didn't do much for my already agitated mood. Then, I looked at my meal. It was a far cry from fulfilling my needs—and it was bleh. I wasn't expecting quesadillas or loaded fries, but I expected a *few* goodies. My plate was carrot sticks and hummus, and with it was cucumber water and a "dessert plate" of berries and cheese.

The waiter left, and the four of us looked at the plates.

I was seriously starting to question our decision to stay here at the spa. It wasn't bad enough that I'd starve, but the meals were depressing, too. Allie ended up with what looked like raw steak with a raw egg and onions draped over. That was it. Raw steak and cucumber water.

"Steak tartare," Allie offered with a grimace. "Good for iron and protein. . . I guess I need that to recover from the extra I'll need to feed you, boss."

"Blanched chicken, broccoli, and spinach," Christy offered gesturing at her plate. "And a cheese plate."

"Four bean salad." Sera smiled at her heaping plate. "Did you tell them I was a vegetarian?"

Allie shook her head, poking a fork at her raw meat as if she could threaten it into being edible. "So, everyone is getting iron-rich, high protein meals?"

"Everyone but me. I got *carrots*," I muttered. "Why carrots? Do I look like a bunny?"

"I'll take them!" Allie offered. "You can have this bloody mess . . ."

I winced. I might drink blood in my breakfast smoothies, but I wasn't going to eat raw meat. "Hard pass."

"Maybe they expect us to collect nuts and berries or catch a lobster at the beach," Allie muttered before pushing away from the table.

"Not going to do much for my 'specific nutritional needs,' but I could certainly catch food for the rest of you," I offered. "I'm more than fast enough to—"

"This will not do!" Allie interrupted. "I *own* this place. I *will* have real food and liquor, damn it. And so will you."

The next thing I knew Allie tossed me a blood slushy from her carry-on and ripped open a candy bar she'd stashed in there. That bag was a veritable cornucopia of surprises.

"Either of you need anything?" Allie looked at Sera and Christy.

They shook their heads and dug into their dinners.

After a moment, Christy swallowed the first bite and asked hopefully, "Salt? Hot sauce?"

Allie pulled out a tiny restaurant packet of salt and a little jar of hot sauce. Then she withdrew a small airplane bottle of brown liquor of some sort. Rum? Whiskey? Bourbon? I had no idea. Mostly, we were all just marveling at the variety.

"I just need to grab a few things," she muttered, pulling out a pair of tweezers, a jar of moisturizer, and a fig bar. She set them all aside. Finally, she pulled out a roll of duct tape with a victorious, "A-ha!"

"Do you want me to go with you?"

"Eat." Alice plopped an airplane bottle of bourbon beside the slushy bag of blood. "Get a facial. I'm going up to the office to explain the errors of their ways. I'll be back before"—she glanced at the wall schedule—"our scheduled 'relaxing group beach walk.'"

After Allie marched out, duct tape in hand, Christy whistled. "Man, if Lady B ever transfuses *that* one, Allie could run the whole hemisphere."

We observed a moment of quiet while I searched for a tumbler to use for my blood and bourbon slushy. Honestly, I thought Alice had every right to be pissed off. It was a spa. *Her* spa. She came stealthily to investigate, and what she'd learned was worth a bit of yelling.

"Should we go after her?" I asked, thinking about the no cell phones policy. I had figured the phones would work in the rooms, but so far, I had no signal here either.

"She'll come get us if there's trouble." Sera pointed out.

It wasn't as if we lived in a city that lacked trouble, and Alice Chaddock was not a stranger to conflict, handguns, or pushy people. She was fierce and smart—and armed. I trusted her, but I was used to being the one marching into conflict.

"One hour," Christy suggested. "She'll yell. They'll fix it. She *bought* this place, so they'll get a quick lecture. If she's not back after our 'whirlpool or sauna session,' we go after her. Her idea of waiting until the beach walk . . ."

"Three hours is way too long," Sera agreed.

I wasn't sure if it was paranoia, but I suggested, "Do you mind if I put all of our things—including shoes and keys—under a stasis spell?"

The relief in their expressions told me that I wasn't the only person with a sliver of paranoia. I didn't want to tote our belongings everywhere, but I was starting to have doubts about the staff.

"Please do! No shoes. No cell signal. No booze." Christy met my gaze. "I'd feel better knowing our weapons were secure."

I pulled on the magic that I could summon. I might not be able to raise the dead, but the *draugr*-blood made for a nourishing slushie. It was one of the more rejuvenating things I'd tried. I made a mental note to pay a visit to my grandmother to thank her for sending blood once we all returned to New Orleans, and then I heaped all of our things in one corner. I placed both a security layer—strong electrical charges on anyone my magic didn't recognize—and a concealment layer over the luggage, weapons, and shoes.

Plan and spells in place, we finished our odd lunch, although I skipped the berries this time. I had a prickling feeling that being tipsy wasn't ideal. Maybe I was overreacting. Allie was probably just dressing down her staff, possibly firing people or explaining that we needed proper meals. I was so used to threats that I saw danger everywhere. Sure, the spa was a little weird, but that wasn't *dangerous*.

Twenty minutes later, Allie wasn't back, but a guide with a satchel popped into the casita without so much as a knock or word.

Christy and I already had weapons drawn.

"Knock first." I pointed my sword tip at him. "Make a note. What if we'd been changing or . . ."

"This is a *spa*, madam. You will be unclothed quite often. The staff is unaware of nakedness." He sounded like he was mocking me, but not in any overt way that I could address. It was that passive-aggressive thing that always made me want to jab people the way Allie had with her raw meat meal.

"Knock," I repeated. "Because I'm not always quick to ask questions before shooting."

At first, he said nothing in reply, merely gestured toward the door with a calm, "I am here to escort you for the scheduled soothing spa or sauna session. Please join me."

As we approached him, he offered us each a bundle with beige robes and some sort of woven thong-sandal things. "We are without shoes or wear *only* these on this ground in order to respect the soil."

"Let us grab our suits, and we'll be right with you." Christy turned to walk into her bedroom.

"That won't be necessary. Material has chemicals, and chemicals could create imbalance in the hot spring that we draw our water from." The guide smiled beatifically. "Simply unburden yourselves of clothing, and we can depart."

Silently, I sent a little magical buzz his way, just to "taste test" to see what he was. If he were a regular human, he wouldn't react. If he was something else, I'd know—at least I would if my magic answered.

It fizzled before I could read him. Still no reliable access to my magic.

"Are there other people there?" I asked, worrying about my friends' privacy. I was a witch, so being skyclad—naked—was as comfortable for me as dressed. But I wasn't sure Christy was entirely at ease with walking around naked, and *that* was enough of a reason for me to object.

"You will have a towel for the sauna if you opt for steam over the hot pools. The spa is heated with the same water, so you will be purified either way." He smiled again, and I was tempted to ask what he'd been smoking. The man was too damned chill.

Shoes left behind, wearing the least comfortable woven footwear I'd ever put on, we hobbled through the garden toward the spa. Weirdly, this was our second time walking outside, and we still hadn't seen another soul.

"Is the spa always this empty?" I asked.

"Empty?"

"You know, no guests. *Empty.*"

He gave us another vacant smile. "We are at capacity, madam. Our guests are simply enjoying the benefits of a peaceful existence."

"Okaaaay." I glanced at my friends. They weren't buying it either.

We walked in silence that felt eerie now, and that creeping feeling of dread didn't relax when we stepped into a vacant spa.

"I'll leave you in the care of your personal spa guide." The man turned and left—after collecting our footwear.

"Select a pair of spa shoes," the vacant-eyed spa guide said as she approached. "They are separated into size bins."

We looked at each other as we collected our shoes. This time, we were given what appeared to be pea-soup green, tissue-paper "shoes." They would do exactly nothing to protect our feet.

"Seriously?" Christy whispered.

"They're crafted of pressed leaves," the vacant-eyed spa guide said. "They'll melt into the pools or protect your feet at the spa. When they fully vanish, it's time to step out of the steam." She gave us a wide-eyed smile. "Isn't that clever? You don't even need to watch the time. We like our guests to be freed of all responsibility."

I'd never wanted a sturdy pair of sandals as much as I did today.

"They *melt*?" Sera echoed.

"It opens your pores, so when you depart the spa center you can absorb the earth," the smiling woman added.

"So, we'll be naked, wet, and barefoot?" Christy prompted.

"Isn't it wonderful?" the woman said.

I think we were all too horrified to answer. This was turning into a vacation focused more on torture than relaxation.

"I'm Misty, your spa guide." She smiled at each of us. "Let us begin."

# CHAPTER 7

After Misty, the vacant-eyed spa guide watched us put on our shoes, she announced in an unsettlingly calm voice, "Who will be steaming?"

"Steaming?" Sera echoed.

"Hot steam will open your pores and soul," Misty explained. "Calming scents will add to the rejuvenation."

"And we keep a towel?" Christy clarified.

"Oh yes, you can sit on it or cover the softer parts from steam." The young woman looked so earnest that I wanted to ask if they were steaming high grade marijuana or something else in the vents, but I was *really* trying to believe that this place was just extra-eco, extra-earthy, not corrupt. It was San Diego, for goodness' sake! They didn't even have *draugr* here.

"I'll do the hot springs," I said. "See you two after."

Sera and Christy opted for the sauna, but I felt relatively certain that one of us ought to investigate the hot pool. I hoped I was being paranoid, but I was starting to have a strong suspicion that the employees were all high or drugged. I kept trying to explain it away as hippie-dom gone wild. But . . . Maybe it wasn't simply *extra*.

Maybe something was actually off here, and although I had no idea what it was, I wanted to ease my potential paranoia.

I waited in my robe and tissue paper shoes until Misty returned. Then, I followed her through a pair of wooden doors into a freezing cold room with a burbling steamy pool about the size of an extended, rectangular dining room table. The room was absent of plants, but the scent of something sweet was just this side of nauseating. Was *that* the drug? It was so sugary that I could taste it in the humidity.

I walked over to the hot spring and dropped my robe.

The smiling spa guide said, "When your shoes fully melt, you are allowed to exit."

"Allowed?" I echoed.

She just nodded, even as I gave her a questioning look. Paper shoes in near-boiling water? They'd melt as soon as I entered the pool. But whatever. There was a hot spring, and flaky spa staff or not, the feeling of sinking into that hot water was like dropping into peace.

Within moments my muscles relaxed, and I sighed.

For the first time since we left the resort lobby, I felt truly relaxed. The extra-hot, bubbling water seemed to sluice in and out around me like waves. Giant rocks rimmed the pool like strange seats. And whatever that scent was, it was calming. Not too sweet. Not too anything. It was like inhaling peace.

I stayed like that, submerged up to my shoulders and feeling calm enough to nap, right up to the moment that my head slipped under water and hit a rock. The shock and pain of it jolted me upright and out of the stone tub.

Why was I here? Why was I relaxing so much? Something was definitely wrong. Whatever peace I'd felt quickly vanished.

Naked as the day I was born, shoeless and dripping wet, I walked out of the hot springs room and to the front desk. As I did, I saw an older suit-clad man dart away.

No. Not dart. I saw a man *flow*. Only one creature did that.

*Draugr.* There was a *draugr* here.

My peace was all sorts of gone.

Misty the spa guide stepped up to me in a flurry. "Are you unwell? Would you like a soothing glass of cucumber water?"

"Who was that?" I asked, nodding toward the doorway where the man had vanished.

"There was no one here." Misty frowned, giving me a baffled look that seemed genuine. Had she not seen him?

"Dead guy in a suit," I clarified. *"Draugr.* Right here, plain as murder."

"No. There are no *draugr* in San Diego." Misty shook her head. "How could there be? We check everyone at the gates."

"I saw him."

"No." She glared at me and repeated, "There are no *draugr* in San Diego."

I couldn't tell if she was afraid or angry. Either way, she obviously wasn't a fan of questions.

I looked around, cursing my continued lack of necromancy. I wanted my magic back. All of it. It shouldn't still be an empty reserve inside me. Weeks of this had worn on me—enough that I was apparently on a hell-vacation.

"There was a *draugr* here. Just now," I said calmly. "You were *just* talking to him."

*"Draugr* don't live in San Diego." This time, Misty laughed like I'd told a joke, but then she said, "Were you in the spring too long, ma'am? Oh no! Let's get you hydrated, mmm?"

She tried to reach out to check my temperature, like a mother putting a wrist to a child's fevered forehead.

I swatted her away. "Stop that."

"You must have been faint. Drink this!" She poured a tall glass of that now-tepid water.

"You drink it." I stepped back.

And she did. She blinked. Then she lifted the glass and drained the whole thing. Then she re-filled it and held it out.

"Cucumber mint water?" She gave me another beatific smile. "Or I have celery if you're hungry."

"Hop."

Still holding the glass of tepid water, Misty started hopping. "Drink the water, ma'am. It'll clear your mind of all troubles."

"Sauna," I managed to say.

Misty scrunched up her face like I'd confused her, and then she started hopping toward the sauna.

"Stop hopping," I whispered.

"I thought . . . weren't you going to the pool?" Misty blinked at me several times before whispering, "You're all wet, you know?"

I bit back my frustrated yell and said, "Misty, I am looking for the sauna. *Walk* me to the sauna."

"Oh. Are you scheduled for it?"

I paused. I hoped she was drugged, not naturally this daft. I smiled as calmly as I could. "Why yes, I am scheduled for it. I was late. Swimming, you know."

A flicker of terror went over her, and her mouth opened wide like she was going to scream, but then she blinked. The fear and pending scream vanished. The words looked like they were a struggle to get out, but she managed to say, "Stay away from the beach. They'll get you."

There was something wrong here—beyond the celery and carrots and weird-assed shoes.

Just then, Allie burst through the door, purse bulging, a trash bag over her shoulder, and bloody hands gripping what looked like a broom handle. Her feet were bloody, and all she said was, "Boss! Weapon."

She tossed me her back-up gun, a tiny .22 that was perfect for concealing in your cleavage, but not exactly high-powered.

"News?" I gripped the gun, just as Allie swung the broom at Misty, who dropped the syringe she'd had concealed in her hand.

"I'll take that." Allie scooped up the syringe, wrapped it in a couple pairs of the tissue paper shoes, and stuffed it all into what looked like an empty blood bag.

She met my gaze and announced, "*Draugr*. Witches. I don't even *know*, but talking to the staff was like talking to a bunch of drunk bunnies!"

I nodded; not-interrupting was often best with Alice.

"They locked me in a supply cabinet. Can you believe that? As if that would cage me! I whacked my head hard when they shoved me in there. But that meant I was clear-headed long enough to grab some stuff before escaping."

"Are you—"

"I figure I bought the resort already, so I'm not *actually* stealing!" Alice tapped her broom handle on the floor like she was some old, wizard with a staff. "Let's get the others."

"Right." I sort of blinked, realizing that I was still a little woozy from the hot spring. "Get them. Go outside to get fresh air."

We walked through the spa center, guns and broom handle at the ready. No one was there. Anywhere. The first few treatment rooms were empty. As we walked further, we discovered that a few rooms had people--*comatose* people--stretched out on the massage tables. They all seemed alive, but more than a few had been there long enough that their muscles were significantly atrophied.

"They won't wake," Allie said. "I tried to wake one I saw beside the pool on a lounger."

"What in the name of duck gizzards is going on here?" I muttered.

Allie shook her head. "We need to get out of here, and . . . I'll need a well-armed cleaning crew for this place. First, though, it's rescue-and-run time."

After several more minutes, we found Sera and Christy, giggling uproariously in the vanilla and fruit-scented sauna.

"Gen!" Sera yelled cheerily.

We tugged them out of the sauna, but they were giggling like they had been smoking *all* the drugs at the same time.

"Why are you taking out trash?" Christy pointed at Allie's bag. "Are there chores?"

"Pain helps shock you out, but . . . I cannot hit *them*," Allie motioned at them.

"Bee!" I yelled. "Get it, Sera! On Christy's cheek."

Sera slapped Christy's face, and Christy shoved Sera backwards. Sera kicked Christy, taking her legs out. I let one friend smash into the wall, and the other crumple to the ground. I felt a flicker of guilt.

Then Sera blinked. "What . . . where? Huh?"

"Why are we naked?" Christy asked, wrapping a towel more firmly around her.

"*Draugr.* Possibly magic. Drugs in the steam, I think . . ." I ticked it off. "The flowery, fruity scent."

Sera grabbed robes and handed one to Christy—and then she started going through cupboards until she found one for me. "Clothes, Gen."

I grinned. Right. Fighting while naked could get super awkward.

Allie had opened the trash bag, although her gun was still in reach if she needed it. She pulled out several cans of aerosol cleaner. "Here. Aim for the eyes."

Sera and Christy each stuffed cans of cleaner into one of their robe pockets. Then Allie pulled out a long-necked lighter. Grinning, she held it up. "Fire balls, anyone?"

She pulled out several glass jars, each filled with a yellow liquid, thumb tacks, nails, and a floating candle. The candles' wicks were sticking out of holes at the top and black electrical tape covered them. "Pull off the tape, light, toss, and *boom.*"

Christy shook her head. "You and me need to have a *long* chat, Tennessee."

Allie beamed. "Nicknames imply friendship."

"Give me some bombs, Tennessee. I played softball." Christy

held out a hand, and Allie, smiling widely, gave her the three improvised bombs.

"I'd feel a whole lot better with my swords," I admitted.

Allie looked at me. "I can't give you my favorite gun, but you can have my staff."

Now someone who had no martial arts training might not realize that a broom stick—a staff—was a worthy weapon, but a staff was able to execute all the primary blows a sword was. The difference was that the sword would slice flesh, and a staff would pummel the bones and organs.

I twirled my new weapon. Up close, a staff was just as good as a sword. And at a distance, we had improvised bombs, two guns, and homemade fire balls.

"Shall we go get our clothes, and get up out of this place?" Sera asked.

"Sounds like a plan," I agreed.

"But, you know, try not to set it *all* on fire," Allie said. "I *did* buy it."

"Come on, Tennessee. Let's test your bombs." Christy grinned at Allie.

And while it wasn't *exactly* a weekend that matched our plans, I felt good seeing them get along. It was a Girls' Weekend . . . but our way.

# CHAPTER 8

We walked into the lobby, watching for lurking *draugr*, human staff, or witches. Honestly, I had no idea what all sorts of trouble we had to face, and the one certainty was that the air was toxic.

The groggy-but-upright Misty looked horrified to see us—and I was fairly sure it wasn't just the fact that Allie was bloody. She stared at us like she was trying to speak and couldn't. I didn't know if she was drugged or enthralled to the *draugr* I'd seen or maybe just blackmailed. Either way, she stared at us and twisted her hands together.

"Windows," Sera muttered. She was swaying like she'd been on a bourbon tasting marathon.

I stepped around the hand-wringing spa guide and started shattering windows. The staff gave me reach, and there was something satisfying about bashing them. Glass tinkled down around me like a localized ice storm.

"Wait!" Misty suddenly grabbed at me, trying to grab the staff that I was currently using as a baseball bat, and in the process hanging onto me like an angry koala. "The raw air is deadly!"

Allie stepped back as Christy detached the worried woman

from my back and arms. Misty was struggling, though. She was convinced that the air *outside* was deadly, and in her attempts to rescue us, she kept trying to cover our mouths and noses as if to save us.

"Hit . . . her," Sera suggested between clearing breaths of fresh air. "Seriously. . . some . . . one . . . just *hit* her."

Christy was trying to hold the woman while avoiding getting clawed in the face, and Sera was struggling to speak. That left me or Allie.

Before I could figure out how to safely hit Misty, who was clearly drugged, Allie—still holding her gun--punched Misty in the temple.

Misty dropped like dead weight.

We dragged the now-unconscious Misty with us as we went outside. Her legs were being scratched all to hell by plants and rocks as she was half-dragged half-carried across the ground.

An alarm sounded and a series of sprinkler heads shot out of the ground. The misters that were strung through the trees and the sprinklers all started spewing a pinkish mist.

"Cover your mouth!" Sera gasped, putting her robe-covered arm over her mouth and nose.

"Bombs," Allie gasped. "Blow it all up!"

Christy shoved the unconscious spa guide toward Allie, who more or less caught Misty. Within moments, Christy started lighting and launching bomb after bomb as we ran through the garden. Small fires started and flashed to life, burning away the scent of sugary toxic air.

But too soon, the misters were switched to full-on geysers. Pink water fountained upward, putting out fires and creating a tinted floral fog that seemed to linger over everything. Allie's homemade IEDs were overkill on sprinkler heads, and someone was watching closely enough to turn mist into fountains.

I would have loved to take down whatever security system our unseen assailants had, but for now we had no targets other than mist, and *that* was impossible to counter without a few industrial fans.

We ran toward the casita, slower since Sera was now dragging Misty along with us. Christy still tossed the occasional bomb, and I played whack-a-mole with sprinkler heads. Everyone tried to avoid the hot, steaming pink water that spurted up at odd intervals.

"Don't stop running!" Sera ordered. "Almost there. Any corpse armies, Gen?"

"No!" I tried, but I wasn't able to summon anything large. Plus, short of dead crustaceans, I wasn't finding any corpses within range. I felt the edges of my magic flickering like the energy wanted to surface, but that wasn't terribly useful without corpses. Right now, my best options were assorted crustaceans, a few fish, and some jellyfish. Typically, I could summon both human and animal corpses, create an undead fighting force to attack enemies or defend me. Being magically depleted meant that I had no juice to summon much of anything, but even I did . . . well, let's just say that dead fish and invertebrates weren't as helpful as wolves, coyotes, or even the occasional yappy dog.

I had no army to bring to our aid.

We were all stumbling, and when we reached the casita we found several angry spa employees waiting, I wanted to cry. Beyond them were our weapons, keys, and clothes.

Christy tossed two bombs in short order, and as the smoke and fire overpowered the mist, I surged forward with my staff, bashing and shoving them with all my remaining energy.

As they fell, we stumbled into the casita. I watched as my friends stepped over the fallen spa employees. Then I followed, slamming the door as if it would protect us.

"Sewer weasels. . ." I leaned my whole body up against the door. There was no steam here, but the sugared scent was so strong that I wasn't sure if it was in the casita or if it was all over us.

"We need to get out of here." Christy watched the door. "If this place is really run by *draugr* . . . we have until nightfall."

"Weapon check?" I pulled the magic away from our belongings.

"We can't shoot our way through steam, boss." Allie pulled her sopping wet hair into a messy bun. "I can make more Molotov cocktail bombs, but . . . it's not enough."

"So how do we get to the rental car?" Sera was tossing clothes at all of us.

She paused to grimace at our thrashed feet. We weren't exactly used to barefoot living. As a child in the Outs, I had soles as tough as leather, but these days, I lived in the city.

"Beach?" I suggested.

The spa guide blinked up at us. "I was sea kayaking when they caught me."

"What?" Sera asked.

"Tossed a net over me, drugged me, and . . ." Misty touched her temple, wincing. "Thank you for clearing my head."

"So not by sea." Sera paced as Christy watched the door.

"The walked right out of the ocean, set up camp, captured us and drained us." Misty shuddered. "Then they set up here and victims just check in. No one ever leaves."

"You need a *juice,* boss." Allie looked over the woman we'd rescued, and I knew what she was saying.

I couldn't, though. Not her. Not here in front of someone who'd been so victimized by *draugr.* The poor thing had been captured, brainwashed, and undoubtedly used as a walking juice box already.

"What we need," Christy pronounced, "is a way out. I don't think we can reach the lobby, get to the car, and not get drugged up. Maybe Gen can, but not all of us."

I turned my back to Misty and whispered, "I can *flow* with one of you, then come back and—"

"Or you could rip a hole in the air and take us to Elphame," Christy suggested. "Doorway, Gen. We need a door out of here."

"There are a lot of rules," I hedged. "Mortals brought there are required to stay unless they are cleared prior to arrival."

I tried not to look at the stranger in the room. The reality was that if I took her over there, she was staying. No negotiation would change certain laws, not with the fae.

Sera and Christy were pre-cleared because they were in my wedding party. Allie wasn't, not yet.

"Allie . . ." I met her gaze. "You don't currently have clearance."

My fiery assistant gave me a look that could undoubtedly quell small nations. "Darlin, I'm not a person. I'm a *lunchbox*. Call me the red platelet special, but that man—any man—isn't going to keep me from my vow to you. He might be the fae king, but I go where you go, when you go, if you need. I'm like a part of you."

Sera snorted, gathering our bags up and shoving one toward Alice. The thought of Allie facing off against the king of the fae made me wince, but I couldn't image leaving her. Marcus would be reasonable. He *had* to be.

Misty flinched as something broke a skylight.

A canister of pink smoke clattered from the ceiling.

"Prisoner here or prisoner there," Misty muttered. "Which is worse?"

"Here." I reached out into the air with one hand, pulling on the part of my energy that I thought of as an extension of Eli and seeking a grip. I didn't want to open my mouth and inhale that toxic fruit and flower scent again, but I did yell, "Bags."

Then I found what I was seeking My hands parted the air as if it had become a heavy curtain that I could grab. I wondered briefly if it was easier to tap *this* magic because my life had always been magical. Being a witch-*draugr* meant I'd always had magic. *All* fae could open a doorway home, though. Now that I'd married Eli, I was included in that tradition.

The air took form and separated at my will.

"Go." I held the intangible curtain aside as if it had actual form, and Christy stepped into the other world with her luggage. Sera followed with her bags. Allie carried my weapons bag, her handbag, and her gun—outstretched as if she might need to shoot her way through enemies. She didn't bother with her suitcase. Priorities.

Misty paused. "Will it be better with the fae?"

I nodded, hoping I wasn't wrong, and she followed my friends in *Elphame*.

Then I stepped through, leaving the pink smell behind.

We all paused, gasping the clean air, and I waited for the inevitable fae assembly to arrive. I wasn't going to take one more step into *Elphame* until traditions were met.

# CHAPTER 9

"Geneviève of Stonehaven," the king of *Elphame* greeted as he stepped into the clearing with a group of fae soldiers.

"Crowe," I corrected. "Greetings to you, Marcus, King of *Elphame*."

The king smiled but it was a tense expression. He was put-together as always. If my husband had an older brother who had just slain an army single-handedly, the king of *Elphame* would be that man. I trusted him as much as I trusted any faery or politician—which is to say that I felt as wary as he looked.

"Be welcome tonight, bride of my nephew." The king met my gaze. The assembled guards, easily fifteen people, kept their silence. Swords were at the ready, and several were looking far too eager to draw them.

I sighed and dropped to a not-awful curtsy; my friends followed suit. Misty looked around like a drunk at an open bar. Allie held her gun loosely, ready but not starting trouble so far. Sera silently dropped our bags and handed me a sword.

"I seek haven for my friends . . . and a victim we rescued. We were attacked." I was suddenly hyper-aware that we were bedraggled and pinkish. "We are safe, but . . . there was no way out."

The assembled guards looked far from calm suddenly. They awaited orders, perhaps a rescue attempt.

"My nephew?" Marcus asked.

"Eli is at home, safe and blissfully unaware. I'd like to keep it that way." I gave him a wry smile.

"Oh, Death Maiden, I think my nephew has more than met his match in you, hasn't he?" The king didn't stifle a smile that looked a lot like a laugh in waiting. "I shan't be the one to tell him."

The king stepped forward as if I wasn't clutching a steel sword, and then the king of all fae in his world or mine kissed my cheeks in what appeared like fondness. I didn't exactly trust that it was. The fae were nothing if not political.

"Welcome home, niece," he whispered.

When he stepped back, I motioned to Sera, Christy, and Allie—naming each as I gestured their way. Then I added, "My friends and I were on holiday at the coast."

"Roisin had mentioned an inability to reach you." Marcus glanced at the fae guards. "There was a failure to update your travel plans for some reason. She was pursuing consent to forcibly enter the buildings where you were housed."

"I told you something was wrong," Roisin grumbled, sounding uncharacteristically human.

"You were correct, Roisin." Marcus grinned. "Shall we prepare for battle, Death Maiden? I've not had a skirmish in quite an age. Let us roust those who have cast insult on my family."

I tried to reply and choked on my words. "Roust?"

"I thought you said he was stuffy," Alice whispered far-too-loudly in the silence.

And the king of *Elphame* laughed as if a grand joke had been shared. Then Marcus looked at Alice and said, "There are quite a few changes in my mood since my nephew has accepted his duty—subsequently marrying the prophesied Death that I thought would steal my throne. As a faery, Alice, I had thought that *my own death* would come if I grew too attached to a woman."

"That's so sad!" Alice stepped forward and hugged him.

As she did so a dozen guards surged toward her, and I stepped forward in answer. I was but one sword against fifteen, though. Rage bubbled in my belly.

"Boss?" Allie called. She was clasped in the king's embrace, watching armed warriors aim weapons at her.

And in that moment, the magic I hadn't been able to access since I'd raised a cemetery to fight woke with a roar.

"*Mine!*" The word echoed across the ground like a quake. A surge of almost maternal affection rose up—as did the very ground around us. The king and Alice were suddenly atop a tall hill where the ground had been flat.

Walls of soil encased Sera and Christy, and by proximity, Misty. They were safe from harm.

And Allie was out of reach of the guards with swords.

From atop the newly formed hill, Marcus stared down at me with a curious expression. He raised his voice and asked, "Yours *how?*"

Allie smacked him. G-d help me, she smacked the king.

"Don't be a perv! She's family," Allie shouted at him. "I wouldn't be fool enough to bed her even if she wasn't twenty-seven kinds of drunk on Prince Eli. She takes a lot of work emotionally, and that's just being her assistant . . . and platelet supplier."

Marcus made a gesture and stone steps appeared, carved into the soil and sod of the new hill. He offered Alice his elbow.

His words were clear as day as he asked, "Platelet supplier?"

"When boss almost died, she sprouted fangs you know? Lady B —she's like you but fangier and scary but not quite as sexy—she said I need to feed the boss."

They descended the steps as everyone there stared.

Allie continued, "So, Prince Eli tricked Gen into drinking blood. Not like all throat-bitey, though. That seems . . . intimate, and not really for me. I have a siphon and--"

"Allie, dear? Shut up," Sera said calmly.

Alice snapped her mouth shut and nodded.

"Is she addled?" Roisin asked from my side.

"*Such* a good question," Sera muttered.

Alice raised her hand—the one that was still holding a gun—like a pupil in a classroom.

"Yes Alice?"

"Can we get a meal and some liquor for you before we go kick in the doors? And can we bring the faery lady who is staring at Sera?" Allie paused and grinned at Roisin. "Was that too blunt? I'm not sure of the etiquette. She's single, though, Miss Faery Lady."

Roisin folded her arms. "Not addled at all, is she? Sly."

Sera grinned. "Try dealing with her regularly."

"Food and refreshment sounds lovely," I said loudly. "Then I will go deal with whatever monsters are there. If I could leave my friends here while I—"

"I go where you go, boss." Allie still had a hand on the king's arm, and he made no move to dislodge her.

"We will bring a squadron or two to handle this, niece of mine." Marcus made eye contact with several guards, and they departed. Whatever orders he passed were handled so subtly that it was as if it hadn't happened.

"Can we message Lady B?" Allie added. "I bet she'd love an excuse to come to San Diego. Plus, she loves a good fight."

Marcus patted Allie's hand. "So do I, my dear. So do I."

I paused. "Alice, did my grandmother know about the spa?"

Alice paused, frowned, and then said, "She's how I discovered it. Her legal team knew a guy, and we bought it from the original owners who had gone missing."

I sighed, suspecting that my dear dead gran knew that there were *draugr* operating in San Diego. She couldn't go there herself, because of the no-*draugr* policy the city had, but I had to wonder if she'd intentionally sent me as her emissary. If so, although I might not have known it, she'd dispatched me like a rabid hunting dog.

The king met my gaze, and I knew he'd made the same connection I had. "I'll be at your side, Geneviève of Stonehaven."

"Crowe," I muttered. Then I added, "I look forward to a battle at your side."

By the time I'd taken my friends to Eli's house, which was also mine now that we were married, I felt the awkward need to ask my uncle-by-marriage what his intentions toward Allie were. There was no mistaking that spark of interest in his eye, and I wasn't sure Alice was in the right frame of mind to be seduced by a faery king.

Once the guards had left, and Misty was sent off to wherever mortals who stumbled into *Elphame* went, I was ready to pull the king aside for a little chat.

"Misty will be okay, right?" Allie prompted again.

"I swear she will." I gave Alice a reassuring look. "They treat humans well. She'll have all her needs met, and she'll build a life with the other humans. It's sort of a forever-cossetted thing here. She can work—or not. She can date—or not. The only rule is that she can't leave."

Allie nodded. "Marcus is so sweet. I probably shouldn't worry."

Christy snorted. "Sweet on you is more like it. Human or fae, people are people, and *that* man was panting at you so hard he was practically tripping on his tongue."

Allie sniffed as if dismissing Christy's words. "He was just kind. Friendly. Being a good host. Right, boss?"

I met her gaze. "Allie, the king wants you. It was as obvious as the way Roisin watched Sera. The fae might not be blunt, but they are believers in enjoying love and sex. So, in that area . . ." I shrugged. "Eli likely slept his way through half the city. Beautiful, eternal, and sexual. It's what they are."

Allie walked over and started to clear the table when we saw trays of food being carried toward the house. "Well, I think you're wrong," she said primly. "I'm a *widow*. He was just being a gentleman."

I exchanged a look with Christy. Clearly, I would be having a super awkward chat with my new uncle. Maybe reaching out to Eli —and asking him to handle it--wasn't such a bad idea after all.

# CHAPTER 10

Once we'd tucked into the sort of meal that vacations actually require—complete with a decadent dessert tray filled with everything from apple pie to crème brûlée to a Chantilly cream cake to a four-layer trifle and a selection of truffles—the dishes simply vanished.

"I'm feeling significantly less sympathy for you today, Gen." Sera stretched. "That was amazing. This place is . . ."

"Gorgeous," Christy finished.

"No *draugr* either," Sera added. "Would it be so bad to live here?"

I shook my head. It was a complicated question, which I wasn't entirely sure I could answer. Being here *was* incredible, and the best part was that it meant that I was now bonded with the only person who had ever made me feel whole. I'd always thought that "you complete me" business was silly, but then I melded with Eli. He *literally* completed me. Our souls were fused; our lifespans now tied together. I would die when he did—or the inverse. It was both terrifying and wonderful.

"It's incredible here, but I have a duty in New Orleans," I started. "Each person should leave the world better than how they came into it. That's my faith. It's as much a fact to me as anything science or magic can prove."

"So basically, you can't let yourself be happy because it's your duty to behead monsters?" Sera gave me the sort of stink eye that highlighted the increasingly difficult issue in our friendship of late. She didn't like what I did. Never had. Never would.

"Yes." I met her gaze head-on. "You don't have to like it—"

"Good. I don't." She folded her arms. "Why can't you just be a faery princess, Gen? You love Eli, and being his wife creates *other* responsibilities that you could spend eternity working on. That would be making *this* world better, and you'd be safer!"

"Eli knew who I was when he chose me, and he accepts it." I tried to keep my temper contained, but this had been the elephant-in-the-room for us for years. "This is me. Warts and all. You don't have to like it, but you need to accept it."

Sera pressed her lips together and walked out.

I sighed, hating the threat of tears I felt in the corner of my eyes. I wasn't a crier, hadn't ever been, but there were moments I wished I could be softer. I was happy with my life, loved my job—or *jobs* as the case now was—and I looked forward to my life with Eli. That didn't erase my identity. That was not the point of marriage, at least not the point of my marriage.

"She just worries," Christy said.

A thousand words wanted to come out, but it wasn't Christy who needed to hear them. And I didn't think Sera could, no matter how many times I tried to explain. Sure, she worried. She didn't see the world as I did—and that was fine. However, it wasn't my responsibility to change her mind.

I shoved the hurt away. It was time to focus on what I could do.

"So, my magic appears to have found its way home," I started. "And the king is kindly offering me a few fighters. I'd like you to stay here. Enjoy *Elphame*. With fae back-up, I'll get things sorted out over in San Diego."

"With minimal damage, please!" Allie interjected. "Maybe I should tell Marcus . . ."

That was that. I was taking the king. The last thing I wanted was to leave him and Allie alone. They were both adults, but Allie was my responsibility.

And, of course, starting a fight with the king of the fae when he broke her heart would be . . . complicated. I wasn't fae by birth, but I was fae enough to open doorways here now that I'd melded with Eli. I was, technically, a subject of *Elphame*. A citizen. Being the wife of the future king didn't change that.

Of course, it also didn't mean that I would stand by and let a friend be hurt.

"Marcus will be with me," I pointed out. "You, Alice Chaddock, will be staying here with Christy and Sera. Relax. Sunbath. Eat desserts."

Allie twisted her hands together. "I hate not being with you. What if you need me?"

"I do need you. Make me a pretty platelet smoothie, Allie, for when I return," I said in my mothering-est voice. "I won't be gone long."

Then I left to find the king and troops. My magic was itching to be used, and I was ready to kick some ass.

WHEN I REACHED the path that led to the palace, Marcus was outside. No crown. No guards. Instead, he was a man with a broadsword and a grin. A chain shirt covered his tunic, and thick leather gloves dangled at his belt like a sporran on a Highland clansman. He wore weathered boots, and his hair was braided back.

"Are we going to a medieval war?" I teased.

Marcus laughed. "I haven't fed my blade for a few decades, Death Maiden. Duty to the crown, to the people. Now if I fall to a foe . . . this"—he gestured around us—"is all Eli's responsibility. It's freeing to have an heir willing to fulfill his duty."

I nodded and drew the blade he'd gifted me when I wed Eli. "Freeing in all sorts of ways, I'd wager..."

Marcus bowed and lifted his blade. "Help an old man stretch before battle?"

I snorted. He might be a few centuries old, but the king of the fae looked to be only a few years older than me. This man was not a creaking old grandpa—and I was glad of it. I wanted him to live and age, wed and breed. I wanted him to have an heir, so Eli and I were never required to take the throne.

I bowed my head and waited for his first attack.

"So . . . does this mean you're going to take a bride?" I asked as I parried his *oberhau* strike.

"Indeed."

Since he volunteered nothing, I pushed the topic. "Shouldn't you be casting your eye toward fae maidens? I recall quite a few beautiful women lining up to offer to marry my husband."

Marcus grinned again. "Couldn't wed the prince, so they'll settle for the king. I suppose I could glance that direction."

I decided to be blunt. Time was short when it came to private conversations with the king. "Alice is a widow, Marcus. She loved her husband, and he was murdered last year. That's how we met. She hired me, tried to kill me, and the rest"—I lunged at the king—"is history."

He blocked. "She's a mortal in Elphame, Geneviève of Stone-haven. I am within my rights to keep her here, and I find that I'd like that."

"Crowe." I attacked with a series of *mittelhau* strikes, all of which he deftly parried. "I'd like to see you try. King or not, you don't want me as an enemy. Kidnapping Allie would create a problem for you. Don't do it."

We fought in silence for several moments.

Finally, Marcus offered, "*If* I break this law for you now, you will bring Alice for visits, Geneviève of Stonehaven. I offer you this bargain in kindness and familial regard." The king lowered his blade. "You shall not speak of the terms of this faery bargain to anyone save for your husband."

Unfortunately, I couldn't strike him unless we were exercising—and I couldn't actually refuse his bargain. I might be his niece by matrimony, part-fae because of my meld with Eli, but Marcus was the king of the fae. He was not one to be outwitted or outmaneuvered.

And we both knew it.

"I will only accept this bargain if I have your word that you do not intend to harm or use Alice. Romance? Fine. Seduce her *if* she understands your intentions are temporary? That, too, would be fine, but she's mine to protect as surely as every faery here or in my world."

Marcus looked at me curiously. "What makes you think my intentions are fleeting? My family always knows when we meet our destined bride. I knew she was in *your* world, as did my sibling and my nephew. So, I simply stayed in *Elphame* to avoid meeting her. And yet . . . you brought her to me."

I opened my mouth, but no words came out.

"Alice is beautiful, clever, and charming. Anyone would be lucky to know her." He gazed in the direction of the cottage where she waited. "Your loyalty is admirable, Geneviève, but your opinion of our kind could benefit from a bit less bias."

"Oh."

Marcus sheathed his sword, raised a hand in a gesture, and then added, "I believe mortals speak to the parental figure before beginning a courtship. This I have done with you. Do you accept our bargain?"

He paused until I nodded.

Once I did so, he continued, "I will allow my future bride to depart back to your world, but you are bound by our bargain to bring her here to know this world and people. In due time I shall inform her of our future."

"I don't know whether to feel tricked or simply worried for

you," I admitted, thinking about the fury that Alice would direct at the king when she discovered his intentions. She could, of course, refuse him—and it would serve him right. I met his gaze and said only, "So mote it be, Marcus of Stonehaven, King of *Elphame*. This bargain is accepted."

"So mote it be," he repeated with a cheerful grin.

In the next moment, twenty-odd guards joined us. And in another blink Marcus had rent a hole in the air. Unlike mine, his gate was instant, elegant, and shimmering like opals had been drawn from the soil to create a stately archway.

"Together into the battle?" Marcus offered.

"With pleasure," I agreed, but this time I was grinning in anticipation.

I had monsters to slay and magic to use.

# CHAPTER 11

W e stepped out of *Elphame* onto the beach in San Diego. The waves slammed against the shore, and birds of some sort seemed to cartwheel through the sky, riding currents in the air. The taste of salt lingered in the air, and a glance at the horizon told me that the ocean truly did seem to end the world. It was a lovely stretch of sand, spotted with large rocks and sprinkled with tidal pools.

"They wouldn't have had to drug me to keep me here if they'd simply showed me this," I murmured, partly to myself.

"We have a sea at home," one of the guards pointed out.

"*Elphame* is still new to me. As a girl, I used to dream of pirate ships and lost islands. Foes to fight and sea creatures to discover." I smiled briefly, thinking back to books I'd devoured. "When both the fae and the *draugr* are normal to you, when magic is in your veins, sometimes it's nature that holds the most allure."

"Indeed," Marcus said in an odd tone. There were secrets hidden in that word that I wanted to ask him to explain, but now was not the time. He added, "This nature has allowed the dead to invade their shore. Man has forgotten to learn his history. The *draugr* do not need air as we do. They can walk out of the sea."

"So the gates . . ."

"Are useless," Marcus finished. He gave me a look. "They do not stop *your* kind, Death Maiden."

"Classy," I muttered. Louder, I added, "I'm not dead, Marcus. Not all *draugr*. I need air, just like you."

Then I turned away from the faery king and let my magic roll out in front of me like a wave, and with disuse or perhaps with the added juice of my new genetics, my wave was neither gentle nor subtle. My magic rolled like a tsunami across the beach, the spa, the city as a whole.

*I could summon armies,* I thought with a shiver of something that felt more like pleasure than fear.

*"Daughter of Mine?"* Beatrice's voice filled my mind. *"Are you unwell? Imperiled?"*

*"San Diego. Girls' Weekend. Spa is run by* draugr *that have magic and drugs."* I continued to walk, feeling the dead in the distance awaiting my summons. *"Got my juice back. Could raise a city . . ."*

*"Please do not."* My dead grandmother sounded worried. *"Are you alone?"*

*"Nope. Uncle Marcus popped out of* Elphame *to wage war at my side. Brought a wee army. We're family bonding with swords and violence."* I glanced at the king, who looked at me curiously.

*"Fight well.* Draugr, *even those with magic, are susceptible to your will. Speak if you have need of my aid."*

Then I felt her withdraw from my mind. Whatever secrets she had were not ones she was sharing today. Perhaps she was envious. She *did* like a good fight.

Or she might be possessive. My grandmother was not entirely fond of the fae.

Or perhaps she knew what *draugr* were here and intended that I resolve this issue.

I made a mental note to talk to Beatrice. Dear old gran wasn't above using me as a weapon, and typically I might not object. This time, though, she'd sent me to battle alongside my very human friends and *without* my magic.

I concentrated, sending what I thought of as tendrils of curiosity out toward the spa. Six *draugr* were here. They were old, but not ancient. Two were magical.

"Six dead biters," I said to the fae. "Two work energy."

"You didn't plan to tell us about that until now?" a guard asked.

"Had to be here to feel them." I shrugged. "Death Maiden thing."

We ascended the cliff from sea to spa. My foot slipped a few times on the loose rocks and sand, but no one else seemed to struggle. They lived in nature. I'd spent the last few years on concrete sidewalks or dodging the roots of old oaks in the cemetery.

At the top, a man in a linen suit of some sort, yoga teacher meets lost-in-the-desert prophet, stood waiting.

"Friends," he started. "Such violence is not welcome here."

"Dead," I announced. "Old dead if he's in the sun like this."

The man gave me a pitying smile. "Oh, child. Not at all. I've simply found enlightenment. Breathe peace with me."

"You trap people here. Fruity drugs or whatever." I gestured to the pink-tinted water that sprayed from the misters.

"I encourage peace through natural—"

"Nope." I sent a thought toward the misters, freezing them, stopping the toxins. "Not stalling while you wait for everyone to 'breathe peace.'"

The beatific expression vanished. Fangs dropped. And he charged—toward the king. The dead guy clearly thought he could *flow* and latch onto Marcus' throat before anything happened. No older *draugr* at home would make such a mistake, so it was nice to have my draugr-traits as a surprise for a change.

I *flowed*, almost as fast as the *draugr* yoga-preacher.

My back was to Marcus' chest before anyone could blink. My own fangs were sticking out as my temper sparked. Magic made my bright blue hair shiver as if actual serpents extended from my scalp.

"My family is off limits," I said as I shoved magic into the *draugr*.

I was surprised when he simply blinked at me and said, "Mistress?"

"Not the leader," I explained. "Too weak."

"Mistress, how may I serve your guests?" the now befuddled fanger asked.

With a sigh I stepped away, and in the next heartbeat, Roisin had severed his head. Another guard kicked the head away.

"He attempted injury to the king," Roisin explained with a shrug.

We continued onward, quickly dispatching the next two *draugr*. Marcus and I beheaded one each. He chortled happily when his quarry put up a decent fight. Truthfully, I thought he missed several obvious openings to end the fight, and I said as much.

"Why not extend a fight for your joy if it's not truly dangerous to do so?" he asked.

I couldn't fault his logic. My own fight was far easier than I wanted. This entire excursion felt like the proverbial walk in the park--and not just because we traveled with armed fae guards. My magic was back awake inside of me. I felt like I could stay awake for years, take on hordes. I couldn't fault a king who had missed the fields of battle.

We made our way toward the spa building. I felt at least one more *draugr* there, but as we were walking through the garden, I felt multiple new dead signatures. Gaps where there hadn't been any. Early on in my life, I'd thought that meant a new *draugr* had arrived, but now that I was older, I realized it was something worse: new death.

People were dying, murdered. I felt sick enough that I stumbled as the number of gaps continued. I couldn't get to all of them in time, no matter what I did. How was I to choose? All life mattered, and I felt suddenly helpless.

"Niece?" the king prompted.

"Murders," I managed. "Rooms."

"*Draugr?*" Marcus asked, eyes gleaming in anticipation of a fight. "How many?"

"Two *draugr.* Killing." I shook my head, trying to focus. Was it better to go to the rooms? Or the spa? There were three *draugr* on site here, and they all needed to be stopped.

"You know these monsters better than I, Geneviève. What do you need?" Marcus asked.

"Stay."

The king quirked his brow at me, but he gave orders, sending fae guards to the rooms as we continued toward the spa.

Once it was just us, he murmured, "Most fae wouldn't speak to me like a disobedient hound."

I scoffed. He was lucky I could speak at all. My senses were all screaming as body after body died. The spa obviously *had* been at capacity. All of those people gone. All of those lives ended.

I hoped the fae warriors were prepared to handle the *draugr* there. My heart ached at the thought of their deaths, but my magic screamed that the *draugr* at the spa was stronger. They could likely handle the others. I had to go to the spa. Magic recognized its own, and now that I was back in possession of all of my capacities, I knew this *draugr* was one of my kind: magic and death.

I glanced at Marcus before we entered the lobby. "This is my fight, uncle. I need you to defend yourself and take the head if you can."

Marcus gave a curt nod. "Why?"

"Death magic." I jerked the door open and let my magic roll out like a hammer seeking a target. No subtlety. "Hey, asshole! I'm here for your head."

At my side, Marcus made a noise that might've been a laugh.

We stalked past the front desk where a man was slumped over, blood not yet congealing on the savaged wound on his neck.

"All I wanted was a relaxing weekend," I called out. "Some fruity drinks and beach time. A massage. But nooooo, you ruined it."

I slammed open the locker room, heading toward the *draugr*

with the unerring focus of a bloodhound on a scent trail. I felt his dead presence as surely as any corpse. This one, though shimmered in a way that only Beatrice did—and my great-times-great grandmother was the only other magical *draugr* I knew.

"Come out, come out, frog nuts!"

I kicked open the door to the spa where I'd been half-high on that fruity fog earlier, and there stood the tallest man I'd ever seen. At almost seven foot and change, the *draugr* standing in the steamy room looked like he'd done a few turns on a medieval torture rack and stepped off. His eyes widened at the site of Marcus, and without using whatever magic he had been utilizing to control the people enslaved at this toxic hell-spa, the lanky *draugr* wrongly assumed that the faery king was the biggest threat.

"You come here, onto my ground, with your fae magic and—"

"Way to be sexist," I interrupted the villain monologue he was about to spout.

"You." The *draugr* studied me. "Why is your heart beating if you are of us?"

"Because I'm alive." I shoved my death magic into my blade . . . accidentally . . . and for a blink I faltered. That hadn't been what I meant to do, but now my fae-wrought sword was glowing like some sort of bad special effect in an 80s movie.

"You're a *draugr*. Submit to my authority. I am William of Diego, regent of this place." The too-tall dead guy flashed fang at me, as if it was some official dead person greeting. Hell, maybe it was, but I wasn't here to chat.

I *flowed*, stopping across the pool from him. "Not really looking for a king, Billy."

"I am the *draugr* ruler of this—"

"I'm a necromantic witch, and I'm full up on regents ordering me around." I flashed my own fangs, though, as if in a reactive response. Behind me I heard Marcus moving, and I knew he was looking for an opening.

"Get rid of the steam, Marcus," I called, hoping fae magic was as powerful here as in *Elphame*.

As I felt magic that felt like summer fill the hot springs room, Tall Bill lunged to try to steal my sword or bite me. I honestly couldn't tell because when he got closer, the magic in my sword flashed out like a shield and enclosed the two of us in a bubble of magic.

I made a mental note to figure out what that was because being trapped with the thing trying to kill me wasn't exactly ideal. For now, I just hoped that the magical bubble wouldn't drop out from under us.

"Okay, Bill, you can either surrender or—"

He snapped again, like a rabid dog who'd forgotten his remaining manners. This time his teeth caught my shoulder and tore into the meat of my arm.

"Or, I can make you," I finished, reaching out mentally to try something that suddenly seemed possible. I shoved life into Bill, mentally massaging his heart, coaxing it to beat, and filling his lungs with air. I pulled the fae magic into my necromancy, and in that moment, I tugged a half-century old *draugr* into living.

He stepped back, throwing himself at the magical bubble in horror, clutching his chest as he noticed the long-silent heart begin to beat.

"Stop. Stop this," Bill begged me, voice sounding older, weaker by the second.

And something cold inside me smiled. "Certainly."

I tugged all of my magic back, and Bill's centuries of existing as a walking, biting dead man caught up in front of my eyes. Bill aged rapidly, and as mortal men can't live for centuries, Bill withered, died, and floated away in dust.

My magic retracted into my body, dropping the bubble from under my feet, and I fell in an ungraceful crash into the hot spring.

"Son of a monkey!" I stood up, sopping wet and trying to scramble out before the toxins made me high.

"I purified it," Marcus offered as he extended a hand.

Embarrassed, wet, and a little mortified at the joy I felt in ending Dead Bill's un-life, I stepped out of the hot spring and shoved my wet hair back.

We made it as far as the front desk before we were met by the same son-of-a-weasel who had been at Tomes and Tea arguing with Jesse. He was stacking files, shredding some, and singing what sounded like a sea shanty.

"Ms. Crowe," he greeted. "I had thought that the stories were exaggerated."

"What? How?" I blinked at him. Of all the things I'd dealt with of late, this one was the first to surprise me.

Marcus raised his sword. "What are you doing here, Chester?"

"Chester?" I echoed.

The man raised a hand. "Please skip the prurient jokes, Ms. Crowe."

I wanted to object, but I resembled that remark. A lot. So I simply said, "Who are you? Why are you here? And why does he"—I motioned to Marcus—"know you?"

"You are far more adept than anyone had reported." Chester tapped the files in his hands like an orderly office manager. "For an untrained Hexen, you're capable."

I flinched. Capable? That was the sort of flattering that sat next to "nice." And while I didn't think I was the best thing since sliced bread, I was a lot more than merely capable. I was an original. I was a half-*draugr* witch who melded with a faery prince. *The* faery prince, as a matter of fact. I opened my mouth, temper getting ahead of logic.

"You knew about this?" Marcus said, forcing focus back to the matter at hand.

Chester shrugged. "It wasn't sanctioned if that's what you're asking."

I watched him, still fairly in the dark, and realized that the little tiff at the bookstore was an act. He was powerful enough that the King of *Elphame* was being cautious.

"Who are you?" I asked again. "*What* are you?"

Chester straightened his impeccable suit before he smiled. "I maintain balances, educate, and sometimes assassinate. You made a mess of this place."

"They were keeping people in . . . vegetative states." I stepped closer. "And they attacked me and mine."

"And yet . . . here you are." Chester made a *tsk*-ing noise. "You seem unharmed." He shoved the files in a drab leather briefcase and snapped it shut. "And you restored a deceased Hexen. Granddaughter to a *draugr*. Niece of a king. That's a lot of influence for one . . . woman."

Marcus put a restraining hand on my arm, which Chester noted. Then the man—*being?*—departed with a poof of jasmine scented pink smoke.

I looked at Marcus. "He? That? He was involved?"

"Perhaps." Marcus released my arm. "But . . . Geneviève?"

"Hmmm?" I met the king's gaze.

"You're a terrifying being." The king held my hand as he spoke. "Know that if I had knowledge of the power level that you'd achieve by melding with Eli, I'd have killed you. Chester, however, is liable to do so if you provoke him. Be cautious with your choices."

I swallowed. I wasn't sure what Chester was, but I knew I *really* didn't want to fight with the king of *Elphame*. Carefully, I explained, "I had no idea that the trio of . . . heritages? . . . That being *this* would be so unstable."

Marcus nodded. "I believe you, but know that if you ever try to wrest power from me or threaten my people, you will not survive."

"You think you could kill me?" The question was out before I could think about what I was saying.

"Spouses are bound in life span. To kill my nephew is to kill you." Marcus released my hand finally. "It would be wise to remember that if you face enemies who do not hold him in the same high regard that I do."

And I heard that both as the wisdom it was—that I ought to make sure my spouse knew everything, and so was able to keep himself protected—and as the threat that it was. If he thought it was necessary, the king of *Elphame* would kill his nephew to save his people.

We walked out of the spa building in tense silence, only to be greeted by the rest of the fae soldiers.

They gave reports to the king as we all made our way to a good spot to return to *Elphame*. Only Roisin was bold enough to ask if I was well, but the best I could do was nod. My magic was back, and it had brought new tricks with it. I needed time to think and process—and I needed my husband at my side.

My "Girls Weekend" wasn't anywhere near what I'd expected, but obviously it had achieved the unspoken goal: I had relaxed enough that my magic was back.

# CHAPTER 12

When we returned to *Elphame*, my husband was standing there looking far-from- cheerful. His gaze took me in, which was fairly normal. Pre-matrimony, Eli had stitched me up so often that I thought he'd earned an honorary field medicine degree.

"Geneviève." He bowed his head to the king then. "Uncle."

Marcus looked at me. "Someone's apparently in trouble."

"Did no one think it prudent to notify me that my *wife* and my *king* were off in a skirmish?" Eli's formal tone said more about his mood than anything else could. He reverted to increasingly fae mannerisms when he was upset.

"It was *six draugr*." I gave a little twirl. "Barely a scratch."

Marcus met Eli's gaze. "I do not twirl."

Then the king bowed to me. "You are a worthy warrior, Death Maiden." He paused, eyes still holding mine, and added, "Do not forget our conversations."

Without another word, the King of *Elphame* departed, his soldiers dipping their heads to me as they trailed the king.

When it was just the two of us, Eli sighed. "Bonbon. Really? Even at a spa in a *draugr*-free city?"

I shrugged. "They came out of the ocean, apparently."

We walked to the house. *Our* house. And I tried not to smile at the sheer joy I felt. Successful battle. Magic back. Husband here.

"Where are the others?" I asked.

"Sera and Christy are on a beach, and when I left them, Allie was trying to convince a kelpie to give her a ride." Eli sounded amused, so I figured that despite their reputation for being monstrous, the kelpies in *Elphame* were not murderous water horses.

"The king thinks he's going to marry her."

"A kelpie?" Eli stopped mid-step. "Because you certainly cannot mean that he wants to wed the widow Chaddock."

"Destiny," I offered as we reached the cottage. I stripped outside the door, leaving my pile of toxin-covered clothes on the ground to be destroyed. It was a casualty of the job, but I still frowned at losing another pair of reliable boots. "I really liked those boots."

Eli said nothing as we walked to the shower.

"I spend an awful lot of time cleaning away my work," I muttered.

My husband held his words, simply looking me over as if I'd hidden injuries. As the grime washed away, as the flecks of blood washed away, Eli relaxed. "You are uninjured."

"I am." I softened as he visibly relaxed.

"Geneviève . . . you weren't here. You had no magic. And my uncle, who has not left *Elphame* in at least a century and change, was in San Diego. I was . . . alarmed. What foe would be so fierce that the king himself would take up arms? What danger were you, without your fierce magic, facing?"

He stripped as I stared at him, understanding dawning on me. I hadn't realized exactly how serious it was that the king had joined me.

"My magic is back," I whispered, summoning it to my will to touch him without moving a muscle. The very air stiffened into intangible hands that brushed along his bare chest, marveling that a man like him was mine forever.

"Shouldn't I want you less now that we're an old married couple?" I whispered.

Eli laughed. "Never. I think my need and love grow stronger by the day."

I nodded, words failing as he stepped into the shower with me. His hands were curled around my hips, and finally we were kissing.

It had only been two days, but just then, two days felt like an eternity.

When he pulled back, I teased, "I have it on good authority that Girls' Weekends often include someone 'hooking up' with a gorgeous stranger . . ."

"Hello, I'm Eli. We've never met before, but would you mind if I ravished you now?"

"Yes, please. I'm . . ." I managed to whisper as he parted my legs. My attempt to role play failed instantly as he slid two fingers inside me. "I'm . . . I'm *yours*, Eli."

AFTER OUR NOT-REALLY-MAKE-UP SEX, Eli left me there with my friends for the next two days to enjoy a proper Girls' Weekend. Wined, dined, and sun-soaked, my friends were relaxed. Although after the first twenty-four hours, we'd all given up on convincing Allie that the fact that magical creatures suddenly obeyed her was because Marcus told them to do so.

"Did you know that if a kelpie chooses to do so you can breathe under the sea?" Allie was explaining.

"Yes."

"And did you know that the village for mortals here is just . . . basically . . . like a big artist colony?" Allie was carefully packing a blown-glass kelpie in her luggage.

"Yes."

"And did you know that know that Marcus says I can just pop in here whenever I want?" Allie paused, fidgeting with an embroidered linen dress.

I glanced at her. "Did he offer that to the others?"

She shook her head.

"I see." My faery bargain was making my tongue feel twisted. There were things I wanted to say but couldn't.

"You think he likes me . . ." Allie held my gaze. "Why aren't you saying anything, boss?"

"You're very likeable," I said, sounding as cheery as her.

And the often-underestimated Alice Chaddock crossed her arms and pronounced, "You know something."

I'd been thinking on it since the conversation with Marcus. I could not tell her the bargain, his interest, or that he'd made a bargain with me. I could, however, think like the fae and talk around it.

"Do you recall how I ended up married?"

Alice's eyes grew comically wide.

"And do you know how sometimes an eternal being . . . like say my grandmother can be clever and outwit mortals?"

Allie nodded.

With carefully chosen words, I warned, "It's wise to be careful, Alice Chaddock. I am, and yet, I have been *accidentally* married to a faery. . . and probably manipulated into going to San Diego to kill off *draugr* who were behaving badly but out of Beatrice's reach."

Allie looked around as if there were potential spies, and then whispered, "So you think Marcus has plans to manipulate me?"

It was far too direct of a question, so I looked at her, hoping she was clever enough to hear what I was really saying, "I *cannot* say, Alice. I simply *can not say*. But"—I shrugged as if was no big deal—"I know I ended up where I am because I made faery bargains with Eli."

"Well, I won't be doing that." Allie hmphed, and I repressed a sigh. She wasn't getting what I was saying, and the bargain prevented me from outright telling her—or anyone else. It wasn't my future on the line, but I wasn't going to let Allie stumble into something she didn't want.

Later, when I was back in New Orleans, I'd come up with a plan to help her without breaking my faery bargain—right after I went to see my great-times-great grandmother Beatrice and pointed out that I wasn't a hunting dog to be sent out at her will.

"Gen?" Sera called as she came into the room. "Alice, come on! Pack later! Drink now!"

"Coming!" I grabbed a parasol, another of the things Allie had stocked up on, and Allie and I headed outside to join Sera and Christy for a glass of faery-made whisky or two at the firepit. It might not be the spa weekend we'd planned, but we were together, and laughing.

Christy looked up from her lounger. "Fruit bowl for you on the table . . ."

Then Sera added, "And a beautiful shawl for you, Allie." She pointed to the delicate pink thing. "Just you."

The shawl was in a box with a tag in what looked like calligraphy but was probably just Marcus' handwriting. "To Alice, for cold nights when you are far away."

Alice looked at it, looked at me, and said, "He *like* likes me, doesn't he?"

I couldn't reply because of the faery bargain, but Sera and Christy simply said "yes." And I took a long drink to cover for my silence. After all the faery bargains that I'd made, this one was proving more complicated than I expected.

"I made some ice for you." Alice plopped several blood cubes in my whisky before settling in with her drink in a chair beside Sera.

We weren't living in a perfect world, but I realized I'd lucked out on friends. I lifted my glass and said, "To sisters!"

"To sisters!" Sera, Christy, and Allie echoed back at me.

We drank, relaxing until Alice said, "So is it weird that you and Sera used to boink? But you're like sisters?"

"Not literal sisters, we just--" Sera started.

"Shut up, Allie," Christy interrupted.

And Alice grinned at us as she settled back with her drink.

"I love you people," I added, looking at them one after the other. "Best Girls' Weekend ever because you were with me."

Maybe Alice's influence was wearing off on me because I sat back with my drink and relished the stunned looks on all three faces. I could totally be sappy if I had to, and honestly, if it shocked everyone *that* much, I might just do it more often.

Our weekend was a little off plan, but it truly had been exactly the beach trip I'd needed. I felt ready and able to handle whatever challenges life threw my way next. Good friends, good booze, and the occasional beheading were my sort of weekend.

# EPILOGUE

I left *Elphame* and returned to New Orleans with a bounce in my step that I attributed to the holiday as much as the return of my magic. It was evening, so Christy and Sera headed to their jobs.

Allie and I exchanged a look, but she didn't ask any awkward questions.

"Can I borrow a car to go to the Outs?" I asked Allie. My first order of business was visiting my grandmother.

My assistant gave me another odd look, but she handed me her keys. "Try not to break it. I'll get Tres to fetch me so I can go home."

I nodded. I hated keeping the secrets I was—not just about Marcus' interest in her and what that meant, but the Chester situation, too. Hopefully, no one would need to know about the odd man, but if so, I'd tell them when it was necessary. Not today. *This* was my work: figuring out threats and handling them.

As I drove toward what was once called Slidell, I tried to think of ways that the Chester situation wasn't alarming. There weren't many. He was a stranger who knew far more than he ought to about me.

When I arrived at the castle that Beatrice called home, I stepped into the familiar humid air, loud with the chorus of frogs singing and mosquitoes buzzing.

"Lady Beatrice is expecting you," my gran's assistant said, appearing seemingly out of nowhere. Eleanor was maybe fifteen upon her death, and she was dressed in her usual Renaissance garb.

Inside, Eleanor guided me to a library where Beatrice was standing in front of a giant fireplace. She didn't turn to face me even as she greeted me: "Geneviève. Daughter of Mine."

I was usually patient with her, attempting to forge a relationship. She was, after all, my ancestor and one of only two blood relations in my life. Tonight, though, I was tired of etiquette.

"Did you know about the spa?"

Beatrice didn't insult me by pretending not to understand. Her back was still to me. "I did."

"And you didn't think to warn me?" I asked.

The fierce ruler of the fanged monsters that plagued my city-- my *world* in fact—finally turned to face me. Her eyes were swollen and blackened. Her lips were bruised and cracked, and her left arm dangled at an angle that was far from natural.

"I could not," she said.

I was across the room in a blink, *flowing* to her. Gently, I steered her to a chair. "Who did this? Did you kill them? If no I w--"

Her hand covered my mouth, stopping the word. "I am fine. Healing. Chester was most upset that I ruined his little seaside venture."

"Who *is* he?"

Beatrice offered me a terrifying smile. "My creator. The one who saw fit to hand me to a group of *draugr* to create a hybrid."

I froze, pondering the appearance of *humanness* in the suit-clad man. He had seemed innocuous. Human. Weak. Uninteresting.

"He did this?"

She gave a single nod. "He's the oldest living human, Daughter of Mine. An alchemist who made a crossroads deal if you ask him. I don't honestly know, but I know you need to stay away from him.

If I'd known that it was his business . . . I didn't, though." She took my hand in hers. "Please, Geneviève, heed me on this. The last person to cross him was Iggy. And he died for it."

Iggy. The Hexen I'd restored to life.

"Please?" she repeated. "I'm fine. Healing . . . I was simply not expecting him. Chester brings up difficult memories. You must stay away from him, Geneviève."

"I hear you." I felt a wave of tenderness toward her. Sure, she was a monster in her own right, but she was my family, too.

"I've asked Lauren to stay with me," Beatrice mentioned, tone falsely calm. "You and Eli, Alice, you're all welcome here. Tres is watching over Allie for now, but . . ."

"I'll talk to Allie. Is Mama Lauren here?" I sat on the floor at Beatrice's feet.

Beatrice, again, smiled, but this—despite the bloodied mouth— looked happier. "She's working on a hydroponic garden I started. She's been crafting herbal drinks to heal me."

I nodded. If there was a garden, it was because Beatrice knew it would entertain my mother. And if there were herbs to heal the already-dead, my mother would find them.

"So . . . aside from the Chester issue, tell me about the trip," Beatrice invited.

"Worst. Spa. *Ever*," I started, offering her the distraction we both needed. "Shoes made of leaves. Pink mist. No booze."

"I'd heard it was hellish, but it was a *dry* spa?" Beatrice grimaced.

"Completely."

"Eleanor!" Beatrice called out. "Daiquiris? And the gifts?"

I regaled my great-times-great grandmother with tales from my trip as her assistant brought in a tray of Blood Daiquiris. Alongside them were two daggers that looked to be the length of my forearm.

"Magic imbued," Beatrice said as if such gifts were minor. "For any future needs. One for you. One for Eli."

I accepted them with the same casual tone. "Daiquiris and daggers? Maybe I ought to visit more often."

"I'd like that," she said, and we left it at that. I may have no choice. For now though, we did as one must when disasters always lurked: we shelved it and shared a drink.

Later we could figure out the looming disasters, but for the moment, I was rejuvenated, magic-wielding, and my friends and family were secure. All was as well in the world as it could get.

The End

# CHAMPAGNE & COMMITMENTS

A Faery Bargains Novella

Set after

Daiquiris & Daggers

# CHAPTER 1

Living in New Orleans meant that the coming of Autumn was synonymous with the coming of Halloween. It was *also* a time filled with the Jewish High Holidays, witchy holidays, and fae holidays. This year, however, was more stressful than usual because I had to plan a wedding—actually, *two weddings.* There were rules about entering the realm of the fae, and I had human guests, so I had to have a ceremony here and one in *Elphame.*

I hated ceremonies.

I hated being the center of attention.

So I was, in typical avoidance tactics, ignoring my wedding planning until I absolutely positively *had* to deal with it.

Plus, I was restless since my magic had settled and my privacy was upended by tourists with phone cameras. I'd spent my entire life trying to hide who—and what—I was. Suddenly being unable to behead a monster without a reel of my actions on social media was creating a bubble of irritation that was starting to feel like it was festering.

Worse yet, I had no one to blame for it, no enemy to slay, no mystery to solve. It was simply a side effect of public interest in the blue-haired witch marrying the crown prince of *Elphame.*

I'd finished working out. Again. Now I'd tackle the wedding plans, at least some of them.

Since my apartment was a ground floor unit with questionable air conditioning and ventilation, I was wearing one of Eli's shirts and nothing else. Not exactly workout clothes or going out clothes or--

"Bonbon?" Eli walked into the bedroom.

I was surrounded by wedding catalogues and hand-drawn illustrations from *Elphame.* Dresses. So many twice-cursed dresses. I had rejected everything from what looked like mermaid tails to cartoon princess gowns I wasn't sure I could walk in without tripping.

"Why?" I gestured, glaring at the images. "I like trousers. I mean, I can deal with leggings and a tunic but—"

"We could go naked . . ."

That caught my attention. I looked up. He was still standing in the doorway of the bedroom, out of reach.

"Tell me more?"

"*Tell* you?" Eli started to remove his shirt, offered me what I used to think of as an innocent smile. I knew better now. There was nothing innocent about the formerly exiled faery prince currently stripping in our doorway. Wiley. Charming. Clever. Gorgeous.

"Show me more," I modified, taking a moment to admire him. The bare expanse of skin he was now exposing was dusky and taut over muscles, a reminder that he was an agile fighter and a tireless lover.

With a flick of my hand, all the catalogues and drawing went flying off the bed. A bit of plaster drifted to the ground as a pen stabbed the wall. My magic was a still a bit erratic since our bonding.

"My lovely witch," he murmured before I could apologize. "My warrior wife."

I watched as his shirt hit the ground. "*More. . .*"

"More explanation?" he teased. "Well, being naked would solve the dress decision for you, too, I suppose."

I looked back up to catch his gaze. His cut glass cheeks and nose were softened by a mouth that made me think of a courtesan's lips. "I can't imagine your uncle would approve of—"

"Bonbon?" Eli's hand passed over his chest and lingered at the top of his trousers.

My brain went completely silent. I met his gaze again with effort. Looking away from bare skin and taut abs required a lot of focus.

"I'd very much like to ravish you now, Geneviève," he announced, stepping closer and unfastening that first button. "Perhaps we could *not* discuss my family now?"

"Mmmmhmmm."

"Shall I take that as a yes?" Slowly, button by button, Eli unfastened his trousers. "To the not talking or the naked? Or the ravishing?"

In the next heartbeat, I'd crossed the room without thought. "Yes, Eli. Whatever you say. Whatever you want . . . *yes.*"

"All I want is you, Geneviève."

I opened my mouth to attempt to reply, but Eli lowered his mouth to mine and saved me from the perpetual embarrassment over how much his words got to me. I'd rather kiss him than fumble at words. With my kisses, I could attempt to tell him just how much I loved him. With my touches, I could try to be eloquent.

I'd never have the constant pretty fae words to share, not like he did, so I set about telling him how I felt with my kisses and caresses.


A few hours later, I wasn't any more capable of speech, especially articulate and flowery words, but Eli understood me all the same. He whispered, "I love you too, Geneviève."

I sighed out loud this time. "No one else has ever . . . known me so easily."

He chuckled. "Easily? Oh, come now, divinity! I have dedicated literal *years* to the Study of Geneviève. Your silences, your expressions, your temper . . ." Eli pulled me closer into his embrace. "I surely have earned degrees in the tilt of your head or the curve of your lips, and I am not done. You are my enigma, my lifetime pursuit."

I flinched guiltily. "I didn't set out to be perplexing to you."

"You didn't set out with a single plan about me," Eli corrected. "But now, you are mine. Unto eternity. My prey caught in a snare . . ."

"Not prey," I muttered.

"And yet, you are captured, are you not?" Eli's words were light—but I heard the question he was truly asking. While I hadn't studied him for quite as long, I had begun to learn to listen to the silences in his statements and the questions he lobbed gently my way.

"I'm happily ensnared," I agreed. Despite being anti-relationship, I'd been stealthily courted and bonded to *the* prince, but as he had reminded me regularly, he'd never *said* he was merely a bar owner. He'd *also* never said he had chosen an exile from his people to stay in New Orleans as my friend while plotting to wear down my resistance to the romance he'd wanted from me.

The fae might not lie, but they weren't always forthright.

Now Eli and I were fae-bonded. It was more permanent, none of this "until death" business. Our lives were connected on a heartbeat-by-heartbeat level. If I died, he died. If he died, I died.

Don't even get me started on how much panic *that* responsibility caused me. It was right though. We were right. And as sappy as it felt, I admitted, "Being bonded to you is the most natural thing I've ever done. I'd rather be with you in a grave than here without you. My pulse is yours, and I wouldn't want it any other way."

"And she says she has no pretty words for me," he murmured,

lifting one of my hands to his lips and kissing my wrist at the pulse point.

I cleared my throat, determined to have this conversation. "So you *know* that avoiding wedding planning isn't cold feet, right?"

"I do." Eli watched me in a way that made me feel like I was a treasure he'd defend, a cause he'd uphold, and a gift he'd cherish.

"I just hate being the center of attention in a crowd," I tried to explain. "And in my defense, I had planned to go over some details with you tonight. Honestly. But then you came home and . . ."

"Bonbon, you were already half-naked when I came home," he pointed out. "It seemed foolish not to join you."

"It's hot, and the apartment was humid."

"Getting naked was simply practical then," he agreed with a laugh.

"*Exactly*. That's me. Practical. And maybe I was hoping you'd be home soon. I feel like any minutes without you are too long lately." I looked up at him, and he answered with another kiss.

"Bonbon? I *adore* your appetite," he reassured me when he pulled away.

Lately, I was fairly sure the only reason we hadn't been arrested for public indecency was that people were too stunned to react when we'd been caught in public. Well, that and the fact that I was witch enough to baffle them with a quick spell long enough to get away, typically with our clothes in hand, although I'd lost at least two pairs of boots this past month.

Tonight, we were inside. *See? I could be practical.* Meeting at my apartment tended to mean we were less likely to get caught naked in public, and the tourists were flooding the city as they did every year in October. Nowhere celebrated as often or as vigorously as New Orleanians did.

"What's your plan for the rest of the night?" Eli stretched as if he were some great cat.

I couldn't tear my eyes away from the fae man who'd plagued my dreams for years. He stared at me as I watched him. Like every faery, he was not shy. He definitely had no reason to be. His lips curved into a smile that said he was well aware of how he looked sprawled out in our sea-blue sheets. His hair—currently coming unbound--could pass for the dark strands of plenty of middle eastern men, but it fell longer than most human men wore theirs.

"Wedding stuff . . .?" I sighed as I caught his gaze. I could see stars, eternity, a universe hidden in the dark braid that twisted across the pillow. *Mine. All mine.* I still had moments of panic that someone or something would tear us apart. I'd never really dared to believe that I could be this happy, that I'd find a person who accepted me as I was—fangs and all.

"You're far away from me, Geneviève."

I slid closer, so I was half draped over him. "Better?"

"Yes, but I meant inside your thoughts, love." He kissed the inside of my wrist. "Trouble with the 'wedding stuff'? I could help."

"No, I was thinking about you."

"Mmmm, tell me more." Eli's eyes glittered in a different sort of interest, a seemingly impossible trait, but I realized it was simply another way to communicate for the fae. My own vision had shifted when we bonded. There were layers to sights, sounds, tastes, and scents that I hadn't know existed, even with my heritage. And touch . . . Eli's skin against mine was a pleasure that I would've called impossible before our bonding.

"Marriage. How it changes everything . . ." I trailed my hand over his stomach. "I'm sorry I wasted all that time running."

"Eh. I like a chase." He pulled me on top of him for a kiss that left me straddling him. Again. He stared up at me and added, "And I have won the prize I desperately wanted. . ."

When I straightened and sat upright, I was breathless at the love in his expression. It wasn't an overstatement to say that I was certain that I was the luckiest woman—of any species, dead or living—in either world. Love is always a gift, and compatibility is precious.

"Faery struck," I whispered as his hands gripped my hips.

"Likewise."

"You can't be! I'm—"

"Fae-bound? As am I, Geneviève. So, whatever could this be? Am I bewitched? Bespelled? Ensorcelled? Addicted?" His teasing laughter made me start to giggle.

A part of me was mortified that I was even *capable* of giggling. I was a witch, a necromancer, and the last sight before the death of many a monster. A half-witch half-*draugr* with spells and weapons ought not giggle!

But the rest of me reveled in feeling safe enough to laugh. Eli was my haven, and I'd do anything in my power to keep this feeling, this man, this love.

"I love you," I murmured, holding his gaze.

"Likewise."

"Show me, *bonbon*." I grinned as his hands tightened on my hips, leaving marks that I'd remember for the next few days.

Both my words and my giggles faded into moans and demands as my beloved did just that.

Later, as Eli drifted toward sleep, he gave me a drowsy smile before his eyes closed. "Good night."

I brushed one last kiss across his lips before I slid out of bed. My nocturnal schedule wasn't ideal for him, as his daylight one had been a struggle for me. Now that we were bonded, I was equally alert at sunlight and sunset, noon and midnight, and everywhere in between.

It had been three days since I last slept.

For most of my life, I'd barely slept at the best of times, but I somehow slept even *less* since my magic had returned. I felt like I was washing down Ritalin with coffee chasers every hour. I could either try to be quiet while Eli slept or I could go find something to do.

Eli was good for my stress. He understood me fundamentally, but since he required sleep and I didn't these days, I had to find things to keep me occupied at night. Patrolling for *draugr* or training were my default options, but maybe I could see if Allie, my assistant, was awake and work on wedding plans.

*Patrol my way to her house. Plan. Patrol more. Wake Eli for mid-morning sex. Train.* I needed to find a hobby or something if there were no new jobs coming in. I'd accumulated more enemies than I needed of late. The peril of power is that having it meant that there were always people trying to kill me for one reason or another, and it had put a dent in my jobs.

Maybe that could be my cookie for getting the weddings planned—start a new hobby or side job. I had too much downtime.

I grabbed a jacket and pulled the bedroom door shut.

As I walked into the main open space of the apartment, I looked for the jeans and boots I'd left in the training area earlier. My apartment didn't scream fae royalty. When I bought it, I had no dream of becoming royal. Hell, I hadn't even known Eli was royalty when I bought this place.

The listing had been a bad area, filled with *draugr*, so I got the first apartment—the one Eli slept in currently—for a steal. Over time, I bought the rest of the apartments on this floor.

I looked around at the mess. Definitely far from royal fae living, but it was still mine. I shimmied into jeans, shoved my feet in a pair of combat boots, and put on holsters. There were things worse than the monsters I had been beheading my teen and adult life, and I didn't leave the house unarmed.

"Ready . . ." I held my hand out, bracing myself before touching the forearm-long dagger on the settee. It was half of the pair of magic imbued daggers the *draugr* queen had given me.

I concentrated on grounding myself.

The sizzle of magic in the dagger had me gasping as if I'd jumped naked into a snowbank. I wasn't sure I could carry both blades, so the other was on the nightstand beside my sleeping husband.

With the dagger, a sword on the other hip, and a pistol in my underarm holster, I slipped out the heavy door into the building's lobby and then stepped onto the sidewalk.

I paced the perimeter of the well-lit lot. My neighbors were tolerant now that I was a princess, and agreed to extra lights, but that didn't mean I wanted to be illuminated like a target.

An engine turned on as I walked toward the sidewalk. Someone had been waiting inside the car because I sure as sugar hadn't seen anyone walk toward it.

I drew my pistol. Not nearly as comforting as a sword, but I wasn't going to get close enough to stab a tire. I stood at the edge of the parking lot outside my building, eyeing the dark-blue SUV.

Engine running.

Lights bright.

Between the glare of the lights and the tint of the windows, I couldn't identify anything about the driver. I tried to think of non-threatening options. Was this a ride for one of the residents on the top floors of the building? Were they simply pulled over to check maps? There were plenty of logical answers, but I still had a welcome flicker of fear.

I stalked toward the SUV, hoping that whoever was inside was not packing venom-filled rounds or something else inconvenient and painful. My bouts of insomnia and extra energy meant that a fight sounded lovely, just a little sparring with a new partner.

But the driver shifted the car out of park and drove toward the exit of the parking lot.

"Weirdo," I grumbled, hoping it wasn't another camera-mad "influencer" determined to catalogue my life for clicks. Honestly, I'd rather have a fight than be in anyone's lens.

I looked away—just as the SUV sped up and swerved toward me.

The grind of tires on pavement was low enough that without my enhanced hearing, I'd be roadkill right about now, but I heard the tires crackling and crunching, and I'd turned at the revving of the engine with a slice of a second to spare.

The mass of blue metal was trying to hit me.

Fortunately, SUVs aren't exactly bullet-speed. I launched myself into the grassy strip alongside the parking lot and landed with a *thunk* as my feet tangled in the tree roots that didn't have the good sense to stay under the sod.

"You badger-bonking jerk!"

The driver backed up and paused. Not departing. Not charging. I was cornered.

The urge to *flow* warred with the logic that my ability to move as fast as the dead was still a secret to most everyone. If the driver had a camera, I'd be exposed if I did that. The mere thought of such hate terrified me.

Being a witch meant I had the occasional death threat or murder attempt. Being a Jewish witch meant that some of those attempts were fueled by the hostility every Jew encountered in their lives. But being a half-living half-*draugr*? That was the sort of thing that landed a person in laboratories. Nightmares of vivisection had plagued me for years.

No *flowing.*

So I stood there, playing chicken with an SUV and debating the options. If I *did* decide to *flow,* I could go over, jerk the door open and ask Mr. Badger Bonker what his issue was.

*And he'd report me . . . unless I kill him.*

*His word against mine.*

*Unless he has one of those dashboard cameras...*

More and more I had to remind myself that a viral video of a living *draugar*, especially one who was also the future queen of *Elphame*, would be deadly.

So my choices were to try to walk away or wait him out. On the upside, unless he planned to ram the oak tree beside me, he wasn't likely to smoosh me even with however-many-pounds of steel.

My phone chimed.

A text from Allie popped up: "Tourists. Gate. Help?"

Decision made, I turned toward the oak and asked permission, "Aid?"

The lowest branches quivered, and a thicker branch slightly above them crackled and stretched toward me. When it was in reach, I wrapped my arms around it, hugging the tree, and held tight as it returned to its position in the leafy boughs.

I looked toward the SUV and gave them a jaunty one-fingered salute.

Then I dropped a big smacking kiss on the oak branch, not feeling the least bit silly despite hugging and kissing a tree.

I hopped over the fence beside the tree. I might still be new to this faery princess gig, but I was a born witch. I already knew nature was the sort of magic that mere mortals—or near-immortals like the fae and *draugr*—couldn't match.

# CHAPTER 3

Safely out of reach of the SUV, I looked again at the text from my assistant. The text was classic Allie in that it included emojis for emphasis: a dagger, a baseball bat, one that was for swearing, and a wine glass. The last image I understood, though. She'd added a castle, which was her way of saying she was at the house I co-owned with Eli.

The rest was a mystery. Honestly, I couldn't tell if Alice thought that I would be swearing and need a drink or if *she* was swearing and drinking. It didn't matter, though: Alice Chaddock was my right-hand-woman: somewhere between a Renfeld and a teenager on her bad days, and somewhere between psychic and best friend on her good days.

"Inbound" was my whole reply.

I flagged down a police cruiser on St. Charles.

"Crowe." The officer, a man I'd met a handful of times, had a name. I was certain of it. That didn't mean I could recall it.

"Distress call from my assistant," I said as I dutifully put on my seatbelt. "Garden District."

I rattled off the address, as if anyone in the city needed to hear it. Eli being outed as the future ruler of *Elphame* had meant that our home was now on every tour and tabloid.

"The prince?" Officer Whatshisname was already reaching for his radio.

"Blissfully unaware at my other home, and I'd like to keep it that way. I just need a lift."

I thought about Eli's reaction to the crowds outside his house. It happened more and more, and Eli was on the verge of agreeing to fae guards—although neither of us wanted that. Any guard was likely also going to report to the king, and while Eli and his uncle were on good terms, I had reason to prefer that the king wasn't in my business more than absolutely necessary.

"I'm hoping they'll go away quietly," I added.

The officer nodded, not quite saying the "are-you-daft" aloud, but his expression covered that part.

What he didn't realize was that now that my magic was back, the city as a whole felt like it was as much my "kingdom" as Elphame did. Eli felt protective of our homes, our friends, me—and I felt like my fae traits had only enhanced my need to keep New Orleans safe. The residents of my city had no idea that I felt like they were my *own* citizens or the lengths I'd go to keep them safe. Of course, I wasn't sure how far I could go. Honestly, I was a little afraid of how easily I now accomplished the same things that used to require concentration.

Sooner or later, I'd have to test the parameters of the new energy that came from being bonded to a faery prince. His energy was life-affirming, and mine . . . well, I was a necromantic witch and the sperm donor who impregnated my mother was already dead when I was conceived. I was complicated.

Neither wholly dead nor alive.

Neither wholly *draugr* nor human.

And that was before a murder attempt when I was injected with *draugr* venom and before adding a bit of fae to my genetic goulash. I wasn't entirely sure what I even was these days. Tonight, though, I was trying to be considerate and patient. That transcended species. Right?

We stayed silent as Officer Probably-Has-A-Name navigated us through the streets of New Orleans. A few human stragglers were out, but fortunately, I saw no *draugr*.

Or faeries.

Just humans, mostly tipsy and laughing.

"Safe?" I texted Allie.

"So far. They're trying to climb the gate. Lots of cameras."

I paused at that. Tourists could definitely be intense, but that was a shade too far.

"Attempted break-in," I told the officer. "Can you get me there faster?"

He sped up but, eyes still on the road, said, "Ma'am, I know you've instructed NOPD not to use your title, but this is a royal residence. You put us in a bad place if I can't call it in and there's trouble."

I grabbed his radio. "Dispatch. This is Crowe. I need Gary Broussard at the castle if he's on duty."

"Blood? Fangers?" was all dispatch asked.

"Tourists." Frustration laced my voice.

The dispatch officer's laughter was muffled, but I caught the edge of it under the cough she tried to use to hide it. "Units en route, Ms. Crowe."

I LET OUT an audible sigh as we stopped half a block from my home. The officer was still fumbling with his seatbelt as I marched toward a building in the Garden District that looked like it could have been one of the first in the city.

*Home.*

As much as my apartment was mine, this house had become my haven—and not just because it was where Eli had lived before we were bonded *or* because it was where we resided most nights. It was magic in a way that felt revitalizing to me.

A fence, stone not iron, surrounded an almost plain house, but as both a witch and the bonded mate of a faery, I could see the shimmer of old magic. My home practically glowed.

The tourists were snapping pictures, even though all they could see was a plain, old house. It had no balcony or gallery, no porch or Ionic columns. It was almost so plain as to be unnoticed—which required a great deal of magic in this area.

Gary Broussard, my "liaison" these days for New Orleans Police Department, stepped out of his car just as we walked up to the back edge of the crowd. Either he was driving like a teenager at curfew, or he'd been in the area.

"Officer Broussard," my ride started to say as he practically ran up beside me.

Gary held up a hand to him. "Crowe. Could you maybe wait in my car?"

I grinned and said, "Nope."

"No beheading tourists." Gary gave me a look that was mostly joking. "Davis, you handle crowd control on the street. We don't need tourist pancakes."

Davis nodded. "Yes, sir."

Gary looked at me. "Can't ever take a back seat can you, kid?"

"My house. My assistant. My city." I shrugged. "Doesn't seem like I need to sit this out."

Gary sighed. He was a sort of father-stand-in for me, and my fondness for him was why I'd done a few weeks of crowd control and monster-mashing earlier in the year. And I suspect it was why I tried to play nice with the city mayor, who oozed political charm but lacked ethical everything.

"Let's get you inside before anyone decides to come make a political moment out of this." Gary motioned me forward. "What do you need?"

I let my magic curl out like a wave that any dead or *draugr* would feel. It used to be a simple thing, but now it felt like a medical assessment of nature, too.

I stumbled as my magic touched the fence that separated my home from the street. It was sturdy, stone with living wood and vine coiled around it currently. That was my magic, not just Eli's. I'd added a layer of natural deterrent that was only triggered by someone attempting to scale it.

Frowning, I reached a hand out toward the vines, feeling the places where someone had tried to cut them. They'd been hacked at, assaulted, and trampled.

"They cut my wood roses," I said, staring at the vine, willing it to expand into the street like a fast-growing hedge.

"That assistant of yours said you got your juice back," Gary half-asked, half-declared as he watched my hedge shove tourists backward into the street. "That's you . . .?"

"Yep."

People—*intruders,* my mind whispered—were yelling and crying out as they swatted at my vines.

*Silly mortals,* an increasingly apathetic voice murmured. *Treading on our territory.*

I shoved that thought back in the box. It was an unwelcome side-effect of my newly fae side cozying up with the witch and *draugr* parts of my genetic soup. Apparently too many supernatural genes in a bowl made for an internal voice leaning toward sociopathic when I used any magic while upset.

My phone buzzed again, drawing me closer to the moment and away from that inner voice.

"Boss! I feel like Briar Rose!" Allie's text had emojis, of course—neon roses and cartoon swords—and then the words, "Rescue me, princess!"

I rolled my eyes, but her Allie-ness made me focus. The wood roses were spreading over the whole of the fence, crawling up the house, and had at least three tourists held aloft as if they were bugs caught by a giant spiderweb.

"Crowe?" Gary said, his voice tilting into a cajoling tone. "Could you put them back down on the ground? Bad press and all that . . ."

I noticed the phones, the recordings, and thought about my vivisection nightmares. With a whisper of a panicked thought, I sent a surge of electricity into every phone within a half block—including my own.

There was a clatter as everyone dropped their phones, which were hot to the touch. My aim was still more akin to an antique Tommy Gun than precision sniper rifle.

"Well then." Gary looked over at his car, which was now smoking. I guess I'd caught more than phones in my surge.

Then the tourists saw me, realizing what had just happened was my doing. The excitement of seeing the fae princess seemed to dim a little. Fear mingled with their awe, but a few foolhardy people still seemed to be on the awe side of the equation.

"Are those silver swords?" one man asked.

Several people were trying to restart their phones, instinct overcoming logic. Others were scrambling for pens.

"Why would my sword be silver?" I asked. "I wasn't *born* fae."

I was astounded that this question was still confusing to them. Someone had read just enough folklore to know that the fae were allergic to iron and steel, but skipped too many science classes. I wasn't born fae but bonded to one.

"I was born to a human. Witch by choice. Bonded to the prince," I said, loudly. That part was all true. I was also born to a *draugr*, but I wasn't sharing that tidbit.

"Does the prince use silver—"

"There is a publicist who schedules questions," I said, still using my crowd-control voice.

"Where is the prince?" another voice yelled.

"Sleeping," I said lightly.

"Does he mind you being a witch?"

"How is he in bed?" someone else called.

I scanned for that one. Eli was bold with me, but he was a

private person. "Rattling a witch's gates isn't terribly safe, and neither is upsetting one."

I smiled so they'd laugh. Mostly all of them did. A few looked at me without even cracking a smile.

Then I drew one of my swords.

No one spoke.

"And intruding on the prince's privacy doesn't bring out my kindness." I summoned the injured roses toward me, and the rose hedge snapped a long, thorny vine out toward me. "Plus, uninvited guests upset the roses."

The vine paused as it touched my fingertips, as if in greeting.

*Mine. My safety. My armor.*

The vine continued to grow, thickening as it wrapped around my arm, crept across my chest and spiraled down my other arm.

The vines encircled my waist, and in the next moment, the vine cut itself away from the hedge. Now that it was separated, the two ends swirled around my legs in perfect matching coils.

In mere moments I was rose-and-thorn-covered, a nature-wrought, magic-altered armor. No weapon could cut through the rose vines when they were around me.

I knew what I looked like: sword in hand, blue hair twisted like tentacles as magic filled me, rose-and-thorn armored.

"Now, if you'll excuse me, this witch needs to ask you to leave peacefully." I smiled. "Enjoy our beautiful city. Buy a book on pirates or plagues. Our city has history on both! Have a chicory coffee. Listen to the amazing musicians. *Enjoy.*"

I strolled forward, my vines lashing out into a fence that burst into blooms as I passed through the natural archway.

# CHAPTER 4

Threats at both of my homes tonight. I pondered the possibilities. SAFARI, the hate group that existed to try to promote laws against *draugr* and fae, was always near the top of my list. The occasional upstart *draugr* who knew that my great-gran was the *draugr* queen could be trying to attack her by way of attacking me. Random relatives of dead folk I'd beheaded? Some obsessive interested in the stunning faery prince I'd supposedly entrapped? And of course, the Hexen Master I'd resurrected from the dead was out there, and his murderer, Chester, who was behind a number of questionable things in the world—and was developing a hatred toward me that I couldn't quite fathom.

My fan club was vast and varied.

I glanced back, scanning the crowd as if I could spot an instigator. Silly, perhaps, but the raw truth was that a certain sort of hatred included wanting to see your victim suffer. And sometimes that meant first-hand, not via photos or video.

"We have trespassing laws," Gary told the crowd sternly, peering at the tourists through the flowering wall of thorns. "Blockading this residence or attempting unlawful entry will land you in jail if you are seen here again."

The officer who'd driven me to the house joined Gary. He held out old-fashioned Polaroid pictures. It might not be high-tech, but today that meant it was exactly the right tech.

"We keep a log on any perceived threats to our resident princess witch," Gary said in a lighter tone.

As the tourists and Officer Davis filtered away, I stepped up to the gate to my property, which opened at my approach.

The vines that covered the gate were seemingly absorbed into my body little-by-little, and tiny thorn-picks of blood dropped onto the soil inside the fence. It was a minimal amount of blood, but it hurt all the same. A thousand thorn pricks as the armor anchored to my flesh. Later, I'd need a tall glass of revitalizing smoothie—blood and herbs—to restore me from that blood loss, but it was a small cost for the layer of magical armor that now coated my skin.

"Gary?" I called as the remaining vines—those covering the rest of the fence—began to grow. Once the gate closed, it would again be thorn and rose covered.

Gary met my gaze. He had stayed outside the gate. "Crowe?"

I beckoned him forward, and the vines lashed out and laced together behind him. A thorn-coated wall started to expand, steering him forward.

When he crossed the threshold into my property, I felt the magic in the soil rise up.

"Hold still for a moment," I ordered.

My land read him as truly as any serum or technic invented by man or magic. If he had threat in his heart directed to me or mine, he'd not take a step closer. I trusted him enough to invite him in, but there were reasons no one came here without a level of trust I rarely bestowed. To enter with violence in heart would result in death. It was a bit of magic I'd recently added to our home.

The shock on Gary's face was enough to make me smile.

When the roses dusted him with deep red petals, I said, "Come into my home, and be welcome here, Gary Broussard."

"You're scarier than you used to be, kid." Gary shook his head, but he strode forward as if he was nonplussed by ancient magic reading his heart.

And though I'd offered him the mildest of formal invitations, and his words were mild, he still looked a bit gobsmacked as he crossed the lawn and approached the vine-draped house where my assistant was waiting.

By the time we went inside, I thought Gary would have something to say, but he was looking around like the mere thought of being inside my house was stunning.

"You okay?" I finally asked.

"Sure, kid. Sure." He cleared his throat. "Can I call you that now that you're all . . ." He motioned around at the hallway as if it was a clarifying word.

I knew what he meant, but I wasn't particularly pleased by it. "In a hallway? Inside? Walking?"

"A damned princess." He bit the words off. "You're a monster-beheading, blue-haired, smart-mouthed witch. I came to terms with all that, but you're not exactly making it easy on me these days. You know how much shit I got shoveled at me over potentially endangering the heir to Elphame? Not just in-house, Crowe. I got feds calling up the boss, and my boss . . ."

His words faded into a sigh as I stared at him.

"You, Gary Broussard, are my friend. And I like working with you, and I'm good at beheading fangers." I crossed my arms. "I'm still me."

He nodded, but he looked about as convinced as I felt.

Then the door to the main living quarters jerked open, and my assistant stood there holding onto what looked like a frozen Bloody Mary.

I stared at the drink and pressed my lips together.

"Oopsie!" Allie backed up. "Didn't know you brought company, boss." She held the frozen *actual* blood concoction out to me like it was a normal greeting. "Can I make you a cocktail, too? I cook when I'm stressed, so I made the boss a drink, you know? It isn't like she always drinks . . . err . . . I mean everyone drinks. Perfectly *normal*, right?" She shook the glass at me. "Bloody Alice, boss."

I closed my eyes and hoped I wasn't about to rattle poor Gary's brain. If he thought me being a princess complicated his life, he'd have a coronary if he discovered what exactly a Bloody Alice was or why I needed one.

"Lots of people drink, Ms. Chaddock," I muttered, pointedly not using her first name.

Gary looked at me. "Crowe, your assistant is going to make me think you're a lush or—" He stopped himself. "Are you Mrs. Chaddock? Widow of Alvin Chaddock."

Allie all but shoved the drink into my hand and tugged Gary into the house. "You knew him? My sweetie?"

"He donated to a lot of charities. His son, your . . ." Gary looked awkwardly at me.

I smothered my amusement in a long drink of my blood smoothie. Like a lot of rich old men, Alvin Chaddock married a woman who was the same age as his kid. I couldn't judge too much; I still had no idea how old Eli was. The question wasn't one he was at ease answering, so I let it go.

At a certain age, I guessed that numbers stopped mattering.

I wasn't sure how old that was for humans, but whatever people thought or accused, Alice Chaddock adored her late husband. *Still.* She'd tried to murder me as a result of her loyalty to him and his son, convinced me to enthrall her dead stepson, and continued to convince me not to behead him. Allie might be a bit intense, but she was one of the most loyal people I'd ever met.

"Tres," I interjected into whatever chatter Allie had been sharing. "Her stepson is Tres."

I met Allie's gaze. "So . . . why were there so many people outside the house? And how did you get trapped in here?"

Allie pouted briefly, which meant that I wasn't going to like the answer. "I reserved the cathedral like you said, to . . . err . . ."

"It's okay," I said. "NOPD needs to know sooner or later."

"Right." Allie gave one sharp nod. "So I reserved the cathedral, asked about setting up a perimeter, booking guards . . . you know. I let on that it was an important event. That I had a *royal* pain of a boss. Not that you're a pain that often, boss. Just trying to be hinty without being too subtle."

Gary's eyes were wide. "You're having the royal wedding *here*? You're. . . that's . . . you're Jewish."

Allie sighed.

"True," I admitted. "People are sometimes daft, though. They aren't thinking that a Jewish witch marrying a faery wouldn't actually be having an indoors wedding ceremony in a Catholic church."

"So, you aren't hiring guards?" Gary asked.

"Oh we are." Allie clapped her hands together. "I'm paying an embarrassing amount to the NOPD to pretend there's a royal wedding, and I'm going to donate the whole thing to some couple who can't afford a big ol' wedding. Like a fairy godmother!"

Gary stared at her and then looked back at me. "It's a distraction."

I nodded.

"And today's little crush of people was just the first bit of madness," he added.

"Yes . . .?" I admitted sheepishly.

Allie put her hands on her hips and launched into a mother hen lecture. "Gen deserves a wedding without paparazzi and tourists and haters and—"

"She does," Gary said, taking the sass out of her voice quickly.

"And the police will get paid the same as if it *was* there, so it's a win-win." Allie didn't sound nearly as chipper or flighty now. She sounded scary as she poked him in the chest with one manicured fingernail. "And you will help us with this ruse, Officer Broussard, or I know people who will make you regret it."

No one laughed, me because I thought she was as endearing as an angry mama bear and Gary because he was used to women with fierce attitudes. Alice Chaddock might be tiny and chirpy, but she was also the kind of woman who knew where bodies were buried, and in that moment, she was in full bridesmaid mode. This wedding would go off without a single error, or Allie might very well feed anyone who mis-stepped to proverbial dragons—or to the actual alligators since we were, in fact, hosting the real wedding out in the bayou.

"I'll happily be point person to coordinate the wedding at the cathedral," Gary said with a flicker of a laugh. "And I'll not tell a soul that the witch will marry her faery prince right here in our own version of a fairy tale castle. I'll nudge and raise a brow and be very subtle."

"Excellent." Allie hugged him. "Gen said you would likely help."

Whatever else she was, Allie was a part of my found family—and although *Allie* had no idea yet, I suspected she'd be literal family in time. The king of all fae had decided to marry her. They hadn't dated or anything, but fae relationship decisions were perplexing to me, even after magically marrying my own faery prince. Take Eli, for instance. For reasons only Eli knew, he'd met my blood-covered, sword-swinging, foul-mouthed self and thought "she's the one." He'd lived in exile, been my friend, and eventually my bonded spouse.

Weird courtship was a fae thing.

Unfortunately, so was the giant wedding celebration I was currently unable to keep avoiding. I had to plan at least one, but probably two wedding ceremonies—which meant that I pulled my notes out of my bag.

"Why didn't you tell me you were doing this tonight?" I asked.

"You're a terrible actress. I needed a scene. A real one. You delivered that because you were stunned." Allie shrugged like her answer made perfect sense.

It didn't, but neither did one of the wealthiest women in the city working as my assistant. Allie did what Allie wanted, and the rest of us just sort of coped as best we could.

"Let me get a drink for you while we get this part sorted out," I told Gary. "Allie, give him your official statement on the attempted break-in."

"Yes, boss." She walked over to sit primly on the sofa as if polite manners would hide the vicious streak she'd just revealed.

"It'll likely be all over the department within forty-eight hours," Gary said. "Don't be too subtle, Mrs. Chaddock. They need a few details to start gossiping."

I tossed back more of my Bloody Alice, as I wandered off to find a bottle of vodka and bowl of fruit.

Might as well multitask.

# CHAPTER 5

Afew days later, I was feeling more capable about the wedding. Allie was working with my mother on the details—public and private ones. Contrary to the rumor mill we'd set in motion, I would not be having my ceremony inside *any* buildings.

Tonight, I was at a restaurant where I'd been meeting my grandmother bi-weekly. The interior was dimly lit, old-European ambiance with eloquence and age vying for dominance. On the wall were carved skulls and several paintings that were from lesser-known Renaissance artists. The chandeliers were old world oil fixtures, but that was not unusual in New Orleans. Flickering flames lit a lot of places in the city. I *suspected* that the décor was my grandmother's property. I *knew* the restaurant was.

"Ms. Crowe?" the waiter came by the table again. "Would you like to order? Or are you still waiting for the lady."

The lady, of course, was my great-times-great grandmother. She closed *Diablerie* for our meetings, allowing us both a privacy that we craved.

Beatrice was usually early, but tonight, I'd been here for an hour, and she still hadn't shown. Admittedly, she could be busy running one of her companies or beheading usurpers or whatever else she did. Still, I worried.

She hadn't mentioned any recent issues, and I tried not to ask too many questions—the secret to successful families, in my experience, was to avoid awkward topics. Sometimes it was belching at dinner, and sometimes it was "please don't send me heads in boxes." We agreed to disagree on the latter last holiday season.

*Grandmother?* I called on whatever "channel" it was that we used to speak at a distance. *Are you well, Beatrice?*

No answer.

I motioned for the waiter. If Beatrice wasn't replying, I was headed to the Outs to check on her.

But before the waiter reached me, Beatrice swept into the restaurant like a small storm. The red and black tablecloths all fluttered in the breeze created by her wake. There was *flowing*, and then there was the speed at which she did so. My bones tingled at the chill she radiated.

"Water," she said as the server paused at our table. To me she said, "My meeting ran late."

We were the only people in *Diablerie* other than the waiter, bartender, and chef.

Beatrice looked like a misplaced warrior. Knee-length leather wrapped her legs. She wore what resembled a traditional Scottish kilt, which was nothing more than a long swath of plaid fabric wrapped artfully around her. It was held at the waist with a length of snakeskin, as if the snake was biting its own tail. Leather gauntlets with metal decorations covered her wrists and throat.

Uncharacteristically, blood streaked her hair like dye, and bloody fangs were woven onto a cord that dangled around her throat. People were terrified of *draugr*, and with good reason. They were dead, and their existence was predicated on drinking the blood of the living. It made them closer to reptilian than human, although they all, in fact, started as human.

"Are those dripping?"

Beatrice smiled. "Someone questioned whether I was fit to serve."

I winced.

"I do dislike spurious challenges to my authority," she said mildly.

The waiter returned with water, as well two glasses of what appeared to be red wine. My glass *was* simply wine. Hers was not.

"Let's talk about flowers," Beatrice said. "Your mother thinks that we ought to ask Marcus if the fae have any bridal flowers of a traditional nature."

"Mmm."

"I think that he can do that in *Elphame*." Beatrice dabbed her lips with her red linen napkin.

"I think that my feet on the soil, and my family present to share my joy is all I want," I explained. "Honestly, I have no opinions on most of it."

"And the cathedral plans?"

"In order." I had no doubt that the wedding Allie was planning at the cathedral would be the dream wedding for whatever couple she'd privately approached. My wedding would be outside, though. In nature. That was the one unifying detail between the ceremony in the Outs and the one in *Elphame*. Well, that and my groom.

"Any word from Chester? Iggy?" Beatrice asked, as she did every time we met.

"Both silent." I sipped my wine. Chester was the oldest living human, and Iggy was a witch I'd brought back from the dead accidentally. The former had threatened me—and a very long time ago murdered Beatrice. The latter was either friend or foe depending on his agenda. "I think we're clear to have a crises free wedding."

She made an indelicate noise. "Between tourists and *men*, I have my doubts."

"You do realize that I'm *marrying a man?*" I asked lightly.

"Eli is acceptable." Beatrice shrugged. "I tire of beheading my enemies, daughter of mine. So often they are men. Our problems . . . so often . . ."

She stared at a spot beyond me. And for a flicker I thought an enemy waited there. Foolish of me. I would feel any dead presence, and all I noticed were her corpse-guards. She looked into her thoughts. I knew that the ancient witch *draugr* who had once been a mere mortal witch had been forced to carry children as Chester plotted to create a witch-*draugr* hybrid. Me. He had plotted to create *me* centuries before I was born, and it cost Beatrice her life. Add to that the fact that her descendant—my mother—was manipulated a couple decades ago to that end, and it was easy to see why Beatrice had some misogyny.

"Cannot feed them to the dragons, cannot turn them into pigs," Beatrice muttered. "Your mother has asked much of me of late. I will be glad when the wedding has passed."

"I do appreciate you not feeding anyone to the gators," I said lightly.

"One pig and you mother threatened to move out." Beatrice held my gaze. "She has such patience, that woman."

I patted Beatrice's hand. "But you did get to rip the fangs from someone tonight . . . that's, err, something . . ."

She smiled, not quite a laugh but more cheerful now. "He was foolish to doubt my ferocity. A woman? A witch? A Jew? Does he think that *I* am stranger to challenges?"

"Underestimated isn't the same as defeated, though." I sipped my wine. "If there is any chance of co-existence with humanity, your path is the right one. Your allies see this."

"You give good counsel, daughter of mine. Perhaps we can stage a small coup after your nuptials. I have been eying what your nation calls Florida. They create so many conflicts."

I made a noncommittal noise, and this time Beatrice laughed genuinely.

By the time I was ready to leave, Beatrice and I had agreed that we would allow my mother her way with the wedding, and I would talk to Mama Lauren if there was anyone who truly would be best served with a stint as a pig—excepting the King of *Elphame.*

After I left Beatrice, I met my groom at his bar, Bill's Tavern, for a drink. He had an incredibly capable manager, my friend Christy, but Eli was still on site frequently the last few weeks. It was Eli's bar, the reason we met and the place I had felt undeniably at home for several years. I used to think it was the ambiance: a polished wooden bar, low bar lights, and a remarkably good liquor collection. Turned out it was Eli.

"Crowe," the doorman called out to me as I approached the line waiting to get into the bar.

"No fair!"

"Hey!"

The doorman shut them all up with a glare. The news of the royal nuptials and the usual Halloween crowd in our fair city made for more of a crush than normal at Bill's Tavern. A part of me rebelled at all the unfamiliar faces as I stepped inside.

"Fangs," Eli murmured as he pulled me in for a polite hug. He was increasingly circumspect in public, and I wasn't sure if it was about protecting my privacy or about dissuading gossip.

I concentrated on retracting the recently acquired fangs. I didn't need them. I wasn't *dead,* so they were an unwelcome surprise. My *draugr* genes disagreed sometimes, though, and fangs extended. I developed an awkward lisp that could give me away, but other than that, it was fine.

Without another word, Eli motioned for a bartender, and in a matter of moments, we were walking to a roped off corner table with a bottle of tequila and a pair of glasses.

"And how is your grandmother?" he asked.

"Dressed in bloody fangs and grumbling at dealing with my far-too-patient mother." I smiled. "I swear that Mama Lauren is the most reasonable of the bunch. Allie is bridesmaid-zilla with her desire that everything be perfect, and Beatrice is irritable. And your uncle . . . apparently he was irate that we were getting married in a church."

"A *church*?" Eli sounded like he might laugh. "He believed that?"

"Many people believe it. It's a historic building, beautiful and—"

"Catholic." Eli chuckled. "Do you think people are that gullible?"

I pulled out my phone and showed him a row of currently trending hashtags. I was simultaneously excoriated under the tags #badwitch and #BadJew and cheered under #faeryweddings and #witchybride.

"This is absurd," he muttered.

"Wait for the #hotfaery and #PrinceEli threads," I teased. "Apparently, there are plenty of people willing and eager to convince you to pick them instead."

He gave me a look that ought not be legal in public. "Impossible. I have everything I need right here."

He didn't look away from my eyes as he lifted my hand and pressed a kiss into my palm; his lips glanced over the edge of the callouses left there by countless hours with swords or axes in my hand.

"My warrior bride," he added. "My long-sought prize. My perfect dessert."

I sighed. "You make me feel speechless when you say things like that." I stepped closer and whispered, "Or like I ought to pull you into the office and ask you to ravish me."

"Good." He looked smug enough that only a fool would mistake him for human. No one does arrogant quite like the fae.

It felt like an absolutely perfect moment, right up to when the screams started.

"Death to monsters!" someone yelled before two other people shoved our bleeding doorman inside.

With a screech that was loud enough to cut through the chaos of a bar full of frightened drunks, a rust-bucket car came slamming into the front door. The hood of the car was covered in crucifixes, and the front window was missing.

Two people in hoods that resembled the ones worn on Mardi Gras floats crouched there with . . . high volume spray guns.

People screamed as they got doused in what smelled like plain water.

All the while, the radio of the car was cranked, and a Latin mass was playing loudly. The sound of a priest intoning prayers as the bar patrons were being doused with water was enough of an oddity that I had to wonder if this was someone's idea of a Halloween prank.

But prank or threat, I wasn't about to let it stand.

Eli was helping the doorman to his feet, and he and Christy were already handling getting people moved to the back of the building. The injured would heal, and even if there were *draugr* in the bar, holy water wouldn't do anything but make them wet.

Aside from the damage to the bar, this wasn't a dangerous situation. There were no fatal injuries. I wasn't feeling forgiving though.

*My home.*

*My people.*

I stomped toward the door, all while sending my grave magic out in waves that rippled and returned to me.

*To me.*

I could feel eyes opened in the soil. Ears listening for my call. Human and rodent and assorted pets. They were all aware of me. They were waking at my summons. No grave soil needed. For much of my life, I'd worked to develop control over my grave magic. It had been my focus since childhood, but since bonding with Eli, I was less about control—and more about testing my limits.

*We come.*

*Mother.*

*We are yours.*

*We protect.*

I invited the corpses to see through my eyes as I stared at the people who were here to cause me and mine harm.

"Get her!"

I felt something hit me, just as I heard the dead fall back to sleep.

Eli yelled, "Geneviève!"

But I was unable to reply to him, to the dead, to anyone.

# CHAPTER 6

"I knew time with you was going to be a wake snakes experience, Miss Crowe," a man said. The voice was familiar, but whatever knocked me out was intense enough that I couldn't focus.

"Wake snakes?" I echoed blearily. My brain felt fuzzy, and my mouth was parched. I tried to reach for my sword as I stepped forward, only to realize that there were metal restraints on my wrists and ankles.

I tried to force my eyes to focus to figure out where I was. I could smell air that felt stale, motionless, and *old*.

*I can't see.*

*I can't move or see. I can speak.*

I sent out a trickle of grave magic to see if I could figure out where I was—or summon the dead to my aid. Old age meant there had to be something or someone dead. If I could wake them, I could—

"Ah-ah-ah," the man said with a laugh. "Bad hexen! No uninvited armies."

I recognized that voice. I'd brought the ghost of the dead Hexen Master to life—and then I'd accidentally resurrected him. He was as alive as I was, but as soon as I got free of the manacles on my arms, I'd set about changing that detail.

"*Iggy.* This is not okay." I tried to call upon the fae nature-affinity, tugging *that* magic to the surface, but that was equally futile. Nothing worked. Not a single magician flicker. I couldn't even pretend to be shocked, though. I was kidnapped by a Hexen Master so powerful that the oldest living human had killed him for amassing too much power. He wasn't likely to underestimate me. I'd been bound. Literally and magically. If I ever had a captive, I'd have to remember this . . . well, assuming I got free.

"What in the name of duck dongles were you thinking, Iggy?"

"I'm not sure why duck genitalia would be a factor, Hexen." Iggy laughed. "However, I was thinking we should talk, so I've brought you here to dis—"

"Phones, Iggy. Modern thing. No kidnapping required, so how about you release me?" I reverted to my former light-hearted manner with him, which was fine when he was a ghost. Right now? A lot less fine. I was angrier than a cat in a shower, but I thought I was hiding it fairly well.

"I know you too well, Hexen." Iggy chuckled. "You underestimated me. I shan't make the same mistake."

"So this isn't just a social call." I glared in the direction of his voice. I didn't need my vision to do that, although it was starting to bother me that I couldn't see. "What did you do to me? I can't see *anything* . . . or feel the dead."

"Bound you," Iggy said simply. "Eyes not working yet?"

"No."

I felt a glimmer of pressure as if someone kissed my eyelids.

When I opened them, I was expecting Iggy to be right there. He wasn't. He sat several yards away, on the opposite side of the room, looking remarkably piratical due to his surroundings. A chest, circa 1700s, was on the earthen ground at his side. What looked like a museum's worth of coins and jewels were heaped in it.

Ignatius Blackwood was more than a little intimidating now

that he was alive again. No longer an old man, he still had his walking stick, topped with ebony handle almost as dark as the night, in one hand. It was more of an affectation now. He still wore the same elegant ring and watch, but his suit was no longer the vintage 1800s garb he'd worn when he was a ghost. In its place was a pair of what looked like designer trousers and a shirt that managed to be loose and yet still highlight more muscles than I recalled him having. I wasn't generally up on names, but my assistant was and this looked a lot like some of the John Varvatos pieces she'd added to Eli's closest. Whatever it was, the resurrected Hexen Master looked sharp and modern.

"Well? Do I pass muster?" he asked. "I've worked hard to restore my body to optimum health since you so kindly rejuvenated me."

"You look better now that you're alive," I allowed.

He'd been in his late-40s to early 50s and . . . well, *dead* when we met. I'd accidentally summoned him from the grave, and since the bit of magic I hadn't controlled very well, he looked a lot better. It was more than being restored to life or exercising. I tried to look past his surface for traces of magic, but my own magical abilities were locked out of my reach.

"Not everyone can pull off a magical facelift, nip and tuck, and turning back the decades," I guessed, but his pleased laughter was proof that I was right.

"Not all of us have the blood of the dead and the fae in our veins to make us youthful," he retorted.

Fear flickered at his words. Iggy didn't have to torment me. He could simply expose my heritage. "You're a monster, Ignatius Blackwood."

"Indeed I am." He bowed his head. "And a liar, Hexen, but as I said when last we parted, let there be peace between us. I truly do not wish you ill at this moment."

"Newsflash, Iggy Pops, kidnapping me isn't exactly how we create peace these days," I tugged the chains that were restraining me.

"Would you have met me for dinner had I called?" He sounded more curious than mocking, which made it hard to maintain my outrage.

"No." I sighed. "Hey, I don't suppose you sent a driver in an SUV with tinted windows to try to smoosh me like a bug?"

"I did not." Iggy shook his head. "You think ill of me, Hexen, but I do not wish for your death. We have shared enemies. I seek to ally with you, protect you—"

"Leech off my magic," I interjected. Then I saw what I'd convinced myself was an illusion. The image of Baron Samedi, loa of the dead, hovered over him briefly, and grinned at me.

Then Samedi was gone, vanished as if the entire image was only in my mind. I supposed it could be a bit of smoke and mirrors, but that didn't seem like Iggy's style.

"Are my eyes working poorly?" I asked.

"No. Geneviève of Crowe, you see what my master allows. I made a vow a long time ago to one who is tied to death, one who leads the way, who can cure and kill. I serve at his pleasure. The transition between dead and alive solidified long-ago vows." Iggy gave me a tired smile. "Once upon a time, fair Geneviève, it was blasphemy to serve him, and so I blasphemed. I was born, like you, with an affinity for the dead. . . although I was alive, wholly and completely . . . unlike you."

"Who *are* you, Iggy?" I tugged on my restraints again, attempting to get comfortable as Iggy watched.

"I've worn many names, but I am but a man who is in your debt."

I shrugged and stretched, the chains jangling again as I tested how much reach I had. "Send flowers. A gift card. Oh! Allie set up a wedding registry at a high-end weaponry retailer and one at a blacksmith."

Iggy laughed. "I do like that woman." He met my eyes. "Vow on your magic that you will not try to escape, and I shall offer you an equal vow that no harm will come to you while you're here."

"Mmmm. No. An eternity in your lair? Not exactly the future I'm planning."

"If you are left to roam, you will die, Geneviève of Crowe, and I find myself uninterested in that resolution." Iggy walked up to me and stood just out of reach. "I cannot allow you to meet that fate. It would not please Baron Samedi either."

Maybe it was living in New Orleans with a bunch of walking dead folk or going toe-to-toe with the king of *Elphame*, but the thought that the loa of the dead had an opinion on my life didn't freak me out as much as maybe it should've. Later, perhaps, it would. In that instant, however, all I could think of was Eli. He had to be worried, and more importantly, if I died Eli died. We were bound.

"Iggy, be reasonable! I cannot stay in your dirt pit, even though I applaud the piratical vibe. Very New Orleans history, there." I lunged as Iggy swayed closer, trying to at least catch an ankle to knock him off-balance. Hexen Master or man, a good length of chair around his throat and I could kill him.

*Kill the man, end the spell. Even a baby witch knows that.*

Iggy stepped back, ignoring my attempt at injuring him, and said, "My heart beats again. For this, I am in your debt. And I find that I like you. You remind me of your—"

"My grandmother?" I interrupted. "Seriously? That's a little gross, you know?"

He shrugged, not looking the least bit sheepish. "I waited over a century to be resurrected, to find someone strong enough to summon me. I played meek to lead you to trust me, to reach a point where you could be convinced to resurrect me. To restore me."

"I'm bonded to Eli. I *love* him," I reminded Iggy.

He brushed my hair gently. "He's granted you near-eternal life. I'm grateful that you bonded to Eli, but I am unparalleled in strength and patience."

I laughed, pushing every mean, spiteful, angry bit of energy I had into it.

"Tell that to Eli, who waited *years* for me. Tell it to Chester, the human who murdered you. Tell it to my grandmother, who watched her family for generations." I spat at him. "I'm surrounded by patient people. I'm not impressed."

I didn't mention that I thought Chester was a terrifying creature —or that I hated saying his name. But I liked the flicker of rage in Iggy's expression when I said Chester's name.

I braced for an argument. I wasn't entirely sure if I wanted to debate because I was angry or because I was bored or because I was hoping Iggy would see reason. It didn't matter, though. Iggy simply strolled away into some dirt-walled tunnel, leaving me there in chains.

# CHAPTER 7

I hadn't ever experienced the humidity of being in the earthen lairs, and I had to say that I wasn't loving it. New Orleans, admittedly, was damp in various ways. Humid air. Wet drizzle. Hurricane season. Bayou waters. There were plenty of ways that water was inevitable. In this pirate cave of Iggy's, the air felt thick. Moldy. Musty. But without the benefit of corpses of any sort that I could summon to me. The absence of the dead felt like a sudden loss of one of my primary senses. For years, I'd wished I could "turn off" my necromancy, but when it was gone after my bonding with Eli, I was miserable. Having it cut off now made me feel panic when I woke up in the same quiet darkened room. My magic was silent. I was still a captive.

This time, at least, I had a much longer chain on my ankles. My hands were free, and I was resting on a mound of blankets. They didn't smell terrible, but there was a damp earth scent that permeated them and the air itself.

At least I wasn't sleeping standing up. That was progress. My hands were free, too. I'd like to think that this meant Iggy was a fool, but he was obviously able to knock me out to change my restraints, so I wasn't arrogant enough to think he was foolish.

*He'll make a mistake sooner or later. He has to.*

I studied the rest of the room where I was caged. For a literal hole in the ground, it had its upsides. There were barrels that may or may not be filled with booze, crates of centuries' old liquor, and in the darkest corner, tucked behind the rest, a few free weights.

*Who said you couldn't teach a dead man new tricks?*

It appeared that my captor spent a not-insignificant amount of time here.

I'd always said that there was nowhere else I'd rather be than New Orleans. Plagues, floods, monsters. New Orleans didn't give up or give in, and I was proud of that. I hadn't meant that I wanted to be entombed under the city.

I tried again to reach for the dead, to reach for some sort of nature. I was inside the earth. That *was* nature. My magic was silent.

*"Can you hear me?"* I called to Beatrice, Eli, the dead.

No one answered.

Whatever Iggy had done when he bound my magic, it was damned effectual. I drifted back to sleep on my pallet of blankets. I might not be as strong as the Hexen Master who'd kidnapped me, but I wasn't going to stop fighting. That meant sleep.

*And food.*

That part wasn't as easily handled. Thanks to recent events, I was pretty reliant on my Bloody Allie drinks, and without regular access to fresh blood, I was going to get weaker and weaker.

*Not helping.*

I shoved that line of thought away. Sometimes in this world, all a girl could do was bop the gators that swam closest to the pirogue —or in this case, the kidnappers in the pirate tunnel.

ON MY NEXT WAKE-UP, I was greeted by the sight of my kidnapper draining blood from his wrist into a coffee mug that looked as old as the crates of liquor.

"Good morning, Hexen."

I said nothing, but it hit me then: I'd slept. *Twice* even. Since I went multiple days without needing even a catnap, I was sure that this was his doing, too.

"How long have I been here?"

"Two weeks." He glanced at me. "Fifteen days to be precise. I could tabulate hours, as well, but—"

"Why?" Muttering even that one word took more energy than seemed rational.

*Cut off from Eli.*

*Cut off from the dead.*

*Cut off from nature.*

The reasons were there, and I could think of them, but I couldn't understand why Iggy was doing this.

"Eli kill you," I swore blearily. "Bea…trice…too."

"Yes, yes, your calvary would try. And yet"—he made a point of looking around the cave-like room—"here we still are."

I glared at him, fighting to keep my eyes open long enough to do that.

"Bourbon?" He held up a bottle that looked almost as old as I thought he was. "There's port and sherry. Rum. You seem more like a bourbon-for-breakfast kind of woman."

I raised both middle fingers in his direction.

"Two fingers of bourbon it is!" Iggy gestured and the cork popped out the bottle.

Despite every bit of willpower that I knew I had, I looked at that bourbon splashing into the antique cup, twining around the blood in there, and I salivated like a starving dog.

Iggy walked over to me and crouched down.

I was too weak to reach the cup, too weak to sit up without his help, and I hated him just then.

He put the cup on the floor and pulled me upright. "Vow on your magic that you will not try to escape, Geneviève of Crowe, and I shall offer you an equal vow that no harm will come to you while you are here."

I coughed like I couldn't speak, and he brought the cup to my lips.

*Ha! Fooled you!* I thought as he tipped the cup and poured that beautiful elixir into my mouth.

Too slowly I realized that *I* was the fool in this situation. This was more than simple blood. I'd watched him, believed my eyes in my state of weakness and exhaustion, but Iggy had put other blood into the cup before I'd woken—and *that* blood was infused with his own magic.

"Mine to protect," Iggy murmured.

He held the cup to my lips, tipping it and me back so it poured down my throat even as I tried to close my mouth.

"My vow to you, Geneviève of Crowe, my apprentice. I Ignatius Blackwood, will guard your life and teach you." He stared at me as I grew stronger, watching his own magic enter my skin and bone. "To Death, we are committed. To this city, we are born again."

I jerked away, reaching up at the same time to grab the cup from his hand. In the next moment, I pulled back and smashed it into his throat.

Iggy fell backward, blood and bourbon dripping across his face, and as he reclined there, I rose up and kneeled down on his chest, pinning him.

Whatever binding he had placed on me was gone.

*Geneviève!* My grandmother's voice was a roar in my mind.

And louder still was Eli's: *Bonbon! Wife! Geneviève of Stonecroft!*

*I am here,* I thought-spoke to both. *Come to me. Please.*

I was not expecting them to arrive so quickly, but in less than five minutes, the wall bowed in. Dirt and rock and dust billowed in like a cloud.

And I was kneeling over a bloody, laughing man. In that flicker, I saw Baron Samedi again, winking at me as if the whole thing was a grand game. His hand—*Iggy's hand or Baron Samedi's, I wasn't sure*

—grabbed my hip as if what was happening was something other than the truth.

To a lot of men, I suspect it would look like infidelity.

I was atop Iggy. Admittedly we were dressed and filthy, but Iggy looked pleased as a cat who'd already had more than a sample of the cream.

"Geneviève!" Eli plucked me from where I kneeled and moved us across the room in the same instant.

His hands were all over me, seeking injuries, verifying that I was there and real.

"You're alive," he said. "I knew you had to be. If not, I'd have died, but . . . fear does things. If anyone could find a way to spare me death despite being soul-bound, it would be you, bonbon."

My grandmother was less effusive, but her affection was equally obvious. She currently had my captor by the throat. "Daughter of Mine," was all she said to me. Her attention was on revenge.

Beatrice shook Iggy like a child's doll. "You dare touch my family, Iggy?"

I watched, and for a flicker of a moment, I thought that Iggy was about to die. I could summon his ghost and ask what in the name of—

"Hexen," he croaked. "Stop her."

And at his order, I was out of Eli's embrace and snarling at my grandmother as I jerked Iggy free of her hold. I wasn't fool enough to grab Beatrice, but I pulled him free of her grip.

# CHAPTER 8

Trickles of blood lined Iggy's neck from where Beatrice's fingernails scored his flesh, and he let them drip. A part of me wanted to lap up that blood, and that part warred with the bond I shared with my partner, my love, who was watching the Master Hexen with a quiet fury that made me wish I could say or do something to defuse the crisis.

"You dare?" Beatrice snarled. She was a vision of terror in her torn medieval gown. She'd been somewhere formal from the looks of that dress and the fire opal and diamond choker that she wore. The dress was filthy and torn, but she looked no less regal for it.

"Dare?" Iggy echoed. "I was summoned from death by this hexen. She called me from my grave, Bea."

To say that Beatrice was furious was underselling the level of rage she all but radiated. Beatrice paced like a caged predator, and her eyes turned red as if blood had actually filled them. "She is *my* family. Are you fool enough to start a war with me, *human?*"

"Human?" Iggy scoffed, straightening his shirt as if he wasn't at all intimidated by the rage rolling off Beatrice. Whether or not it was an act, I had no idea. He was powerful enough to hide me from the queen of the *draugr* in this part of the world *and* my bonded fae spouse. That took a level of juice that deserved a bit of arrogance.

"I'm not a bone to fight over," I started.

Iggy waved my words away. "That's what you choose to insult me with, Bea? *Human?* We both began that way. She didn't. You know she's *more* than us. If Chester gets ahold of her . . . " He took a breath, as if the thought he had was too dark to ponder. "I owe her for my life."

"So you bound her? Daughter of my daughter! *Mine*! What sort of payment is that?" Beatrice snarled, lip curled like an actual animal.

"Please don't bite him," I whispered.

"I'm not daft enough to drink a Master Hexen's blood carelessly! Did you learn nothing with the way you enthralled Chadwick? Or Odem?" Beatrice swung her rage-filled gaze toward me, and I was reminded that my *draugr* genetics originated from something far more primal than I liked to consider of late. We had developed a cultural love for vampires, and the *draugr* queen often played into that with her old-world dress and manner.

She was still the monster that humans had hid from for centuries.

She was still the creature that tore bodies limb from limb.

And I felt a prickle of fear.

"If you attack him," I said, sounding far calmer than I felt, "I'll have to defend him. Please don't make me do that."

It was as close to pleading as I'd ever come with any *draugr*, and the fact that she was my ancestor didn't take the sting of begging away.

"You've enthralled two *draugr* already?" Iggy prompted.

I looked at Iggy, but I didn't feel a whole lot like answering his question. If this was what Tres felt like because of his bond with me, I owed him an apology. I wanted to defend Iggy, protect him, and yes, a part of my mind that I wasn't admitting in public, wanted to lick the blood on his throat.

*It's not real.*

*It's not* my *desire.*

Instead, I said, "I'm not sure what you did, but I hold grudges like it's my fucking job, Iggy. You would be wise to remember that, to ponder it, and *undo this.*"

Beatrice straightened her dust-covered dress and seemingly straightened her temper in the motion. "He cannot. You drank spell-infused blood."

"Not by choice!" I looked at Eli. "I didn't bite him. I swear it."

If I was the easily embarrassed type, this would be a thoroughly mortifying moment, but I was in a room with a man I resurrected, my dead grandmother, and my beloved. And I was as blunt as a drunk co-ed sometimes. "He starved me and then there was a glass, well, a mug really with bourbon and—"

"I trust you," Eli said simply, cutting off my rambling explanation. Then he leveled a look at Iggy that would make a seasoned warrior piss his pants.

And I remembered that Eli could read me.

*He can feel my desire for another man.*

"Eli . . ." I reached out, and he squeezed my hand briefly.

Then he turned icy fury back to Iggy. "I recommend you start explaining your reasoning, Blackwood, because while I may not look as threatening as the young Lady Beatrice"—he glanced at her and bobbed his head briefly in respect before stepping toward Iggy —"I am not as tolerant. You are a *mayfly* in comparison to the fae, and you have attacked a sovereign nation by kidnapping and enslaving our future queen."

"I have afforded her my protection." Iggy frowned at everyone. "She is my—"

Before the word was even fully formed, Eli had Iggy pinned to the wall, using the *draugr* ability to *flow* that he'd gained after we bonded. The earthen wall had an indent in the shape of Iggy's body now. "No. She is very much not *your* anything."

I'd thought I'd seen Eli angry, but in that moment, I realized how much I owed him an apology. My gentle fae lover might speak like a poet and treat me as if I was made of the finest artisan-blown glass, but he was still a man with a possessive streak that made my knees weak and my pulse race.

*And he'd felt my desire for someone else.*

"My wife. My woman. My beloved." Each word was accompanied by a punch. "My warrior. My heart."

Iggy had two already-blackening eyes, and blood trickled from his mouth and nose.

"Do not mistake my words, Ignatius Blackwood: Geneviève of Crowe and Stonecroft is wholly mine until *our* mutual death, and any affront to her—which this was—will not be ignored."

Eli released the bloodied man, who leaned on the wall watching me with a wobbly grin.

"Geneviève, I demand—" Iggy's words once again died, this time because Eli punched him so forcefully that he collapsed and slid down the wall to a heap on the ground.

Then Eli grabbed a flask of bourbon and poured it over his blood-stained hands, so the blood was washed into the dirt.

"If you wouldn't mind?" he asked Beatrice.

"With pleasure." She pulled magic from the air and lit the blood-and-booze-stained earth to fire. It wouldn't spread throughout the cave, and for a flicker of moment I was glad. I didn't want Iggy to die.

I glanced at the unconscious man who had held me captive.

"He's still alive, Geneviève," Eli grumbled.

"I'm sorry," I whispered. "I swear I didn't . . . that . . . *I love you. Only you.*"

"I know." Eli swallowed and looked away.

Guilt filled me. I didn't want to care about Iggy, but I did. Maybe it was the bond—or maybe it was the laundry list of questions I had.

"No one else can tell me what I need to know about my magic," I said quietly. "That doesn't mean I *like* his approach or *wanted* to be enthralled or—"

"It'll fade once his blood-magic is out of your system." Beatrice's tone was so cold that I was worried, and in that observant way of hers, she answered questions I didn't know how to ask: "He did the same to me. We shared a . . . few weeks . . . of . . . fondness."

"That's assault!"

She gave me a quelling look. "He gave me the blood at *my* request, Geneviève. We were experimenting. It was another time, and I was not unwilling in any way. Why he would do so with you without your consent is another matter entirely. Did he take liberties?"

It was Eli I looked at when I said, "No. I had his blood, and the silencing hold on me broke and"—I motioned toward the wall they'd imploded—"then you were here."

Eli gave a single nod. No one addressed the possibility of what would have happened if I hadn't broken that hold. I glanced at Iggy, verifying that he was breathing.

*I shouldn't care.*

In a calmer tone, Eli said, "Blackwood withheld your presence from my life for two weeks, Geneviève. He took you away from me. He held you prisoner when you would leave. That is not forgivable. *None* of it."

He looked back at Iggy, but unlike me, Eli watched the unconscious man as if debating whether or not to strike him again.

"Take me home?" I asked, pulling his gaze to me.

Another terse nod was Eli's entire response, but then he gestured for me to walk forward.

Beatrice stepped in front of me, walking over the rubble and roots as if she were gliding across a ballroom. I stumbled after her. I felt a level of confusion and exhaustion that was atypical.

Behind me Eli was a steady presence. One hand stayed flat on the small of my back as if assuring me that he was there—or perhaps assuring himself that I was. Either way, I felt like that hand was all that tethered me to the world.

Why had Iggy risked his newly-restored life?

What was his agenda?

There was one. I knew that with a certainty that defied everything else. He believed he was helping me, and I had no idea how. He'd not seemed particularly interested in me, aside from as a friend or a means to an end.

What was I missing here?

# CHAPTER 9

When we reached our home, the one that bordered *Elphame,* not my apartment, Beatrice took my face in her hands and held my gaze. "Do not forget who you are, Geneviève." She looked at Eli. "Or allow this wound with Eli to fester."

Then she kissed my forehead as tenderly as any mother ever did and, in a moment that left me thoroughly speechless, kissed Eli on both cheeks.

"I will handle your Alice and your mother," Beatrice said with a tone of voice that every Jewish mother could summon at will.

I smothered the smile that such a guilt-provoking tone brought to my lips. Beatrice had barely had the opportunity to be a mother, and both of the women she was going to "handle" were grown women. But seeing this moment of maternal exasperation was as endearing as seeing the gown-clad monster explode a wall to reach me.

"I am lucky to count you as family," I told her.

"Indeed," was all she said, but she looked pleased as a kitten in a basket of yarn for a sliver of an instant. Then she was gone as quickly as if she'd never been there. The *draugr* gift of speed was so remarkable as to mimic disappearing into thin air.

I took an uncomfortable breath before meeting Eli's gaze. "I don't want anyone but—"

"You are eternally my home, Geneviève of Crowe and Stonecroft. I share with you my hearth and lintel. May you find shelter in my heart and home." He led me to the keystone of the doorway, echoing words he'd said to me several times. "In this world and my home, you are mine to safeguard." He looked like each word was sharp glass on his tongue as he said, "And I failed you."

"No!"

"If you would seek shelter at another hearth, I will release—"

"You will not." I grabbed him. "You are eternally my home, Eli of Stonecroft. I share your hearth and lintel. I find shelter in your heart and home. *You are mine* unto death or beyond."

I felt my birth magic and our fae magic swirl around us, as if we were in the center of a hurricane. Wind whipped around us, and I was no longer certain that the earth was solid.

Arms around his neck, I pressed my lips to his. I wasn't sure if it was magic, love, lust or some twist of the three, but together we *flowed* into the house.

"Geneviève." Eli pushed me back onto the bed and pulled my dirt-and-blood-stained jeans down almost at the same moment.

"*Mine.*" He breathed the word against my bare stomach as he kissed and bit his way up.

I plucked at his shirt, as I promised, "Yes. Yours. *Always* and eternally. Now, touch me. Two weeks apart is too long."

He laughed, low and joyous. "I would free you if you asked, Geneviève. It would kill me, but if that's what you w--"

"Not what I'm asking." I unbuttoned his trousers. "Not what I want *ever.*"

I slipped my hand into his trousers and stroked. "This. I want this."

He leaned down and kissed me speechless.

My other hand slid under his shirt, shoving it up. As soon as it was over his head and out of my way, I kissed his chest, his shoulders, his throat. I nipped gently. "May I?"

"*Geneviève*," he said.

"If you don't want me to since—"

"Bite me. Touch me," Eli ordered, voice low and rough. He shoved his trousers further down giving me unfettered access.

Then he ordered, "Show me."

I let my fangs slide into his skin, and the taste of his blood pouring into my mouth made me whimper even as I swallowed. All the while, I stroked him. Time seemed to melt as my world was reduced to the touch, scent, and taste of Eli.

Eli grabbed my wrist and pulled my hand away.

Straddling me.

Pinning my wrists over my head with one hand.

I felt the hard length of him as he thrust his hips against me. Not entering me, merely taunting.

"Who do you belong to, Geneviève?" he asked, a whisper in my ear since my fangs were in his throat still.

I moaned.

Eli pulled back, moving so his throat was out of my reach and his length was almost where I needed it. "I asked you a question."

I pulled my gaze away from the blood trickling along the column of his throat as he eased forward, barely inside me.

"Geneviève? Tell me." The demand in his voice, the same icy command he'd had in the cave made me try to push my hips upward.

Eli's hand gripped my hip and held me steady, all while his other hand gripped my wrists tightly.

"*You.*"

"Who?" he prompted as he slid home.

"You. Only you." I swore. "Eli of Stonecroft. *You.*"

"No doubts, Geneviève?" He had me pinned, unable to move, unable to do anything but wait.

"None. Please. *Please.*" He held me immobile for several more moments, as if he needed to prove to us both that he had mastery of me.

I could only feel and beg. "More, Eli. Please. *More*."

He was quiet, breathing as needy as mine.

"I love you," I reminded him. "I'm here. I'm home."

I heard the strain in his voice as he half-ordered, half-swore, "No one will ever take you away from me, Geneviève."

Then there were no more words, as we spent the night reminding one another how perfectly we fit.

COME DAWN, I had to disentangle myself from Eli's grip. Quietly, so as not to wake the sleeping prince, I whispered a spell for stealth, so the click of the door closing was muted.

Maybe it was a small bandage on a gaping wound, but I spent the next three hours planning details for the wedding ceremony that we would be having. Between Alice and my mother, the main pieces were pretty much in order—as if they had planned obsessively in my absence.

By the time Eli came into the room, eyes darting around in a panic that made my stomach twist, I had selected two wedding gowns, flowers, and finalized the remaining details.

"Tux for the wedding here or traditional fae garb?" I asked as he stood staring at me. "And did we want to have the royal guards attend both weddings?"

He opened and closed his mouth silently.

"And I was thinking that although I want our wedding to be private, we ought to do a drive by for the paparazzi." I realized I was talking nervously, too quickly and too obviously worried. "You. Me. Marcus and Alice. Maybe she'd get a clue that he wanted to make her his queen. I wish I could tell her or that you—"

"I respect the bargain you made, and as I was privy to the terms, I cannot disrespect you or the king by telling Alice. A faery bargain is sacred," he murmured quietly. "We'll deal with your plot to get around it later."

I met his gaze. "Can *I* create a faery bargain? I mean, since *we* bonded I have some of your fae traits."

Eli nodded, unusually speechless.

"I can then. Interesting." I pondered the language I wanted to use for a moment before asking, "What do you say to a faery bargain, Eli?"

The catch, of course, was that if a bargain is begun, the fae making the bargain knows what the bargainer most desperately wants. And I desperately needed to know what Eli most wanted.

Eli gave me a look that made me want to squirm as he pointed out, "If we agree to make such a bargain, you will know my heart's desire in this instant. Do you want that?"

"Yes, very much so. And I'll give it to you if . . ." I stalked toward him.

"If?" he echoed.

As much as I had enjoyed Eli's need to prove his dominance over me, I wasn't done with atoning. "Does that mean you would like to enter a faery bargain with me, Eli of Stonecroft?"

"Perhaps. What are your proposed terms?" he asked.

I took a deep breath as Eli's desire washed over me. *Eternity. My safety. Not taking the throne. Figuring out what Iggy wanted from me. Chester's death. A baby.* The noise of his mixed and varied desires was daunting. Several sexual scenarios flitted through my mind, and I made a note to examine those more closely later.

"This is how you knew what I liked," I mused.

He offered one of the half-shrugs that meant that he agreed but would not be admitting anything. "The fae do not lie, but that does not mean that we ignore those things we have in our arsenal."

He gave me a look that left me certain that we had always been headed to forever, even when I had the foolish notion that I might maintain my illusion that I could resist him.

"I will offer you a wish, Eli. One unrestricted request when most you want to use it," I said.

"If you do so, you are bound by law to comply." He stared at me, as if his will alone could impress clarity upon me. "Nothing and *no one* could order you otherwise."

"Yes." I took his hands in mine. "Not even your uncle the king, or Beatrice—"

"Or Blackwood," he added because that, of course, was the crux of the wish. We both wanted him to be able to use that wish to free me if the need were to arise.

I understood then that this—this ability to offer a bargain for the other person or for the bargainer to gain a coveted moment or exception to a law—was what he'd been doing all along. Our first faery bargain was for a kiss, which had led to our engagement. The first bargain made him my fiancé, but it allowed him to save my life. The second allowed us to stay engaged without rushing toward an actual marriage. The third led to our bonding.

Until this moment, he'd been giving me the power to control my fate despite the challenges that came from eons of fae tradition and law. And today I was giving him the power to overcome the Hexen magic that Iggy had used to entrap me.

"What terms?" Eli asked.

"I will grant you this wish, Eli, if you take me to Elphame and pronounce me your bride before all of *Elphame*."

"Now?"

"Now." I gathered my wedding plans and dress images. "Take me to your place of birth. I think it's time we had a wedding."

# CHAPTER 10

Over the next two hours, we made hasty plans to gather up my mother, my assistant, and my closest friends: Sera, Jesse, and Christy.

After my last trip to *Elphame*, I wasn't truly eager to leave New Orleans for the realm of the fae, but a mental clock was ticking louder and louder. Now that I was waiting to let Iggy's spell wear off, going to a land where he was not made welcome was all the more reason to get on with the ceremony.

"If I could invite you, I would," I told Beatrice as we stood at her estate, which admittedly seemed to have more feral pigs than it used to. I made a mental note to ask if they all *had* to stay in their porcine states. For now, I simply asked, "Will you have our ceremony here ready within the next week or so?"

"Of course, daughter of mine! I can finish without Fair Alice and Lauren." She sent a glare toward a man currently shaping vast topiaries. "I may find it easier in fact."

"Not all men are pigs," Eli said mildly.

"*You* are on two legs, Eli," Beatrice demurred. Then she offered a cold smile. "Please remind Marcus that as he would deny me the chance to see you wed in his world, I do hope he understands that he will not be welcome *here* on my land where the next ceremony will be."

Eli quirked his brow in her direction. "So, my wedding has become a contest, Beatrice? Truly?"

"Geneviève is more my child than any before her. You know this. Marcus knows this. Iggy knows." She patted my mother's cheek, as Mama Lauren joined our small group. "Lauren has *always* known. She created Geneviève from magic and will, carried a child that was both living and dead in her womb, and despite her ill-conceived affection for that worthless hyena of a creature who impreg—"

"Grandmother," Mama Lauren interrupted. "We agreed not to argue about Geneviève's fath—"

"Not my father," I grumbled. "He was a sperm donor. And I didn't agree not to point out that he was not worth the slime on the bottom of a toad's warty ass."

Mama Lauren looked around, as if someone would step in.

Jesse shrugged. "Don't like the dead."

"Except you Lady B," Allie added. "Right, everyone? And the boss, except Geneviève's not *really* dead, so are you insulted by the *draugr*-opposition, boss?"

I snorted. "What's my job?"

"Right." Allie clapped her hands and looked at the group. "So no, unless the job is a way to kill that part of you by projecting it onto—"

"Alice?" Eli interrupted. "We must depart. I expect that Geneviève would rather we do so without a psychoanalysis of her career path."

Allie grinned and no one did more than roll their eyes. We were family, a mismatched collection of weirdos who had turned friendship and genetics into something wonderful. And this family's shit-stirrer was Allie. Although she'd tried to murder me last year, Allie had more than earned her place at my side.

"Give Marcus my words," Beatrice said with a razor smile.

"Please try to not hex or eat anyone," Mama Lauren whispered.

Beatrice shooed us away with a placid look on her face.

Allie giggled, and I had a moment of gratitude that the queen of the *draugr* had a near-unparalleled fondness for me, but then Eli took my hand and we walked toward the glimmer in the air that was beckoning us to open it.

Allie, Sera, and Christy had been to *Elphame* once, and I suspected Allie had gone over on her own on several occasions. My mother and brother-by-choice had never entered the realm where the fae lived. I was more anxious than I probably ought to be, and Eli's steady hand in mine made me feel less like panicking.

"Only for this day and this time," he reminded our small group, as if he hadn't impressed the rules upon them repeatedly and carefully already. "Today and today alone, you may enter my homeland without restriction. To enter here without such assurances is to be trapped at the will and whim of the regent."

As we walked, a blinding slice appeared as if the air itself had been torn open. It glowed with a light and warmth that would make anyone want to run toward it, and I was glad to see that Jesse took both Christy and my mother's hands protectively. I flashed him a grateful smile as I motioned them forward.

Allie strode through first, as if she was far more at ease with that doorway than I realized.

Sera followed.

Then Christy released Jesse's hand, so she could step through the gateway in front of my mother and Jesse.

Once they were securely through, Eli and I crossed the passageway between this world and *Elphame*.

On the other side the air was as pure as air ought to be. No pollution. Nothing but the sort of air that the human world hadn't known for centuries now, except in the most remote corners.

"Welcome to my home," the king said to all of us, although his gaze lingered on Allie with the sort of proprietary gaze that she somehow *still* wasn't admitting existed.

I had theories as to why, but I'd made a bargain with Marcus not to get in his way . . . more or less. He had considered holding my assistant captive within *Elphame*, as was within his rights for any mortal entering his domain. Our discussion for her release was a combination of epiphanies and insults—and culminated with a vow not to disclose his intentions.

I hadn't found a good way to get around it, but damned if I hadn't tried.

"Nephew of mine," Marcus said with a warm voice. He embraced Eli before meeting my gaze. "Death Maiden."

I accepted his open armed invitation and whispered, "Cradle robber."

He laughed jovially, inviting curious looks from my entire group and a few shocked ones from his retinue. The royal guard was a fierce fighting force, and I'd had the pleasure of their accompaniment when I'd ended up trapped in a spa run by magic users and *draugr*.

A series of dipped heads met my gaze as I looked at the assembled fae warriors.

Then Marcus stepped forward to greet my mother. "It is an honor to meet the mother of my niece to be."

He reached out to lift her hand, expecting her to swoon or whatever it was most mortal women did. Mama Lauren was not most women, though. She turned his hand when he reached out and shook.

Marcus of Stonecroft was handsome and seemingly ageless. The fae didn't age like humans, so I had no real measure of his age—despite asking more than a few questions. Marcus had been king for a lot of years. He had been king when the world learned the fae were real, and he'd been king when they all retreated to *Elphame*.

And yet my mother—who had a few decades of knowing she was raising a mixed species child, and that her own ancestor still walked our world as a blood-drinking, dead, warrior queen—was not easily impressed. She kept hold of Marcus' hand and whispered low enough that only the non-humans heard, "Young Alice may not see the truth of the words between your lines, but I do. The girl has no mother to speak for her, but that child is *our* family. My daughter and my grandmother are quite vicious, you know . . ."

The King of *Elphame* gave her a level look. "I see the trait is hereditary."

"I'm not opposed to outsourcing," she murmured.

Then the awkward moment passed, and everyone other than my mother was whisked away. I thought it best to keep Mama Lauren nearby in hopes of avoiding conflicts.

At Eli's house, my mother explored and then sat outside, marveling at nature as I once had. Unlike in the Outs, there were no random monsters—or the *draugr* or looter variety—roaming in the dark of night. There she'd always risen and slept with the cycle of the sun, and I thought she was enjoying the peace of being able to commune with nature under the moon.

# CHAPTER 11

I slept. That was a weird side effect of whatever Iggy did. I sort of liked it, but it was obviously bothering Eli.

"Are you injured, Geneviève?" He was propped on one arm staring down at me. He touched my forehead carefully, and then took my pulse. It was sweet, if not for the reason. I'd bled all over him, been injected with venom, stabbed, shot, and magically depleted. I was, in sum, accident-prone.

"I don't think so." I didn't feel unwell. "Sleepier than normal, but I feel okay other than that. Honestly, my magic feels . . . *obedient*. It's not overwhelming or humming or anything. Maybe I just finally settled into my bones."

Eli didn't look convinced, but he took my hands and asked, "Shall we stand before the world and proclaim our love?"

I pulled him down and kissed him before slipping by him with a laugh and *flowing* to the main room. Out there, Mama Lauren was waiting with veritable baskets of flowers and hair pins.

I dutifully sat on an ottoman while she started twining blossoms into my hair.

Eli fixed coffee, glorious man that he was, for all of us, and said nothing as my mother fussed and jabbed and twisted my hair into something fitting for the future queen of *Elphame.*

"Boss?" Allie came in with a glass bowl of what appeared to be gemstones. "I have a gift from Lady B."

My mother looked at the cut-glass bowl. "I told her it was too much."

"What?" I looked closer, feeling the magic in the stones calling me. Carefully, I reached out a finger and felt the impossible flutter of ethereal wings.

Looking past the magic I could see gleaming emeralds of a Birdwing, rich sapphire of a Blue Morpho, translucent near-opal Amber Phantom, the ruby Red Lacewing, deep amethyst of the Purple Emperor. They were temporary, neither real nor living, but to create such an illusion was a degree of magical mastery that left me speechless.

The faux jewels were in a net that draped over my hair. The effect of flowers and gems on my already sapphire-hued hair was stunning.

"Time to go, Eli," Jesse called from the doorway. He walked inside and came to a dead stop when he saw me. "You're not as funny looking as you were when we were kids, Gen."

I flipped him off. Then I said, "You're shirking on your man of honor duties."

"What? I thought you said that over here—"

I snorted in laughter at his panic, even though Mama Lauren swatted me. "Geneviève. Behave. Both of you."

My childhood bestie and surrogate brother said, "Yes, Mama Lauren."

"Sorry," I said unapologetically. "But you should see your face."

"Wench." He rolled his eyes and turned to Eli. "Come on, man. Your bride is a vicious thing. You sure you want to do this? We could hit the beach and—"

"I have no doubts," Eli said loudly and clearly. "Eternity will not be enough to make me tire of Geneviève."

"Your life, man. She snores. Cuts her toenail in the kitch—"

"Liar," I said. "That's *you*."

Jesse walked over and stared down at me. "You're gorgeous, Gen. Strong. Kind. Fearless. He's a lucky man, and I'm proud to call him family."

Mama Lauren sniffled.

"No tears!" Jesse and I said in unison.

She gave us a watery smile, pulled me to my feet, and hugged us both. "My babies."

And Jesse and I both did that awkward man-pat on her shoulders. Weepy women were dangerous, especially mothers.

"Right, well, I'll be taking the groom." Jesse backed away quickly. "See you at the . . . wedding."

Once the two men were gone. Allie looked at us and said, "I'll go check on the other bridesmaids."

And then I was alone with my mother, who was still giving me a weepy smile.

"Let me get the dress," I offered and all but ran to the bedroom where the simple unbleached cotton and lace dress was. I'd seen the confectionary-looking dresses online and in stores, as well as in illustrations sent from *Elphame*. They were lovely, but they weren't me. So I'd chosen what looked like a long dress with a slit in case I had to run.

*No, really. I understand people thinking I'm paranoid, but I was just kidnapped and held in a pirate's lair. These things happened.*

So slit, simple, and natural.

Over that was a lace layer that went on a bit like a duster or a cardigan. It added the delicate layer that everyone else seemed to want, and I will admit it made me feel feminine. The hex-woven belt, shot with spun gold, was the only truly extravagant item, but it was commissioned by Eli. He brought me the materials and asked me to create a wedding sash.

He wore a matching one.

I walked toward my mother with the belt in hand. "Will you?"

Silently, aside from stray sniffles, she wrapped it around my natural waist and tied it so that it hung down. It would sway as I walked, but that was fine.

The last touch was the butterfly veil that draped over my hair. My face was uncovered, but the net of gemstones on my hair added a weight to my step. This was it. My wedding. A flicker of panic rose in my throat.

"You love him." My mother kissed my cheek. "And he loves you."

I nodded. We were already bound unto death, but it felt somber to proclaim my tender feelings in front of the whole of *Elphame.* These were mine, and I hating feeling exposed.

We walked toward a field where it felt like the world had gathered. Thousands of faeries gathered. A path of blossoms led me toward Eli, where he stood waiting. My mother walked me to him.

"I give you my child unto your safe-keeping." She took his hand in hers, and then she took mine in her other hand. She pulled them together, so our hands were clasped.

Then Mama Lauren stepped back. Loud enough for all to hear, she pronounced, "There are two paths. One together. One apart."

My bridesmaids and Man of Honor all stood. In this ceremony, they were my witnesses. It was a fae thing.

"Before these witnesses of your life and past, I urge you to choose."

King Marcus and assorted fae stood.

Marcus walked to a central bower of closed flower buds. "Do you bring me a queen of our people, Eli of Stonecroft?"

For a long moment, no one spoke.

Then Eli looked at me. "I offer you my throne, my homes, my last drop of blood, my final gasp of air."

I swallowed.

"Will you join me, Geneviève of Crowe?" He stared into my eyes as if there was any chance that he'd find doubt.

There wasn't.

"I go where you go," I said. "Your people are mine. Your ancestors are mine. All I have to offer in return are my last drop of blood, my last breath of life, and . . . both my grave magic and my blades, for you already have my heart, my body, and my soul."

No one remarked on the modification of our vows, but I was a witch. I would add those aspects to my vows.

Eli smiled. "I will walk whichever path you allow."

I looked at the two paths—away from or toward the king—and then I grabbed Eli's hand and ran toward the king. Hand-in-hand, we *flowed*. It was not a trait I would share so openly in the world of my birth, but here I was willing to show them what I was. If I was going to do this, accept the responsibility of a throne, I was going to be clear on what they were getting as a queen.

Marcus didn't quite muffle his muttered expletive, but Eli looked joyous.

"I was in a hurry," I said loudly.

Laughter fluttered around us, and my groom joined in.

"Are there any objections?" I asked the assembled crowd. "Not to marrying Eli. That is done. But to me being here as your queen-in-waiting alongside him?"

No one objected. Instead, as one, they curtsied or bowed. And I felt a wave of acceptance that was foreign in my life.

"No delicate maiden," Marcus said. "A warrior queen fit for your warrior king."

The butterflies-made-jewels took flight and dispersed.

Still with our hands intertwined, we both knelt—although protocol was such that only Eli was to kneel. I was merely to bow my head.

Then the King of *Elphame* placed crowns gently on both of our heads. "I give you Eli and Geneviève of Crowe and Stonecroft, my heirs."

# CHAPTER 12

Returning to New Orleans was bittersweet this time. I had felt a connection with the land of my husband, and I'd enjoyed yet another mini-honeymoon with him. However, being the officially presented heir and being tour guide for my friends and mother was exhausting.

When we stepped through the gate from *Elphame* to our human-world home city, we paused at Beatrice's estate long enough to deliver my mother there. Jesse and Christy stopped by his mother's home in the Outs, which left Sera and Allie in the car with Eli and me.

"It's not so bad there, is it?" Allie asked Sera. They were both in the backseat of the car we were using. It was modified for fae, of course, but much more spacious than Eli's convertible.

Sera smiled. "It's beautiful."

I'd seen her dancing with one of the fae guards she'd met over the summer. And more than once, I saw them walk away together. Allie, on the other hand, was all but chasing the king away with a rolled-up newspaper. Two of my friends seemed liable to be enmeshed with fae, although neither one quite understood how serious their flirtations were.

"You know, Sera, often the fae select their mates based on weighing criteria that only they know." I tried to stare at Allie as I said it. "Eli chose to marry me years ago. He waited and waited, carefully getting closer . . ."

"True." He reached over to the passenger seat and squeezed my leg. "Worth the wait."

Allie perked up. "Well, I think that's just sweet. Patience and all . . . I can't believe how oblivious you must've been."

I opened my mouth to point out that this was kettle-pot statement because she was somehow not catching on that the King of *Elphame* had her in his sights. No words came. Just a garbled noise as if I was choking. The peril of the faery bargain with Marcus was that I literally couldn't comment.

"Allie . . ." Sera started. "The king looks at you like Eli looks at Gen."

Allie looked at Sera like she was a swamp rat with a piece of trash. "Why would you say such a thing?"

"Because Gen seems to choke when she tries," Sera said, watching me. "Something is preventing her from speaking clearly. Roisin says that's what happens if there's a bargain."

Allie looked between us like Eli and I were betrayers or like Sera was a mad woman.

"Some traditions are magically binding, Alice." Eli shrugged, but he squeezed my knee in a way that I knew meant 'it's fine.'

I was, obviously, frustrated that I couldn't say anything, but at least Allie had a bit of a clue now.

"Well, that devious bastard . . ." Allie muttered.

And finally, I exhaled. Marcus might've led her on a bit of a con, but now that Allie knew his intentions, I almost felt sorry for him.

Testing the boundaries of the faery bargain, I said, "Poor Marcus."

Allie gave me a look that could strike fear into seasoned warriors but all she said was, "I'll be needing a bit of a holiday boss. I'll let you know when."

"Oh?"

"Mmmhmm," she said. "I'm overdue for a trip home to Tennessee."

Eli flinched a little, maybe in empathy for his uncle or maybe at the knowledge that an angry Alice was a terrifying thing to ponder.

"Wedding first," Sera pointed out.

"Of course!" Allie leaned back in her seat.

Prim and proper expression back in place, Alice Chaddock could pass for a sweet Southern lady in that moment. Butter wouldn't even melt in her mouth.

And in that instant, any hope I had of Eli avoiding the throne because his uncle would marry and have a child vanished. The King of *Elphame* had no idea what he'd sparked when he pissed off Allie. I couldn't imagine her forgiving him and marrying him.

ANY THOUGHT I had of the king or Alice or anything else faded as we neared the cathedral. The entire block was filled with tourists. It was like Mardi Gras met Superbowl met Halloween.

"What in the name of sweet baby Jesus is that?" Allie gestured to an effigy that I suspected was to be me because of the garish witch's mask and blue wig. The thing was strapped to a crude post on the street corner. Wood was piled all around it, and what appeared to be tailgaters with coolers were hooting and hollering like it was a pre-game party.

"I think they're . . ." Sera glared out the window. "They're planning to burn you at the stake."

"Well, 'Die Witch Bitch' isn't the cleverest slogan I've ever—"

"Bonbon." Eli interrupted, as he pulled the car to the side of the street to watch the madness. "I do not find this amusing."

The truth was that I didn't either. I felt several dead presences in the crowd, *draugr* who undoubtedly were not sanctioned to be there by the reigning queen—who was, incidentally, hosting my wedding at her home.

I let my grave magic roll out, feeling the age of the enemies stoking the hate. No one under two centuries.

As I realized that the fervor was being stoked by political enemies of my grandmother's, my temper slipped a bit more.

"Do you trust me?" I asked.

"Always," Eli answered.

I reached over and kissed him. "I shall see you at the wedding tomorrow. . . or before. Take my bridesmaids home?"

Eli nodded. He obviously *could* fight, and if I needed him, he would come. Being a few blocks away would be better right now though. I let my grave magic rise up, settle into my bones and skin.

"If you need me—"

"I always need you," I reminded him. "But there are times when your fae energy does not like what I will do."

Sera interjected, "Gen, maybe you could talk to them. . ."

"Hate doesn't listen to words." Eli looked back at her. "SAFARI exists to bring death to fae and *draugr.* And SAFARI is either involved or behind th—"

"*Draugr,*" I interrupted, gesturing toward the pockets of dead that I could feel in the crowd.

"For fucking real?" Allie said.

Eli laughed. "I would feel terrible for my uncle if he didn't create his own bed, as you say."

"Made your bed, lie in it, Prince Eli. That's the phrase. But that man would be so lucky as to lie in a bed with the likes of me," Allie muttered. Then louder, she added, "We'll be at the house, Boss. Go give 'em hell."

"Try talking to them, at least," Sera asked, grabbing my arm.

"That's the plan," I told them both as I got out of the car and grabbed my sword and dagger from the trunk.

*Sharp things. Never go anywhere without them.*

As soon as my beloved and my friends were a block away, I had sheathed my weapons and untethered the grave magic that wanted to be released. It felt like a monsoon surging through a hose. Too much. Too forceful. A part of my mind whispered that my own magic would tear me apart.

Another part stretched like a fighter about to get a little exercise after a dull season.

*Come out, come out, wherever you are.* I summoned the dead, felt them knit bone and flesh together. Heard their voices as one loud symphony in my mind.

"To me." I spoke the words into the air, let magic whip my order across the city.

No part of me was fae in this moment.

No part of me was human.

I was Death Magic given form, and this was *my* city that had been invaded. I strode across the street toward their signs and crude mockery of me. This was hate and ignorance. This was fear whipped into violence. And I had no fucking time for it.

"Do you follow the dead so eagerly?" I said, projecting my voice as I swung up into a balcony on one of the historic homes that had been preserved well.

"It's her!"

"Death to witches!"

"Burn her!"

"You would come to my city with violence at the behest of *draugr*?" I called out. At the same time, I summoned the *draugr* there to me.

I wasn't sure how many of them I could beckon with will and magic while I was raising the dead, but no time like the present to test my limits, right?

One fanger, the youngest, all but threw himself at my feet.

"Well, don't you look human," I murmured. Louder, I ordered, "Teeth. In fact show them what you were like before you were leashed."

And he flashed fang like a child on Halloween.

Then promptly started hissing, slobbering, and generally acting like a newborn fanger.

Apparently, my magic went a little *too* far. Oops.

Tourists screamed, and more than a few took pictures . . . because of course, they did. Social media was its own sort of monster. Why fear death right here hissing and growling if you could pause to photograph it for your feed?

Elsewhere in the crowd, my magic pressed the same command on the other *draugr*.

The eldest of the lot *flowed* to stand in front of me. She was dressed like a Viking playing dress-up as a Goth. An awkward mix of fur and leather and jewelry on a fighter's body that ought to be holding a sword, not a metal chair.

I guess violence is the mother of improvisation or something like that. . .

She swung the folding camp chair at me like it was a bludgeon.

"Stop it." She smacked it into a tourist who went flopping into another, and in short order, we had a riot on our hands as well as an angry dead lady with a camp chair.

"I feel you in my head," she complained, rubbing her temple.

I snorted. "You won't be feeling your head on your dumb shit shoulders if you don't turn around and get out of my city."

"*Your* city?"

"Mine to protect."

Another older dead-dude showed up then, *flowing* up to her side. This one had a golf club.

"Seriously?" I almost regretted drawing a sword, but talking wasn't getting anywhere.

I gave talking one last try, though, and said, "Get out of my city. Don't make trouble for me or Beatrice, and I'll let you keep your heads."

"Your days are limited, child," the golfclub-swinging *draugr* said. "You—"

He stopped talking as my sword sliced through his vocal cords.

Then my army of the dead arrived. Before me and all around us were literal walking corpses that had been knitted together in their moldering graves to do my bidding.

"Remove them from my city unless they swear loyalty to me," I ordered my undead army.

I felt another dead presence to my side and turned, expecting to find one of the other *draugr*.

Instead, there stood Iggy. "Hello, Hexen."

"Take a number, Iggy." I was unexpectedly impressed as a third dead guy appeared and took up the golf club like it was a rapier. He actually took a fencing stance and motioned me forward.

"I swear, some people think that just because I'm a witch I'm going to be a shit swordfighter." I was more longsword or single-hander than rapier, which was suited for thrusts not slicing *and* thrusting like a longsword. "I don't have time for this. I need to sit through a manicure yet."

"A manicure?" Iggy said as he watched me fence with the *draugr*.

"Wedding tomorrow," I called to him. "You aren't invited."

Iggy sighed and with a gesture, the *draugr* froze. Literally. He was encased in ice. "Fix that, Miss Crowe."

I beheaded the fencer and strode into the crowd hunting the other three *draugr*. Even if they weren't starting a hate-Gen party, they were obviously not great people—even by my slightly laxer standards for dead folk these days.

"You are a vexing creature," Iggy pronounced as he walked at my side. "I try to offer you shelter and safety, and you chose this . . ." He paused, drew a knife from his hip and hurled it into the throat of a *draugr* mid-*flow*.

I was reluctantly impressed.

"You choose a *melee* over the sanctuary I offered you," Iggy continued, dodging a pair of 17th century corpses dragging a literal sack of yelling tourists away.

"Leave them at the gate, please!" I called to my army.

Then I turned back to Iggy.

"I'm just tidying up." I motioned to the chaos. "I don't want the monsters—human or *draugr* —running around starting shit on my wedding day."

The formerly-dead Hexen Master frowned. "In my day, we kept women safe. Perhaps not dead women like Beatrice, but aside from her, women knew that they were to stay safely locked away while men sorted out the conflicts."

I paused. "That's why you *kidnapped* me? To keep me safe?"

"I'd heard rumors of this"—he gestured at the chaos around us—"and I wanted to keep you free from harm, talk to you about training, explain the dangers of Chester and . . . well, I do enjoy your company. I had thought that perhaps you would be receptive."

I stared at him.

"It is not an impossible hope," Iggy said, sounding far too sure of himself for someone I had exactly zero interest in as anything other than a magical mentor.

"Bite my freckled fanny," I grumbled.

Then I *flowed* away, forgetting for a moment about the cameras everywhere.

"Oh Hexen," Iggy called.

Then with a snap of his figures, lightning flickered around in a beautiful web to various phones and cameras. People dropped suddenly hot electronics, circuitry fried.

"Blessed nuptials," Iggy said as he strolled past me a few moments later. "You obstreperous woman."

# CHAPTER 13

Later that night I slipped into bed with Eli. The dead were safely nestled back in their graves, and the *draugr* I hadn't beheaded were gone. The tourists who arrived in my city with hatred in their heart were escorted to the city's gates. And Iggy had crawled back into whatever cave he lived with his antiquated notions.

"How was work?" Eli murmured after kissing me hello.

"Dead," I quipped.

Eli, proving yet again that he was the one for me, smiled. "Indeed."

I filled him in, and then snuggled into his arms to rest a bit. It was a bit alarming to suddenly need sleep more often, but that was another question for another week. Tonight was for pre-wedding snuggles and sleep.

THE NEXT MORNING, we woke to the magical alarm that let us know that Allie was here.

"Breakfast!" she called as she let herself into the house.

"Did you forget to lock the door?" I grumbled to Eli.

"I gave her a key," he said cheerily.

Then he escaped my grumpy morning-mood to start to ready himself for the day while I met the chirpy "Helloooo, my bridal birdie" of my assistant.

I swore she was cheerful just to piss me off sometimes.

"Come on," she said, knocking on the bedroom door. "We need to head out so we can get you all beautified. I have a whole team meeting us there."

I jerked open the door. "You're lying, right?"

"Nope."

We arrived at Beatrice's estate. Reflexively, my magic reached out to the dead in the soil, absences in pockets of space. There were a number of graves here. Three women in the bayou. Six more men in the ground closer to the house. A child in a grave. And a tangle of bones in a field . . . sixty. . . maybe up to eighty bodies.

It was as if I greeted them when I visited, reaching out, finding them. Knowing where they were. In the city, the dead were always easy to find. New Orleans was a city of graves. Out here in what was once called Slidell, the dead were often hidden.

Except the *draugr*.

My sense of the dead was always humming at Beatrice's home. Her guards were not *all* walking dead, but they were present enough that I felt hyper-alert the first few times I'd been here. Now, after several visits over the last year, I was getting used to their "signatures." I could identify some of the guests by the way my magic recognized them.

Beatrice swept out the door, and despite her elegant gown, she still looked like she was a moment from declaring war. She was draped in a midnight blue gown with a hundreds of small glinting gems that gave her the appearance of royalty—which she was among her kind.

She wore no shoes. In fact, a pair of employees at her door were collecting and tagging all shoes. There would be no footwear allowed at my wedding.

Fortunately, this was a small, private event, and none of my guests were the sort to disagree. They knew me.

"Your dress awaits," Beatrice said, motioning us forward.

The hallway was covered with a carpet of moss and flowers. Magic or patience could be responsible. I didn't ask which it was. I merely followed her to a medieval-looking room where dresses were hung in waiting.

Light blue and green dresses waited for my bridesmaids. And for me, a mid-tone blue gown that was cut to look a bit like a mermaid's tail. The material was dyed several shades lighter than my hair. Simple, but narrowing at the calf to highlight my shape. It was fancier than I'd thought I wanted, and there was nowhere to hide a sword.

"I'll slaughter the world for you," Beatrice reminded me, noticing my anxiety. "Wear the dress. Relax for these hours."

I nodded and slipped into the dress.

Beatrice stared at me. "I have sent Alice's people away to tend the bridesmaids. I know that is not 'your style.'"

I muffled a laugh.

Then she leaned forward and placed a circlet of gems on my hair. "This is not a veil. It is not a fae crown. It is in place of those things."

Carefully I met her eyes in the mirror. The crown was obviously a gift, but I could not help but suspect that there was more to it. "You're not telling me everything."

Beatrice waved my words away, reminding me of every time my own mother made such a gesture.

"Today is not the day to speak of *everything*," Beatrice said. "Later you may question me."

I nodded.

"Today you celebrate your love before your family, yes?" Beatrice fussed with my hair.

Behind me, by way of the mirror, I saw my mother, who had

just walked into the room. The three of us stood there for a moment.

Then Beatrice kissed Mama Lauren's cheek. Then mine. "You are my greatest achievements in these many centuries of un-living existence."

Before we could think to reply, she *flowed* out of the room.

"She loves the way she can," Mama Lauren said. "I remind myself of that often when she is imperious."

"Sounds like you," I teased.

Mama Lauren swatted my arm lightly. "You are lovely, despite that sass."

"Because of it?" I asked.

"Perhaps." My mother's smile was agreeing, even if her words were tentative. "From my long-ago bargain . . . to this wedding, there has never been a risk too great when it came to your happiness."

We talked and finished getting ready in what felt like minutes, although it was almost two hours later that we walked out of the room and toward the courtyard.

I watched as Allie, Sera, and Christy walked toward Beatrice, who was officiating. Then, Jesse stepped forward. My "Man of Honor" had chosen to wait at the front with the ring. He was also in place to hold my bouquet of vibrant flowers.

Halfway up the aisle, then, was my groom. My already-husband. My bound-unto-death fae prince. Handsome in every way I could dream—and mine. Eli was everything I never dreamed to find.

My mother escorted me toward him, and I could not look away.

"Breathe in and out, Gen," Mama Lauren whispered.

"Trying." I smiled at Eli. "He steals my breath."

I knew there were guests as well, but in that moment, I couldn't tell you who or why they were here.

My mother and I reached Eli's side, and she said, "I give my heart into your possession, Eli. Guard her. Love her."

"I shall," he promised.

"I trust you." She stepped away.

As I placed my hand on his arm, I was trembling. This was it. The last ceremony. The final exchange of vows.

"Three exchanges," I whispered, thinking about the rule of three.

Eli smiled as we walked toward Beatrice.

She looked at us, smiled, and said, "The couple would like to say a few words in the presence of witnesses."

"Eternally yours," he swore. "I've waited years to be able to call myself the luckiest person in either world, Geneviève Crowe."

"I was oblivious so long, I'm glad you thought I was worth the wait."

Friends laughed.

"My heart, my hearth, and my hand are yours, Geneviève Crowe. Unto death I shall live and fight at your side. And in us, the future of my family is bound." Eli stared into my eyes. "It is my privilege to love you, and my great joy to be loved by you."

"My heart, my hearth, and hand are yours, Eli of Stonecroft. Not even death could tear me from your side." I swallowed. "I love you and will be honored to be mother to your child one day, partner on the throne of *Elphame,* and the sword at your side."

Then Eli gave me a wicked smile. "I accept your faery bargain, Geneviève of Crowe and Stonecroft. Your terms are acceptable to me."

I laughed at his going off script this time. "So mote it be, Eli of Crowe and Stonecroft."

Beatrice shook her head at our impromptu modification and then asked, "Do you take this person to be your spouse, your partner, your equal in all ways?"

"Unto death," Eli said.

"Unto death," I echoed.

"By the powers granted me by familial law, as well as my court and kin, I pronounce you wed." Then she swept her arms open and stated, "May I present Geneviève and Eli of Crowe and Stonecroft."

# EPILOGUE

S everal hours later, I found Beatrice outside in her courtyard as dawn was approaching. Everyone else had left, so only family remained. If this had been my first wedding, perhaps I'd have been long gone, but this was the third such event if you counted my bonding—which I did.

"Grandmother of mine," I said quietly, staring at a pig with the jacket. "Does that pig seem familiar?"

"I warned him." She took a delicate sip of the shiraz she was drinking. A bottle and empty glass sat on a pub table with a linen tablecloth. "Drink?"

"You warned the pig . . .?" I gestured toward the angry-looking pig as I accepted a glass of wine from her.

As she poured my drink, Beatrice gave me that look that said I was a little dim. Then her frown of irritation twisted into a cold grin of victory. "Piggy Iggy."

"Ignatius, the Hexen Master, is . . . a pig." I stared at him as he rolled in the water and muck that Beatrice's caterers had poured out into the garden. It was fascinating because I could see Iggy's intellect in the pig's expression, but he was still, in behavior, a *pig*.

"I invited him for a drink, during which I warned him that I was not going to tolerate affronts to my family," Beatrice said in a prim voice, as if centuries had faded from her. Her diction was less crisp as her emotion quarreled with her elocution. "A woman expects more from former paramours. Did I ask for eternity? Did I ask for fidelity?"

"No," I guessed.

"Precisely. I asked for simple respect, and yet he failed. He ought to have understood that making eyes at—"

"Making eyes," I echoed with a forcefully suppressed laugh.

Beatrice waved her hand and stared at me. "It was unseemly, Geneviève."

"To make eyes at me," I clarified, as a member of the catering team chased Iggy away from the door.

"Boorish. He was being boorish." Beatrice cracked a smile. "So . . . *voila*. He is a *boar*. It is a pun, you see? Your mother was telling me of puns."

"Mama Lauren knows you turned Iggy into a . . .pun-pig?" I asked carefully.

My centuries-old grandmother studied her nails as if she were a teenager caught in a lie. "Not precisely. If she weren't so *ethical*, I could tell her. I thought it was best not to mention before the wedding."

So, I did the only possible thing I could--I gave in to my laughter and pulled her into a hug. Then I whispered, "If you were around when I was a kid, I think Mama Lauren would've grounded us both."

When I pulled back from hugging her, she asked, "Piggy Iggy is better than a head in a box, yes? I did not kill him. He is a temporary pig."

She gestured with her glass before topping off both our drinks.

And I thought back to her holiday gift last year: a silver foil-wrapped box with bold blue ribbons. In the box was the severed head of a man who'd shot at me with the broach of a draugr who'd attacked me jabbed into the forehead of the dead man.

"Equally unexpected," I allowed.

Then the wickedest smile came over her. Fangs glinting, she said "We have a family tradition then . . ."

Quashing thoughts of what sort of gifts followed severed heads and pigs, I nodded. "We do, indeed. Perhaps the holiday season will be more interesting for it."

She lifted her glass to me. "To defeating our enemies with festive spirits!"

I lifted my glass to hers. "To family."

She smiled at me, and then she toasted Piggy Iggy with a malicious grin.

As I drained the glass, I couldn't decide whether Eli or I landed the most terrifying in-laws. Fae King or *Draugr* Queen? Both were ferocious.

Either way, I felt certain of both the love and the strength we had at our sides. Whatever came next, we were not alone in facing it.

**The Wicked & The Dead is AVAILABLE NOW!**

"I loved *The Wicked and The Dead*! A sassy, ass-kicking heroine, a deliciously mysterious fae hero, and a wonderful mix of action and romance. Add that to Melissa's usual great world-building, and I'm already looking forward to book 2!"
— Jeaniene Frost, *NYT* Bestselling Author

Geneviève Crowe makes her living beheading the dead. But now, her magic has gone sideways, and the only person strong enough to help her is the one man who could tempt her to think about picket fences: Eli Stonecroft, a faery bar-owner in New Orleans.

When human businessmen start turning up as *draugr*, the queen of the again-walkers and the wealthy son of one of the victims, both hire Geneviève to figure it out. She works to keep her magic in check, the dead from crawling out of their graves, and enough money for a future that might be a lot longer than she'd like. Neither her heart nor her life are safe now that she's juggling a faery, murder, and magic.

EXCERPT OF THE WICKED &
THE DEAD

The Wicked & The Dead
AVAILABLE now!

## Chapter 1

Autumn in the South was still both humid and hot. New Orleans was always a wet city. Wet air. Wet drizzle. Beer soaked streets. *Other* things spilling out from behind trash bins. Sometimes, the heavy air and frequent rain was just this side of too much.

Most nights, there was nowhere else I'd rather be. We were a city risen from the ashes, over and over. Plagues, floods, monsters. New Orleans didn't stop, didn't give up, and I was proud of that. Tonight, though, I watched the fog roll out like a cheap film effect, and a good book in front of a warm fire sounded far better than work. The nonstop rain this month would wash away evidence of the things that happened in New Orleans' darkened corners, but I could prevent bloodshed. It was more or less what I did. Sometimes, I spilled a bit of blood, but if we weighed it all out, I was fairly sure I was one of the good guys.

More curves and sass than actual *guys*, but the point held. White hat. Dingy around the edges. I blame my persistent nagging guilt.

A *thump* on the other side of the wall made me pause.

Could I hurl myself over the wall into Cypress Grove Cemetery? It wasn't the *worst* idea ever—or even this month—which said more about my life than I'd like to admit.

I listened for more sounds. *Nothing*. No scrabbling. No growling.

I needed to be on the other side of the wall where tombs were lined up like miniature houses. The tree branches I'd used last time were gone, probably trimmed by someone who saw their potential. Now, there was no graceful way to hurl myself over the ten-foot wall.

Every cemetery in the nation now had taller walls and plenty of newly-opened space for the dead. Cemeteries had become "stage one" of the verification of death process. Honestly, I guess graves were better than cold storage at the morgue. The lack of heartbeat made it impossible to know if the corpses would walk-again, and those of us who advocated for beheading all corpses were deemed callous.

I wasn't sure I was callous for wanting the dead to stay dead. I knew what they were capable of before the world at large did.

At least I was prepared. A moment or so later, I shoved a metal spike into the wall, cutting my palm in the process.

"Shit. Damn. Monkey balls."

A ripple of light flashed around me the moment my blood dripped to the soil. At least the light was magic, not the police or a tourist with a camera. While the laws were ever-changing, B&E was still illegal. And I was breaking into a cemetery where I might need to carry out a contracted beheading. *That* was illegal, too.

It simply wasn't a photo-ready moment—although with my long dyed-blue hair and nearly translucent skin, I was far too photogenic. I won't say I look like I've been drained of both blood and color, but I will admit that next to a lot of the folks in my city, I look like I've been bleached.

I fumbled with my gloves, trapping my blood inside the thick leather before I resumed shoving climbing cams into gaps in the wall. Normally, cams held the ropes that climbers use. Tonight, they'd be like tiny foot supports. If I were human, this wouldn't work out well.

I'm not.

Mostly, I'd say I am a witch, but that is the polite truth. I am more like witch-with-hard-to-explain-extras. That smidge of blood I'd spilled was enough to send out "wakey, wakey" messages to whatever corpses were listening, but the last time I'd had to bleed for them to rest again, I'd needed to shed more than a cup of blood.

I concentrated on not sending out a second magic flare and continued to insert the cams.

*Rest. Stay.* I felt silly thinking messages to the dead, but better silly than planning for excess bleeding.

At least this job *should* be an easy one. My task was to find out if Alice Navarro was again-walking or if she was securely in her vault. I hoped for the latter. Most people hired me to ease their dearly departed back in the "departed" category, but the Navarro family was the other sort. They missed her, and sometimes grief makes people do things that are on the wrong side of rational.

My pistol had tranquilizer rounds tonight. If Navarro was awake, I'd need to tranq her. If she wasn't, I could call it a night—unless there were other again-walkers. That's where the beheading came in. Straight-forward. Despite the cold and wet, I still hoped for the best. All things considered, I really was an optimist at heart.

At the top of the wall, I swung my leg over the stylish spikes cemented there and dropped into the wet grass. I was braced for it, but when I landed, it wasn't dew or rain that made me land on my ass.

An older man, judging by the tufts of grey hair on the bloodied body, in a security guard uniform had bled out on the ground. Something--most likely an again-walker--had gnawed on the security guard's face. Who had made the decision to have a living man with no special skills stand inside the walls of a cemetery? Now, he was dead.

I whispered a quick prayer before surveying my surroundings. Once I located the *draugr*, I could call in the location of the dead man. First, though, I had to find the face-gnawer who killed him. Since my magic was erratic, I didn't want to send a voluntary pulse out to find my prey. That would wake the truly dead, and there were plenty of them here to wake.

Several rows into the cemetery, I found Alice Navarro's undisturbed grave. No upheaval. No turned soil. Mrs. Navarro was well and truly dead. My clients had their answer—but now, I had a mystery. Which cemetery resident had killed the security guard?

A sound drew my attention. A thin hooded figure, masked like they were off to an early carnival party, stared back at me. They didn't move like they were dead. Too slow. Too human. And *draugr* weren't big on masks.

"Hey!" My voice seemed too loud. "You. What are you . . ."

The figure ran, and several other voices suddenly rang out. Young voices. Teens inside the cemetery.

"Shit cookies!" I ran after the masked person. Who in the name of all reason would be in among the graves at night? I ran through the rows of graves, looking for evidence of waking as I went.

"Bitch!"

The masked figure was climbing over the wall with a ladder, the chain sort you use in home fire-emergencies. Two teens tried to grab the person. One kid was kneeling, hand gripping his shoulder in obvious pain.

And there, several feet away, was Marie and Edward Chevalier's grave. The soil was disturbed, as if a pack of excited dogs had been digging. The person in the mask was not the dead one in the nearby grave. There *was* a recently dead *draugr*.

And kids.

I glanced back at the teens.

A masked stranger, a dead security guard, a *draugr,* and kids. This was a terrible combination.

The masked person dropped something and pulled a gun. The kids backed away quickly, and the masked person glanced at me before scrambling the rest of the way over the wall—all while awkwardly holding a gun.

"Are you okay?" I asked the kids, even as my gaze was scanning for the *draugr.*

"She stabbed Gerry," the girl said, pointing at the kid on the ground.

The tallest of the teens grabbed the thing the intruder dropped and held it up. A syringe.

"She?" I asked.

"Lady chest," the tall one explained. "When I ran into her, I felt her—"

"Got it." I nodded, glad the intruder with the needle was gone, but a quick glance at the stone by the disturbed grave told me that a fresh body had been planted there two days ago. That was the likely cause of the security guard's missing face. I read the dates on the stone: Edward was not yet dead. Marie was.

I was seeking Marie Chevalier.

"Marie?" I whispered loudly as the kids talked among themselves. The last thing I needed right now was a *draugr* arriving to gnaw on the three dumb kids. "Oh, Miss Marie? Where are you?"

Marie wouldn't answer, even if she had been a polite Southern lady. *Draugr* were like big infants for the first decade and change: they ate, yelled, and stumbled around.

"There's a real one?" the girl asked.

I glanced at the kids. I was calling out a thing that would *eat* them if they had been alone with it, and they seemed excited. Best case was a drooling open-mouthed lurch in my direction. Worst case was they all died.

"Go home," I said.

Instead they trailed behind me as I walked around, looking for

Marie. I passed by the front gate—which was now standing wide open.

"Did you do that?" The lock had been removed. The pieces were on the ground. Cut through. Marie was not in the cemetery.

Shaking heads. "No, man. The ladder the bitch used was ours."

Intruder. With a needle. Possibly also the person who left the gate open? Had someone wanted Marie Chevalier released? Or was that a coincidence? Either way, a face-gnawer was loose somewhere in the city, one of the who-knows-how-many *draugr* that hid here or in the nearby suburbs or small towns.

I pushed the gates closed and called it in to the police. "Broken gate at Cypress Grove. Cut in pieces."

"Miss Crowe," the woman on dispatch replied. "Are you injured?"

"No. The *lock* was cut. Bunch of kids here." I shot them a look. "Said it wasn't them."

"I will send a car," she said. A longer than normal pause. "Why are *you* there, Miss Crowe?"

I smothered a sigh. It complicated my life that so many of the cops recognized me, that dispatch did, that the ER folks at the hospital did. It wasn't like New Orleans was *that* small.

"Do you log my number?" I asked. "Or is it my voice?"

Another sigh. Another pause. She ignored my questions. "Details?"

"I was checking on a grave here. It's intact, but the cemetery gate's busted," I explained.

"I noted that," she said mildly. "Are the kids alive?"

"Yeah. A person in a mask tried to inject one of them, and a guard inside is missing a lot of his face. No *draugr* here now, but the grave of Marie and Edward Chevalier is broken out. I'm guessing it was her that killed the guard."

The calm tone was gone. "There's a car about two blocks away. You and the children—"

"I'm good." I interrupted. "Marie's long gone, I guess. I'll be sure the kids are secure, but—"

"Miss Crowe! You don't know if she's still there or nearby. You need to be relocated to safety, too."

"Honest to Pete, you all need to worry a lot less about me," I said.

She made a noise that reminded me of my mother. Mama Lauren could fit a whole lecture in one of those "uh-huh" noises of hers. The woman on dispatch tonight came near to matching my mother.

"Someone *cut* the lock," I told dispatch. "What we need to know is why. And who. And if there are other opened cemeteries." I paused. "And who tried to inject the kid."

I looked at them. They were in a small huddle. One of them dropped and stomped the needle. I winced. That was going to make investigating a lot harder.

*Not my problem,* I reminded myself. I was a hired killer, not a cop, not a detective, not a nanny.

"Kid probably ought to get a tox screen and tetanus shot," I muttered.

Dispatch made an agreeing noise, and said, "Please try not to 'find' more trouble tonight, Miss Crowe."

I made no promises.

When I disconnected, I looked at the kids. "Gerry, right?"

The kid in the middle nodded. White boy. Looking almost as pale as me currently. I was guessing he was terrified.

"Let me see your arm."

He pulled his shirt off. It looked like the skin was torn.

"Do not scream," I said. My eyes shifted into larger versions of a snake's eyes. I knew what it looked like, and maybe a part of me was okay with letting them see because nobody would believe them if they did tell. They were kids, and while a lot had changed in the world, people still doubted kids when they talked.

More practically, though, as my eyes changed I could see in a way humans couldn't.

Green. Glowing like a cheap neon light. The syringe had venom. *Draugr* venom. It wasn't inside the skin. The syringe was either jammed or the kid jerked away.

"Water?"

One of the kids pulled a bottle from his bag, and I washed the wound. "Don't touch the fucking syringe." I pointed at it. "Who stomped on it? Hold your boot up."

I rinsed that, too. Venom wasn't the sort of thing anyone wanted on their skin unless they wanted acid-burn.

"Venom," I said. "That was venom in the needle. You could've died. And"—I pointed behind me—"there was a *draugr* here. Guy got his face chewed off."

They were listening, seeming to at least. I wasn't their family, though. I was a blue-haired woman with some weapons and weird eyes. The best I could do was hand them over to the police and hope they weren't stupid enough to end up in danger again tomorrow.

New Orleans had more than Marie hiding in the shadows. *Draugr* were fast, strong, and difficult to kill. If not for their need to feed on the living like mindless beasts the first few decades after resurrection, I might accept them as the next evolutionary step. But I wasn't a fan of anything—mindless or sentient—that stole blood and life.

Marie might have been an angel in life, but right now she was a killer.

In my city.

If I found the person or people who decided to release Marie— or the woman with the syringe--I'd call the police. I tried to avoid killing the living. But if I found Marie, or others like her, I wasn't calling dispatch. When it came to venomous killers, I tended to be more of a behead first, ask later kind of woman.

∼

*The Kiss & The Killer* **is AVAILABLE NOW!**

Half witch, half killer, wholly unsuccessful at every Faery Bargain so far...

After an accidental engagement, overcoming attempted murder, and discovering a family secret, Geneviève is ready for things to settle down, but carnival season in New Orleans is not the best time of year for "normal."

As the *draugr* mix with the locals and tourists, and bodies start to pile up, Geneviève is enlisted by the New Orleans Police Department to hunt *draugr* all while trying to navigate this latest faery bargain amidst the swirl of parades and parties of carnival season.

When Eli Stonecroft, the faery who has claimed her heart despite her best attempts, offers her a new faery bargain--she's smart enough to say no . . . right up to the point when she has to decide between dealing with the consequence of this faery bargain or facing the killer alone.

**AVAILABLE NOW!**

**How far would you go to escape fate?**

In this prequel to the internationally bestselling WICKED LOVELY series, the Faery Courts collide a century before the mortals in *Wicked Lovely* are born.

Thelma Foy, a jeweler with the Second Sight in iron-bedecked 1890s New Orleans, can see through the glamours faeries wear to hide themselves from mortals,  but if her secret were revealed, the fey would steal her eyes, her life, or her freedom. But when the Dark King, Irial, rescues her, Tam must confront everything she thought she knew about faeries, men, and love.

Too soon, New Orleans is filling with faeries who are looking for her, and Irial is the only one who can keep her safe.

Unbeknownst to Tam, she is the prize in a centuries-old fight between Summer Court and Winter Court. To protect her, Irial must risk a war he can't win--or surrender the first mortal woman he's loved.

**Available now:** *Cursed by Death*!

**The dead don't always stay dead in Claysville . . . and in the afterlife, Death himself can't be trusted.**

Amity Blue has begun to remember strange impossible events, her ex trying to bite her and people vanishing like mist. After a stalker—a dead stalker—appears at the bar where she works, Amity discovers that the dead don't always stay dead in Claysville. Along with the current Graveminder, Rebekkah Barrow, Amity seeks out the enigmatic Mr D, only to discover that the centuries-old contract to protect Claysville has been broken.

Caught between life in a cursed town and Death himself, Amity and Rebekkah must find a way to put the dead where they belong—because if the Hungry Dead keep rising, everyone in town will be lost.

**Return to the world of Graveminder, Goodreads Choice Winner for Best Horror Novel.**

**Available 2022**
**Pre-Order Now**
*The Hexed & The Hunted: Faery Bargains*

The third novel in a new faery and fanged world written by the author of the internationally bestselling Wicked Lovely series.

Half-dead witch Geneviève Crowe makes her living beheading the dead--and trying to juggle her new duties as a faery princess now that she's married Eli Stonecroft, a faery prince who was in self-imposed exile in New Orleans.

But monsters have no patience with royal obligations, and the same creature who once hunted her great-times-great grand-mother is now trying to put Gen in the ground. When the relent-less monster from her family's past decides to hex Geneviève, she's forced to go on the run or expose how much power she's started amassing. Her royally impatient uncle-in-law, the faery king, has already threatened her *and* Eli.

Death or Flight? Hexed or Hunted? This is *not* the honeymoon Gen and Eli were planning .